REBORN HEART

REBORN HEART

Guardians Trilogy — Book 3

Stefanie Dawn

This book is a work of fiction. Any references to real events, real people, and real places are used fictitiously. Other names, characters, places, and incidents are products of the author's imagination, and any resemblance to persons, living or dead, actual events, organizations, or places is entirely coincidental.

Disclaimer: The material in this book contains sexual content and is intended for mature audiences ages 18 and older.

ISBN eBook: 978-1-7636644-7-0

ISBN Paperback: 978-1-7636644-8-7

ISBN Hardcover: 978-1-7638705-3-6

Book Design by Angels and Fire Books

Paperback Cover Design by Artscandare

Hardcover Cover Design by RJ Creatives

Published by Angels and Fire Books

Also by Stefanie Dawn

The Unearthly Sins Novels

The Demon in Me

The Angel in Her

Lure of a Demon

Dark Angel

Touch of a Demon

The Demon in Him

The Elements of Abduction Novels

Savior

Rescuer

Redeemer

Liberator

Releaser

Freer

The Guardians Trilogy

Rogue Heart

Shattered Heart

Reborn Heart

Novellas

Demonic

Daemonia

For Ana and Cael.

Because I felt they, and this story, were worth saving.

Earth is crumbling to pieces as the three realms begin their tumultuous merge into one.

The Balance has shifted. The apocalypse has arrived.

Mankind is being tormented by incessant earthquakes, violent cracks in the Earth's crust, and the collapse of homes and buildings. Lucidians work tirelessly to protect humans, while the roaming Tenebrians gleefully revel in the chaos.

And I... I can do nothing but watch as what is left of the woman I love shrinks into herself, and questions if a world plagued by violence is even worth saving.

She was used as a weapon, and blames herself for bringing the world to this end.

While Samael and I struggle to hold everything together, fighting an uphill battle to correct the Shift before it completes and all is lost, I must make a terrible decision.

If Ana was the key to destroying the world, perhaps she's also the key to restoring it.

But will I be faced with the choice between saving her life, or saving everything?

Contents

Chapter One

Roger

Forty Years Ago...

Every shift of my foot caused another cascade of bark chips to fall across my shoes. The low retaining wall surrounding the small playground was in disrepair and had begun to collapse due to age. The smell of damp wood drifted around me in the afternoon breeze, and given the recent rain, the playground was almost empty.

Empty save for my six-year-old daughter, Anahera, and her mother, Bronte. They played on the swing set, which creaked with every movement, and Ana's laughter filled the air as Bronte would tickle her every time the swing was high in the arc.

John glanced at me, and my lips curved as his face lit with a grin he couldn't contain. He could rarely suppress the emotions he was still learning to harness when he was around Ana, whom he'd unofficially adopted as his niece. Family values were foreign to him. As far as I knew, we were the closest thing he'd ever had to a family. I suspected beyond the lack of connection he'd lived with in Tenebris, John had experienced heartache on Earth, though he'd never told me the whole story.

Whatever happened, he blamed himself.

But John would protect us to the ends of the Earth and beyond, and we would do the same for him.

My gleeful expression fell because this was all temporary. Surely John knew we couldn't keep going like this, and at some point, I would have to make the difficult decision.

A choice I'd already made, if I were honest with myself about it.

I managed to hold a small smile as I returned John's gaze, but as soon as he looked back at Bronte and Ana, I couldn't keep it for more than a few lingering moments.

"What's wrong?" John asked me as a furrow formed between his dark brows. A hint of frustration flickered within me, and I didn't need my senses to see the resentment that bubbled with his words. I had a beautiful family, and I wasn't appreciating it enough in John's eyes.

We turned back to Ana. She squealed with delight as the swing took her higher, and Bronte fumbled to slow her incline. John chuckled, and I released a low laugh. Ana was fine, but the momentary panic on Bronte's face was priceless.

Silence ebbed between John and me as I watched Bronte's face. When the swing had returned to an acceptable momentum, her deep brown eyes found mine, and she smiled. There was sunshine in her smile, and her pale blonde hair cascaded over her shoulders and caught what little sun showed between the dark clouds.

I loved her. With everything I had and more. A love I didn't know I was even capable of.

When I thought I couldn't fit any more love inside me, Ana came into the world, and my perceptions of the emotions I was capable of feeling were shattered again.

After a moment, I broke the silence. "I want Ana to stay in this realm, on Earth with the humans."

"And she will. Look at her, she's human," John said. I nodded as John turned to me to asses my expression before he continued, "You should be proud of her mixed genes. Who knows what she can achieve?"

"I don't want her to be an outcast."

"You worry too much," John grunted out. "She's a goddamn miracle. You need to see that." He watched me consider his words, and John's annoyance was evident in his features. "You can't protect her from who she is."

"No…" I sighed. "But maybe I can protect her from who I am."

John stared at me for a beat longer as I watched my family, not really seeing them. John tried his best to understand my inner conflict, but as much as he loved Ana, she wasn't his daughter. He'd burn down the world to save her, as would I.

But I'd also burn myself with it.

As Ana and Bronte laughed, John's expression flickered, and I reached out and grabbed his shoulder. He knew what I was about to do but let me do it anyway. When he wouldn't talk, I would read his imprint.

Uncertainty. Confusion. Pain.

Understanding.

John's sigh was heavy and purposeful. "You're trying to put her well-being above everything else, I get that."

"John…" I waited until he looked at me. I needed him to understand that it would be for good if I were to leave. "If Ana constantly battles between the two beings that make her whole, she will never feel complete in this world. Without Guardian influence, without..." I cleared my throat. "Without *my* influence, she will grow and live as a human. She may never even need to know the truth of her heritage. She could have a life, friends, and love without complications."

"There's no such thing as love without complications."

"I know." I huffed out a humorless laugh as I caught Bronte's eye. "What if our continued presence in her life alters her appearance as she grows? What if she is never truly accepted by others?" I shook my head. She wouldn't be allowed to move freely between the realms—she had to live in one or the other, and I'd rather she were here with her mother. I wanted her to have the life I never could. "Is that a life I can knowingly create for her, when I *know* I could make it better if I simply stepped away?"

John nodded slowly, his lips twisted in pain.

I didn't slip up in what I said. I meant every word.

What if our *presence...*

John was a Guardian, too, and his influence could be as potent as mine simply by being present.

We both turned back as Bronte flashed us a smile that radiated from her, bright and full of love and promise. I truly smiled then. I couldn't help it. A genuine smile that drew Ana to look at me and respond with one of her own. She jumped off the swing, ignored her mother's flailing arms as she attempted to catch her daughter, and ran toward me as her ponytail flowed out behind her. Ana threw herself at me and wrapped her little arms around my waist. I peeled her from me only long enough to kneel before I hugged her back, and pressed her against me while internally I continued to fight a battle that would change her future.

I would sacrifice myself and *everything* for her in a fraction of a heartbeat, but could I forgive myself if I needed to make the ultimate sacrifice?

Could Ana forgive me if I chose her path for her?

I'd loved Bronte longer than I knew what love was. She would understand, but she would still hurt.

Leaning back, I assessed Ana as I held her shoulders. She giggled, and my smile dropped when a blue glow radiated from her skin. I glanced at John as panic gripped me, and John's face betrayed his conflict and a hint of pride. I slowly removed my hand from Ana's arm in an experimental move. The blue glow eased, and I frowned and placed my hand back on her arm.

The glow returned with intensity, and my eyes widened as a crack ruptured my chest.

Proof I could no longer hide from the truth.

The realization hit me like a punch in the gut, and I wheezed as the weight of the world fell on top of me. I *knew*, but to see it was an entirely different type of torture. As though there had been a small part of me that secretly hoped my fears were baseless.

But Ana glowed because of my proximity, as my Guardian called to hers.

Bronte chuckled at my reaction, misinterpreting my concern as she hid her beautiful smile behind her hand and giggled at my shock. She didn't see what I saw—Bronte saw our beautiful daughter and all the magic she offered, with powers she still didn't fully understand.

Tonight, I would need to tell Bronte I couldn't stay. She already accepted that I could only be around for a few days at a time.

Subconsciously, I had already been increasing the duration between my visits.

Surely, she would understand.

She must.

Over time, I would have to limit my interactions with Ana, until eventually, when I found the strength, I would have to leave them both.

Forever.

Chapter Two

Ana

Now…

Pain ricocheted through my body as I collapsed into a heap.

The Tenebrians had lost interest in me the moment the Shift began, and moved away to enjoy the chaos while the Balance completed its demise. A world that was already tipping over the edge no longer held consequences, and I had no doubt they planned to enjoy it before the final fall, which would force their survival instincts to kick in.

Survival of the fittest.

I managed to drag myself unnoticed some distance away from the group as they began to make efforts to move through to Earth. Gateways opened and closed rapidly around them, and they seemed unable to control them. Many leapt through gleefully without caring where they ended up.

We had that in common.

A Gateway opened near me, and the muscles in my arm screamed in protest as I reached for it. I didn't care where on Earth it took me, I wanted to be out of this realm. Though the uncomfortable prickling of my skin had eased once the Shift had begun, I still wanted *out.*

But the Gateway snapped shut before I could reach it, and a sob was dragged from my throat as I dropped my forehead against the warm ground.

A whimper drew my attention, and I raised my head to watch as a Tenebrian stood over a human Reflection. The Reflection lay bloodied and beaten, his eyes hollow as he stared into the distance. Bile churned in my stomach, and I had to remind myself they weren't *real.* The Tenebrian scoffed as the Reflection begged and pleaded for its life, before his head turned slowly as if finally noticing me. His gaze flickered from the group of Tenebrians in the distance as they fought to make their way to Earth. When his gums pulled back into a lazy smile and exposed his fangs, I gasped and struggled to move away. But my grip on the ground was lost in the churning dust, and the Tenebrian was above me in three large steps. I huddled against myself, giving up on my quest to escape as he crouched beside me.

His grip on my waist was unnecessarily harsh as he dug his claws into me and rolled me onto my back.

"I have a cage," he started thoughtfully as he looked down upon me. "Nails on the floor and sides, and a ceiling too high to reach. Slowly, you'd relinquish your fight and sink onto the metal." I closed my eyes as he spoke, until with a hiss, he slapped me across the face. "In the past, the Elders told us not to torture the Reflections, and that the essence of our realm was enough to feed the negative energy back to humanity." He traced a claw down my cheek. "I bet you'd scream so pretty for me."

As I whimpered, a quake rocked the ground beneath us, and the Tenebrian shifted his pose to keep his balance. He leaned down to dance his tongue across my ear lobe and whispered, "Scream for me now."

I opened my mouth, but no sound came, and when I stared into his eyes, I realized I had no will to fight. My body slumped as the tension left me, and I allowed my head to loll to the side. The Tenebrian gripped my chin between his thumb and forefinger and turned my face until I looked at him with unfocused eyes.

He scoffed again before dropping his grip from me. "No will. No fun," he muttered.

Our attention was drawn as there was a loud crack, before the Reflection beside us vanished. The Tenebrian's eyebrows raised as he turned slowly to look back at what was left of the group. "They did it..." He shook his head before he laughed. "Oh, this is going to be fun."

A gust of wind blasted through the air, and I rolled to the side to avoid dust stinging my eyes. A Gateway opened next to me, but the Tenebrian kicked me to the side before I could reach for it and leapt through it himself. The Gateway closed before I could get closer, and my arm dropped uselessly against the dust.

Ultimately, my human form prevailed, and I scoffed quietly as I watched my weak human fingers flex in the dirt. The irony that my dominant form was human wasn't lost on me. After a moment of absolute power when I tore apart the very fabric of the world, I was forced into this image. The part of me that had caused the damage—the weaker, the complicated part—had conquered.

Rolling onto my side, I curled up and huffed air from my nose. Technically, it wasn't my human half that was to blame—it was the combination of my halves and the battle between them. But thinking about it while I lay in the dirt of Tenebris wasn't what I wanted to do, so I closed my eyes and stilled.

I was doomed to be a danger from the day I was born.

What was left to do but lie in the wake of the destruction, and let what remained of the world consume me?

The air sucked around me like a vortex as Gateways opened and closed, and if they were too close they caused my eardrums to pop. Although no Guardians were left near me, the Gateways continued to open and close.

I stopped trying to reach them.

My hands clamped over my ears as I pressed my forehead on the soil, closed my eyes, and prayed to a deity I wasn't sure I even believed in. Praying for forgiveness and absolution for what I'd done. For the pain I'd already caused, and all the pain which was to follow.

All the death.

It was my fault. Thousands of years of the Guardians maintaining the Balance, and I had destroyed it in minutes. My lifetime was a blip on the universe, but it was the ultimate undoing of life itself.

It was a lot to take in.

Too much to take in.

Curling further into myself as another quake rocked the ground, I almost wished for the physical pain to return. Anything to distract me from the thoughts as they swirled around in my mind.

The world was better off without me.

If it was even worth saving.

If the Tenebrians had taught me anything, it was that

they would never stop. They'd pile into Earth uncontrolled, without a care for consequences, and wreak havoc on innocent people. Humanity would suffer, *had been* suffering because of them. Shouldn't life balance itself out? Without the Tenebrians prodding and poking and influencing, the Lucidians wouldn't have to work half as hard to keep things together. All the while, humans suffered physical, emotional, and mental pain. Suffering that cut so deep they'd walk the remainder of their lives with their heart barely held together by the will to keep breathing another day.

And now the Balance wouldn't be there to save the delicate realms, and whatever thin leash of responsibility that held the Tenebrians in check had snapped.

What kind of world was that to look forward to?

Was this just a cycle destined to repeat? If we managed to correct the Balance somehow, there would eventually be those who tried to shift it again. All the while, humans would continue to be hurt and killed, innocent bystanders to a war they weren't even aware of.

Maybe we were no better than tools all along.

Guilt and self-hatred consumed me, and despite the ebbing and flowing of my powers through my being, I felt the hard shell of negative energy as it forged around me. I stayed curled in a ball and waited for death, however long it would take to reach me.

Would I die of starvation or dehydration? Would I be in the way when an uncontrolled Gateway opened and dropped me off a cliff's edge somewhere? Would some Tenebrians find me and finish what they started with my mother?

I can't wait to see you, Mom.

Instinct had me shielding my head when another Gateway opened so close to me, I felt the teeth-chattering cold that radiated from the opening. It pulsated with unstable force, growing and shrinking inches at a time, and the power skid me across the ground a few feet. But I didn't look up or release myself from my self-preserving position.

I'd stay here until I died.

My chest throbbed from a wound that no longer existed where I'd come so close to death decades before. Perhaps I had died, and all of this had been a horrible nightmare, where Samael and Cael were bright lights, there only to distract me from my impending destiny to doom us all. I sobbed and ducked my head against my chest. I'd seen Cael in the final moments before the Balance shifted, and the look on his face was imprinted in my mind. He'd witnessed what I'd done and the realization that crossed his features when he *knew* I could tell what was happening, but was too weak to stop it, shattered me. Despite all my strength and the Elders' concerns about me being *too* powerful, I was too weak to control myself when it mattered. Without Cael there to be my balancing force, I was as unpredictable and useless as the Elders had warned I would be. Cael was the calm to my inner storm, and I'd failed him and Samael and sentenced them all to an early death.

They must hate me.

What was there left to fight for?

"Ana!"

I flinched at the sound of my name, but didn't look up. Whether the voice was in my head or not, I couldn't tell. It was distorted and faded like an out-of-tune radio. Static and wind. It wasn't real.

I must be going crazy.

"Ana, give me your hand."

Tears stung my eyes as I whispered against the dirt, "Cael?"

Why would he come for me? I'd let him down, let them all down. If there were any chance he could save the world and undo what I had done, that's where his focus should be.

"There's not much time, Ana." Desperation clawed at the edges of the voice through the distorted sound, and it continued to say my name as though trying to remind me of who I was.

No one knew who I truly was, but now I did. Only a monster could do this.

Still, my name was called.

Slowly, with my limbs shaking from the physical and mental effort it took me to respond, I lifted an arm and reached toward the voice. A strong hand clasped around my wrist, and I allowed myself to be dragged across the dirt and through the Gateway, keeping my head down. The Gateway felt different. Wrong. It was unstable, like being pulled through a bath where the hot and cold water were still mingling rather than the sheet of ice it usually was, and every inch of my skin was at a different temperature. It offered none of the healing powers Gateways usually held, and I gasped at the change in air between the realms. I was as weak when I reached Earth as I had been in Tenebris. My body was limp as Earth's familiar essence surrounded me. As my feet slipped through, the Gateway warped and changed before it snapped closed in a cloud of white and orange dust.

My body was heavy, and as I collapsed on top of my rescuer, strong arms stopped me from hitting the ground. Another pair of hands steadied me and held me under my arms, but I stayed limp as I was dragged to my feet.

"Ana, you have to stand up. Please. We need to get you somewhere safe."

"Nowhere is safe..." I whispered as my feet moved uselessly against the ground. The sound was familiar and grated against my senses. Asphalt. I was on a road. "Nowhere is safe anymore."

Why was the sun so bright? How could there be sunlight anymore? Squeezing my eyes shut, I managed to maintain some semblance of control and allowed myself to be led as I took small, unsteady steps. I barely had the energy left to assess my own body, and noticed enough to realize my emotional imprint had weakened to the point I could almost pass as human again. All the power and energy built up in my body over the years, untrained and unused, had burst forth and been used to bring on the Shift, and I was left an empty shell.

My pendant was warm on my skin, but its proximity didn't carry its usual reassuring presence.

"It's a goddamn miracle we were able to pinpoint her location at all," a rough voice came from my left, and the arm that held me up adjusted as he grunted.

A small bell chimed, and as a door was opened, a rush of air-conditioned air hit me, making me stumble. The light behind my eyelids changed as I was led out of the sun and seated on cool, polished concrete. It seemed strange that there were still sensations to feel, air to breathe, and light in the world when I could find none within.

The chaos from the street was shut out as the door clicked closed, and a warm palm caressed my cheek. "Ana," he whispered. "Come back to us, please."

Fluttering my eyes open, I kept my head down and lifted

my hands. My palms and fingernails were caked in the red dirt of Tenebris, and I slapped them against each other to shift it. When it didn't work, I rubbed my hands roughly and frantically against my jeans, but all that did was add red smudges to my clothes. I couldn't rid myself of Tenebris from my skin, nor my being, and when I took a breath to steady myself, it shuddered in and out of my lungs. The air was crisp and thick, and I squeezed my eyes shut again to remind myself I was on Earth. I hadn't realized until I sat and pressed my palms to the floor that I had feared Earth would cease to exist when the Balance shifted. The fear lingered, and a sob jerked out of me as I tried again to wipe the dirt from my hands.

It may as well be blood, and I didn't want to look at it.

A thumb wiped away a stray tear as it escaped and ran down my cheek, and the moisture smeared the dirt on my face farther. When a hand gently cupped my chin and tilted my head up, I gazed into the blue eyes of a stranger.

Not a stranger.

My chest felt as though it were caving in on itself, and I took sharp and urgent breaths.

"Shhh, Ana, please calm down."

I knew those eyes and that voice, but they'd been buried deep inside my memories.

Was this real?

"Dad?" I whispered, and the tears escaped in earnest, leaving trails and creating a mosaic of dust against my skin as each one fought its way through the grime. I cleared my throat, and the sound ended with a hiccup. "Roger," I stated, and his jaw clenched.

He nodded, and his emotions bubbled up through his body

and escaped from his eyes, surrounded by fine wrinkles of time but kept youthful by his Lucidian genes. My lip trembled as I looked over his shoulder and spotted John.

Uncle John.

I reached out a hand to him, but curled my fingers in before I fully extended. John took my hand anyway, and squeezed it gently, appearing on the verge of tears as his beard twitched, but he stubbornly held his emotions back. Ripples came through the air, though, slowly and hesitantly, due to either my powers fading or the beginnings of the Shift, as though the emotions themselves were hesitating because they had nowhere to go.

Letting my fingers slide from John's grip, I dropped my hand back to my lap. Roger remained kneeling as I leaned against a display case in the small boutique shop they had carried me into. I stared hard at Roger, and my lips pressed firmly together as I tried to hold back the flood that threatened to overwhelm me. A few tears came through, and when he reached up to brush them away again, I swiped his hand away. Hurt bloomed in his eyes, followed by understanding. I felt I should be angry, but couldn't find the will to draw the emotion forth.

In the past, I'd run through my mind a thousand times what I'd say if or when I ever found my father. A thousand different scenarios had been acted out in my mind before and after discovering the truth about my parentage. Some were happy prospects where we embraced and connected as if no time had passed, and the hurt from the past was nothing more than a discarded memory. Others were fantasies of me shouting at him, verbally releasing all my rage and betrayal. Making sure he sat there and absorbed it all, knowing he could not only hear the words, but *feel* my pain.

On top of these ideas now sat so many additional questions, and I had no idea where to start.

Why did he come back?

Why now?

How did he find me?

Why did he leave me alone in a world where I belonged nowhere?

Mostly... *why?*

Dad, where were you when I needed you?

My lip trembled with the break in my willpower. I wanted to hate him, to *loathe* him. I wanted him to feel a fraction of the pain I'd felt. Every thought blurred into a confused mess in my head.

If you were there, would Mom have not been where she was? Would she still be alive?

With a wail that held all the words I couldn't find and had no energy to say, I threw myself into Roger's arms. His reaction was instant and unhindered, and he held me with untamed strength, as though trying to hug away all the years of pain and torment he blamed himself for as much as I blamed him.

Would things have been different if he had taken me home to Lucidis?

Did any of it even matter now?

I squeezed my arms around his shoulders and buried what remained of my senses into him. His powers had faded over the years, until they were almost nonexistent, but there were flickers there. Brighter and with hints of help, as though he'd used John to reenergize himself. Or they'd used each other. I imagine that's how they'd found me.

I wanted to know if John had punched Roger in the nose

the moment he'd seen him. It seemed unlikely, but the image still pulled a reluctant and single watery chuckle from my lips. Roger squeezed me harder, and I let him. When John's hand landed on my shoulder and squeezed slightly, I flinched before I relaxed into his touch. The energy flow between us increased, and I didn't think I could fight it even if I wanted to.

Physically, I started to feel better, but with increased strength, the ache in my chest only got larger, as though my weakness was holding me back from the full realization of what had happened.

Of what I'd done.

"I'm so glad you're safe, angel," John whispered, a slight crack to his voice he couldn't hide. "We didn't know how long we had to find you before you became unreachable."

I flinched again as there was an explosion from outside. Within seconds, a gateway opened and closed, and the force set off car alarms and enticed screams from people in the area before they ran for safety.

With it, the moment shattered, and I pulled away from Roger.

He let me go reluctantly and held my shoulders until I shrugged away his touch. I used the energy they'd given me to build a wall around myself, and as my initial reaction to seeing my Dad and my weakness of nostalgia passed, I steeled myself. No doubt sensing the change in me, Roger gently brushed my moonstone necklace my mother had given me.

That *he'd* given *her*.

I pushed his hand away slowly and with a delicate touch of my fingers, but it was a deliberate move. "Don't. That was my mother's."

"I know, I gave it to her."

I shook my head. "It was my mother's."

The silence stretched out between us, then, "Ana..."

I raised my eyes to his. "Did you know they killed her?"

"Who?"

"The Tenebrians. They killed Mom. They made a man crash his car into her. They took her from me." I glanced outside again as footsteps pounded as a group of people ran past the window, before I returned my gaze to my hands. "They took everything from me."

Roger struggled with the information, and I felt him trying to hide his struggle from me. But I wanted him to feel it. He wasn't there when she died, and I had no one to grieve with. After a beat, he said, "I didn't know that."

"I hope the Shift kills them all," I muttered, almost to myself.

"Ana—"

"You left me all alone," I spat out, looking up at him. "You left *us.*" The words died into a whisper as the accusation flashed in my eyes. "Didn't you love her? Didn't you love *me?*"

"I did love you, Ana, and I love you still, and I love Bronte even though she is gone. I have so much love it hurts."

"But—"

"Ana, Anahera." Roger took my hands in his, and he sighed as I tried to pull my hands from his grip. His fingers tightened around mine, and I glared at him as I stopped resisting. "You were named because you were my angel, *our* angel." His lip lifted into a slight smirk before it dropped. "I can almost see you trying to resist the urge to roll your eyes, it's corny, I know, but Bronte loved corny." My eyes narrowed, and he sighed again. "You were a sign of a fresh start I didn't know was possible." He opened and closed his mouth several times. "I've spent years—decades—thinking about what I would say to you, about how I would even try to find the words to explain what needed to be said." Roger watched my eyes. "Your eyes are exactly like Bronte's..." his chuckle was hollow, "and it's like you're both looking at me right now and demanding answers for my actions."

"So," I snapped. "Give us the answers."

"As you grew, it became evident that my presence alone brought out your Guardian side. I wanted you to grow up as a human. Not because I was or am ashamed of what I am, but because I wanted you to grow with the love I'd only just begun to feel for myself."

He still hadn't let go of my hands, but finally relented when I tugged harder, and I brushed my hands on my jeans as if trying to rid myself of the contact. "Why didn't you come back when Mom died?"

Tears swam in his eyes, and the hints of anger I didn't have the energy to express flickered to life again. "I didn't know if you would forgive me for not being there. Every day I stayed away made it harder to come back. I didn't think you would let me, or even want me to explain—"

"You didn't even give me a *chance*!" I yelled, and allowed my gaze to drift out the window as another Gateway snapped open and shut, and a small group of people ran across the street as the ground trembled. "Maybe things could have been different," I whispered.

"I'm sorry—"

"You're a coward."

Roger waited until I met his eyes before saying, "Yes."

I scoffed and looked down again to trace lines in the dirt on my jeans. Emotion bubbled inside me, and I didn't want to feel it. I didn't want to feel *any* of it. I wanted to yell *How dare you?* But I wouldn't be telling him anything he didn't already know.

But it *hurt*. All of it hurt.

"There are not enough words, or time in the world, to tell you how sorry I am, Ana. I was, and still am, learning to be human. I'm in a world I think I understand so well, and then humans show me something else that surprises me. I'm far from perfect, but I never stopped loving you or your mother." His eyes pleaded with mine. "Please, forgive me."

An earthy sob wrenched from my throat, and when I tried to hide the outburst, another crept up and burst forth. Roger watched the strain in my face before I crumpled and turned away from him. "I needed you."

"I know, I know you did, and I'm so sorry. I thought I was doing the right thing."

Roger reached out to me, and I tilted where I sat and allowed myself to be drawn into another hug. He did it hesitantly, ready for me to pull away at any moment. When I didn't, he held me against him, my small frame against his chest. Cautiously, I lowered the block between us and felt Roger's essence, and he experienced my energies as they flowed through me. All my guilt mingled with his and crashed over us in waves.

Maybe in a small way, we began to heal.

Maybe.

I sniffled, pulled away, and again, Roger's arms only unwrapped from me hesitantly. "What now?" I asked.

"We stop this," John said from where he faced toward the window, the fear in his eyes betrayed his usual calm demeanor.

"How?" I asked, tears blurring my vision as my voice broke again. "I've done so much damage."

"It's not your fault, Ana. It was the Tenebrians."

"It *is* my fault. They couldn't have done this without me."

"They would have, eventually."

"You don't know that."

John sighed. "There's still time to make this right."

Roger took my hand and pulled my arm gently as he stood. "Let's go."

I resisted his pull as the urge to sink down and wait for death flooded me again, and I allowed my body to become a dead weight. I didn't want to move from this spot. Roger looked at me, probably seeing a broken shell of the daughter he had left behind. "Ana, come with me."

I lifted my eyes to his. "*If I want to live*?" I whispered.

"Just come." Roger's mouth twitched as I let him pull me to my feet. When we were face to face, he touched my cheek. "You're still in there somewhere, aren't you?"

I shook my head, regretting the urge to quote *The Terminator* I hadn't been able to squash down quickly enough. Even with resignation bearing down upon me from all sides, old habits die hard. I could see the hope in Roger's eyes as he looked at me, as though my humor was a sign that I was whoever he remembered I was, or who he wanted me to be. But it was nothing more than autopilot, a memory of the Ana who had existed before this, before I was taken by the Tenebrians and flicked the switch that kick-started the end of the world.

That Ana didn't exist anymore. She was still in Tenebris, lying in the dirt.

Roger's hope was short-lived, and I could almost see his heart break when whatever he thought he saw in me vanished, and was replaced by a dark cloud.

Hopelessness.

He searched my eyes for a sign I was fighting the fog that had built around me, and when he saw none, he sighed, squeezed my hand, and led me out of the shop.

As I looked around the street, it was almost empty of the vibrant human life that usually littered the city. The only people in sight fled for their safety, and the fog around me increased.

I didn't see how we could fix what I'd done.

It was over.

Chapter Three

Cael

Until today, I'd never felt unsafe in Lucidis. But the knowledge that this was my *home* mingled with the fear, and I rubbed my arm as if that could take away the uncomfortable crawling of unease.

I lifted my hands and tried again, but the failed Gateways sparked one after another as they fell from my fingertips in a shower of glowing dust. The fabric between the realms was no longer still, and as it was in constant motion, I couldn't maintain grip long enough to open a way through. Guardians had attempted to link together to focus our power. Still, even that hadn't resulted in an accurate Gateway, and most had given up and jumped through to Earth in the spontaneous Gateways.

They could help from wherever they ended up on Earth.

But I didn't want to be *anywhere* on Earth. I needed to be near where Ana was taken.

As my frustration grew, whatever little accuracy I'd had wavered further, and after yet another attempt which left my fingers burning, I roared and punched a nearby tree to release some of the rage before it overtook me. The bark of the tree cracked before bits fell to the ground. I stared at them with my shoulders heaving and closed my eyes as I heard yet another Gateway fizzle out as Samael continued to try.

Throwing my arms up, I recommenced my earlier pacing and rubbed my temples.

The Reflections had vanished when the Shift began and blinked out of existence. In turn, the entire feel of the realm had changed. Positive energies were no longer feeding into and out of Lucidis as the cycle was broken. Lucidis became earthlier and darker in its feel, and everywhere I looked, it was as though I was trying to see through a haze of dust caught in sunlight. The constant push and pull between positive and negative no longer only affected Earth as the world's energies moved freely between the realms. Mid-step, I found myself slapped with a wall of negative energy and the hot air of Tenebris, which broke and dissipated as quickly as it had stopped me in my tracks.

If the Shift were completed, there would be no difference between the realms, and they would all become one world. My home, and everyone else's as we knew it, would cease to exist.

"Dad," Samael said, and I stilled, closed my eyes, and I willed my emotions under control. Samael had been trying to reason with me, but I'd been stuck in a spiral since seeing Ana through the Porthole from Tenebris. The rush of panic and rage only increased with every unsuccessful Gateway, and several times I'd lashed out at Samael the moment he spoke. I looked at him and saw the muscles in his cheeks tense as he grounded himself. I closed my eyes for a moment longer. Samael was maintaining control. I needed to try harder. "Dad," he started again, "Why don't we take one of the open Gateways to Earth and go from there?"

"Because I don't know if I can *find* her from Earth! Because *those* Gateways..." I indicated the ones that continued to open and close in random intervals, "... are unpredictable and unstable. What if we end up stuck on Earth?"

"But what if we try to redirect one that's already open? We could at least have a chance of getting close."

My lip lifted into a snarl. "You don't know what you're talking about," I shouted.

Samael rounded on me and shoved me hard in the shoulder with his palm. "And neither do *you.*" When rage contorted my features, Samael held his hands up, but his expression remained hard. He continued gently, "This is new territory for all of us. I know you're desperate to get to Mother, I am too, but your way is *not working,* and you're wasting time." Samael reached out and grabbed my wrist before I started pacing again. Before I could stop him, he shared his calming influences through the skin-on-skin contact. "Can we just try it my way? Please."

It felt selfish to take energy from my son when we didn't know when we'd be able to replenish our powers, or what effect the Shift would have on them, but greedily, I took what he offered. My blood changed from a boil to a simmer, and I pulled in a shuddering breath. "What if it doesn't work?" I whispered, and Samael tilted his head with concern as though the broken quiet of my voice was more devastating than the uproar.

"We'll find a way and won't give up." Samael sighed and looked across the now near-empty community. He'd already sent Sasha and the others through to Earth as he feared for the humans. With the Tenebrians on the loose without consequence, he wanted as much backup as he could arrange to be there for them.

He'd chosen his duty to watch over the humans first, and I sagged under the weight of my shortfalls. Of course, he wanted Ana safe, too, but he hadn't forgotten everything else. The Gateway Sasha had disappeared through *seemed* as though it might lead them to the correct city. But it wasn't close enough to where Ana was taken, and I'd refused to go with them.

I regretted it now.

Keeping my head down, I nodded as I accepted the clothes Samael handed me, and once I was dressed, we waited for a Gateway to appear. We didn't have to wait long, and sprinted six feet to the left when one burst into existence, its light bright and blinding. But its outline wavered and disappeared before we could refocus its energies.

After this happened for the fourth time, my grip on what was left of my control was a barely-there thread that threatened to snap at any moment. To my right, I sensed Samael centering himself again, rather than sinking into a pit of self-loathing and anger, and I closed my eyes and tried to do the same. The sun wasn't as bright, the air was not as clear, and I could no longer rely on the healing energies of my home realm to bring me back into line. I needed to search for them. After pulling from deep within myself, I opened my eyes and held my hand out again. Samael clasped his palm in mine, and we allowed a free flow of our energy between us in preparation for the next Gateway.

One appeared, and Samael and I spun around in unison to face it. Immediately, we put our free hands out and focused on reinforcing the Gateway. It held, but I dared not breathe a sigh of relief, and barely dared to breathe at all. Shifting our focus, we released our clasped hands, and Samael focused his power on keeping the Gateway open, while I adjusted its position.

The sense of Ana's imprint passed through me like a ghost, and I cried out. Samael released a grunt, and I pulled myself together and focused, shifting the location back until I felt her again.

"Dad..." Samael warned. The energy of the Gateway began to fade, and Samael planted his feet in the grass, desperately trying to earth himself in the realm and draw from whatever dwindling power was left.

"I've almost got her," I said through gritted teeth. Each time I got close, there would be another shift in the air, and the location would be pushed violently to the side, sometimes only by a mile, sometimes by several.

"Dad!" Samael cried out.

"Almost."

"Dad, now!" Samael reached out and grabbed the collar of my shirt before he tugged and shoved me hard through the Gateway. He flung himself in after me and hastily changed to his human form before we crashed onto the road as the Gateway closed with force. The aftershock knocked Samael aside, and he dropped to one knee, and I stumbled in my steps but managed to stay upright. There were several screams from around us before humans fled the area, and I winced, not wishing to cause them any more fear than they were already feeling.

Brushing himself off, Samael stood and choked out a gasp when he looked up at me. "*Dad,*" he whispered urgently as I straightened, and grabbed me by the elbow before he dragged me off the street behind a nearby tree line. I followed with uncertain steps, and only when I caught a glance at my skin did I relent to his insistent tugging and understand why Samael forced me to hide. Although I had no doubt humans had now seen Guardians, even if they didn't understand what they were, I didn't want to cause any additional alarm or pain if I could avoid it.

My fingertips were human, but my skin maintained the blue glow, and my Guardian form held strong on the back of my hands and lower arms. I lifted my hands to my face and hissed as I felt the rough texture of my skin. "Fuck," I muttered. I hated to admit weakness, but I was beyond compromised. When it came to Ana, I could be more animal than human or Guardian. My thoughts were engaged only with her, and I hadn't managed to complete my change into my human form. Whether that was the fault of the Shift or my weakness, I didn't care to look into it further.

My body resisted as I forced the change to complete, but once there, I used both hands to tuck my hair behind my ears and strode purposefully back onto the street. The road was clear of humans. Several cars had been abandoned as people had run from the quakes and rips in the air, and perhaps Tenebrians. What had they seen? Humans couldn't see Gateways, but if Guardians had emerged from them, either Lucidian or Tenebrian, it would be terrifying for them. But all the rules seemed to have changed, and maybe humans *could* see Gateways now as we did.

All this fear would do nothing to help us repair this damage, and would only push the Shift further and faster. I hoped we could salvage the situation, but that hope dwindled with each slap in the face by the reality of what was happening.

I closed my eyes as my body hummed in rebellion against the lack of energy and essence to draw from. However much time I thought we might have had, it was less. I hated to think of what the Tenebrians had already gotten up to, even in this short time, and how much more damage they could do.

Kneeling, I placed a palm on the road and used the earth itself to assist me in tracking Ana's essence. I was positive I'd felt her imprint while working on the Gateway, and although the imprint was a shadow of its previous strength, it was her. She *must* be on Earth. Somehow, she'd escaped Tenebris. Otherwise, I wouldn't have been able to sense her from Lucidis at all.

I could only hope I'd worked quickly enough to re-center the Gateway.

Samael stood, closed his eyes, and raised his hands to feel the air, seeking a trace of her. "Dad, I can feel her."

My brows furrowed as I nodded. "Me too."

She was close.

"Ana!" I called out as I stood.

There was no verbal response, but something flickered in my chest as her imprint called to mine. I followed the feeling, and my heart pounded as we moved from walking to running when the sense increased in intensity. My hands clenched as though I could grasp onto Ana through the air and pull her closer to me.

"*Ana,*" My voice cracked with strain when I saw her. She whirled around, still covered in the red dust of Tenebris except for the tracks made through the dirt from her tears. John was next to her, but I had no idea who the other man with her was. He looked around the same age as John, tall and svelte but with recognizable muscle definition, striking blue eyes, and chestnut brown hair in what would have been a businesslike cut, had it not been ruffled with stress and sweat.

I didn't care who he was because my feet carried me toward Ana as she turned and ran for me. A sob I refused to let loose made my chest cave as I felt her energy drain from the physical exertion of reaching me. Ana's knees buckled as she got closer, and she groaned and twisted her body to keep moving. I sprinted to meet her, Samael right behind me.

"*Ca—,*" she cried out for me, and her voice cut out before she could finish my name or call for Samael. Her eyes darted to his before falling back on mine, and her face screwed up with emotion. Her chest heaved as though she simply didn't have the energy left to cry.

When I reached her, Ana's legs gave out, and I caught her before she collapsed. Enveloping her in my arms, I spun her around in a half-circle to release the momentum from her fall. Lowering us both gently to the road, I held onto her like I never wanted to let her go again.

I should never have let her go before.

Her entire body trembled as she collapsed into my arms, weak and drowning in pain. Samael came up behind where I knelt and wrapped his arms around us as we stilled. Ana snapped, and the cry that escaped her was a sorrowful howl that encased Samael and me in the dome of her pain as we held her. But we didn't let go, and instead worked to fill her with calm and positive energy, whatever we could spare, to re-energize her as best we could while trying to hold ourselves together as her pain radiated out across the city.

She was still so powerful.

"I'm sorry," she cried, feeding off our energies for a few minutes before she closed the connection and refused our help. "I'm sorry. I'm so sorry."

I shook my head and held her tighter, my lips pressed firmly into a thin line. I didn't trust myself to hold it together if I were to speak.

I thought I'd lost her, *again,* and my heart couldn't take it.

There was the slightest flicker of hope from within Ana in our embrace.

But then it was gone.

Her breathing was steady and even, and I wondered if she'd fallen asleep. Despite the present dangers and the work to be done, I was hesitant to move, and Samael seemed to be of the same mindset. Although I could feel him shifting as he kept a lookout, he didn't release his arms from around us. The voices, which were nothing more than droning sounds, snatched enough of my concentration for me to turn my head slightly, where my chin rested on Ana's head.

The drone of the radio from the café next to us drifted out the open door, and my chest squeezed as the reporter tried to hastily summarize all the events and disasters occurring across the globe. Earthquakes, stirrings of what could be a pending tsunami off the coast, and an avalanche were all listed by the breathy reporter, and even as they maintained their professional voice, it was clear they were trying to hold themselves together.

Thousands were dead already. A dam has broken and flooded several small towns, which had no hope of evacuation. Two bridges had collapsed, sending hundreds of cars into churning water.

"Oh, God," Ana croaked out, and I drew my arms around her as regret swirled inside me. I didn't know she was listening. "What have I done?"

Before I could even attempt a response while the pain and death of thousands swirled around my mind, John and the stranger approached. Samael and I didn't let go of Ana, though my arms continued to tremble. Not from any physical effort, but the willpower it took me not to whisk her away somewhere safe and keep her there forever.

But where was safe now?

John placed a hand on my shoulder, and I looked up at him before we nodded silently to each other. John then brushed Ana's hair gently before he moved to the side, and the stranger came closer. I moved to my feet and brought Ana with me, her arms still wrapped around my waist and mine around her body. Samael watched the stranger cautiously, as did I, and almost subconsciously, I shifted Ana from view as he drew near. A sad smile played across the man's face at the display of protective instinct, and as he approached me, he held out his hand.

Reluctantly, I released an arm from around Ana to take it. "Cael."

"Roger..." he paused. "I'm Ana's father."

At this, I increased my grip on Roger's hand, not realizing I had done it. But when the change became a conscious effort, I didn't release my hold and gripped harder than necessary, causing Roger to grunt, but he didn't pull away. He knew what I was about to do and let me flow my senses through the physical contact. I felt Roger's being, learnt about who he was, and searched for any hint of intended betrayal. If there were something he was hiding, something about him that couldn't be trusted, I would find it.

Samael slid his hand on top of mine and Roger's, still clasped tightly. The energy transfer between the three of us pulsed around our skin and distorted the image of our hands. Roger took the opportunity to recharge his powers, and he watched my face as I arched a brow, but I allowed it. The exchange benefited us all, and the longer I could read the man in front of me, the better.

Sorrow, guilt, wistfulness.

Love.

Withdrawing my hand, I returned my arm to where it belonged—around Ana.

"I can only assume that because I'm not face down on the asphalt, you accepted what you sensed of me."

I grunted. "How did you save her?"

Roger glanced at John. "A bit of teamwork, moonstone, and a lot of determination and dumb luck." He looked at Ana, who had her face nuzzled into my chest. "And enough hope and love to tie it all together."

My eyes narrowed. "Honestly, that sounds rehearsed."

"Maybe just in my head while I was walking toward you." Roger smiled sadly.

John cleared his throat. "We need to work on fixing this."

Ana sobbed quietly into my chest again, but said nothing, and I squeezed her tighter against me as I nodded at John.

"We have friends here," Samael said, and answering my questioning look, he added, "You know I told them to come here to protect any humans that could get caught in the crossfire, I don't know where exactly, but they're close enough for me to feel them. So, they either landed here or have since made their way." He lifted a shoulder, and I was flooded again with gratitude for my son and his ability to balance his duty as a Guardian and his desire to protect his family.

Samael may be part human, but it seemed he was more Guardian than I.

"Let's find them, then," Roger said. "I might have some

ideas of where we can go from here, but let's get everyone we can together first." He looked at Ana, and his arm twitched as though he was going to reach out to her, but thought the better of it. "Ana, my angel... We'll need your help."

Ana tore herself away from me, but I kept my arm possessively around her waist and tightened it as she twisted so her hips fit snugly against me. Even as she stared at her father, she leaned back against me, and I relished the contact.

Somewhere inside her was the Ana I knew I loved.

She needed saving as much as everyone else did.

Samael also hadn't moved far from her side, as if we could shield her from the dangers of the outside world simply by staying close.

"I can't help," she said as her fingers squeezed my arm where it was wrapped around her stomach. "I'll only make things worse."

Roger touched her shoulder, and his eyes darted to my arm when I tensed protectively around her. "You *can* help. You have strength and power within you that can reverse this."

Ana shook her head and looked at the ground.

Samael stepped in. "Let's find the others."

Roger opened his mouth, noted my scowl and Ana's downturned expression, and relented as he nodded. He continued to look at Ana, as if he could will her to lift her head and meet his eyes again. But she remained staring determinedly at the ground, and Roger squeezed her shoulder lightly before we all came together, and combined our powers to trace the others.

Chapter Four

Esco

Everything was too much.

I was needed everywhere, all at once.

Once on Earth, Sasha and I had decided to part ways and help as many as we could, as quickly as we could. But I found myself drawn from one area to another, helping people, and then, as soon as I had arrived, being tugged somewhere else. There were so many humans who needed help, and I could mostly keep control of myself.

But hopelessness lingered in the back of my mind and the pit of my stomach.

We didn't have much of a plan—there *was* no plan for this—so we did the best we could. A brief discussion with Monia before we came to Earth had concluded that humans were safer in groups. Whatever lingering positive energy they could muster would, in theory, create a bubble around them and keep them safer for longer.

The bigger the group, the safer they were.

For how long, though, we had no way of knowing.

But moving through the city was dangerous. Tenebrians ran

wild, and I'd sensed more than one hiding in parklands and buildings. As though this were all a big game to them, and not the end-of-the-world disaster that could destroy us all.

I took a heavy breath and tried once again to explain the situation to the police officers. I knew enough about human culture to come here, but their distrust of me was clear, as I had been unable to shift into my human form.

If not through their imprint, then through their expressions.

And the guns they had pointed at me.

"I'm here to help," I said, calming my voice. I was hesitant to use my influence. Would my powers be the same now that the Shift had begun? "Please. We need to gather people in groups."

The officer closest to me lifted his hand from his weapon long enough to wipe the sweat from his forehead before his trembling fingers landed back upon the gun he held in front of him.

I'd come in through a side entrance, which apparently, I wasn't meant to do. The officers were immediately on alert, but were stunned enough by my appearance to pause after they drew their weapons. They hadn't shouted, nor set off any alarm, and I hadn't yet decided if I should draw attention to myself or try to get these three on board first.

No one else had seen me, and I was stuck here with three humans with fear practically dripping from them when all I wanted to do was help.

I wished Cael were here. He would know what to do, and he understood humans in a way I never did.

A sense of inferiority washed over me, and I rolled my shoulders as if that could rid me of the feeling. *Feeling* things was strange, and while I'd experienced flickers inside me over the years, in Lucidis, I'd been able to ignore them.

Until things started changing—Sasha, Cael, and then Ana.

I'd begun to question everything.

"Please calm down. I can tell you all what is happening and how we can help."

One of the officers lowered his weapon slightly and straightened it only when the third glared at him. He stared at her, uncertainty etched into his features. "Something weird is going on, Mel. Perhaps we should listen to her?"

Mel's gun lowered before she shook her head and re-aimed, and I tensed again.

Of course, they were frightened, but this was something else. The Shift in the Balance also threw human emotions and perceptions off—they all felt something was *wrong* without being able to explain it. They couldn't find a way to deal with the fear that flooded them at my appearance, so we stood frozen while I waited and hoped they managed to control themselves without me attempting to influence them.

I didn't know how much power I had on Earth, nor how long it would last.

A human burst into the station, and we all turned as he stumbled and barely regained his footing before he scrambled across the floor toward the counter.

"Can I help you, sir? Are you okay?" the officer at the desk asked, standing from her chair.

I was mostly obscured from his view, and was thankful for that. The man lifted his shirt and wiped his brow before letting it drop, and didn't bother tucking it in again. He leaned heavily against the counter and ran his fingers through his hair. "I swear I'm not crazy..." he said as he opened his hands and looked pleadingly at the officer. "... But I just saw a demon outside my office."

"A demon?"

He scrunched his face up at the skepticism in her voice.

"I know how crazy it sounds, believe me. But it just... stepped out of thin air and onto the street. It looked like it was made of embers and ashes. I've never seen anything like it."

"Where was this?" Her eyebrow remained perpetually arched.

"One block over. When it saw me, it gave chase. I don't know if it followed me all the way here." He looked over his shoulder.

My brow furrowed, and I moved to step forward. The officers who held me at gunpoint shifted and offered grunts of warning, but said nothing.

"Please," I said again, pressing the urgency. "This is the danger I warned you of. The demon he speaks of is a Tenebrian, and I'm here to stop them."

"Aside from the blue skin, she could be a demon," one muttered.

"Let me pass," I hissed out, and pushed some influence into my voice.

Their guns lowered slightly, but not enough.

The officer at the counter leaned to the side and looked out the glass doors to the seemingly empty street. The man slapped his palms against the counter. "*Don't* you tell me there's nothing! You've seen all the shit on the news, let alone whatever-the-fuck is going on in this very city. Blue alien things walking around, earthquakes, and you're *skeptical* about a demon?"

Her eyebrow remained arched, and slowly she lifted a form

from under the counter without breaking eye contact. "If you'll complete this, sir, I'll report it for you."

Gavin swept the form off the counter. "I don't want to fill out any *goddamn paperwork.*"

"Sir, you need to remain calm."

"Why don't you go outside and take a look?" he drawled, and after a moment, she nodded.

"Tina, wait!" One of the officers near me broke from his stupor, and I released a long sigh. As he lowered his gun, and the two followed suit, I nodded gently at them, but didn't move yet. He hurried past me and placed a hand on Tina's shoulder. "He's telling the truth, I think."

"You're messing with me, right? Is this some haze-the-rookie thing?"

"No, no. Listen..."

He didn't seem to be able to find the words, and in the ensuing silence, when Tina again looked out past the man's shoulder into the street, I took the opportunity to move forward into the foyer. Tina screamed and scrambled back from me, and the man shouted something and bolted out the door. I hissed through my teeth and held my hands up in an attempt to look non-threatening.

"I'm here to help. The demon that man saw is a Tenebrian. I'm trying to stop them."

"What in the good goddamn hell is a Telebrian?" Tina shouted.

Before I could explain further, a shriek from outside made all the officers flinch, and I spun on my heel. A Tenebrian chuckled as it held the man who'd run from the station by the throat. I rushed toward the Tenebrian, and when he saw me out of the corner of his eye, he gripped the man's neck and twisted. His gasps for breath cut off sharply at the snap of his neck, and I cried out in rage as I tackled the Tenebrian. The man's limp body fell to the ground, and the Tenebrian and I thrashed around in a mess of claws and teeth.

His fangs closed around my shoulder, and I cried out as I gripped the quills on the back of his neck and tugged *hard.* He came away from me with a snarl, landed a foot in my stomach, and bolted as I pushed myself to my feet. The officers rushed out into the street, but didn't come any closer to me.

"Are you okay?" one called.

I nodded even as I sucked a breath in when the air stung the wound on my shoulder. "Yes." When I pulled myself to my full height, I took a moment to survey the street for other Tenebrians, and finding none, I faced the officers. "Are you ready to listen to me now?"

"Yes, ma'am... whatever you are," Tina squeaked out.

I sighed. "Gather the others, and I'll explain what to do."

They scurried back into the building, and I followed at a slower pace. Stopping, I turned and bent over the man's body. He was dead, and I sighed again and lifted his body before I placed it gently on a nearby bench and laid his hands flat on his chest. When I turned, Tina watched me through the glass doors, and she moved away quickly when my gaze landed on hers.

Gather humans together.

Don't trust the red creatures.

Don't let yourself lose hope.

Think happy thoughts.

It wasn't much of a plan, but it was all we had.

"I know it is scary, but you must trust me." I raised my hands in what I hoped was a calming gesture, forcing influence into my voice.

After leaving the police station, I crossed the city blocks, gathering any humans I could get close enough to talk to. Some I sent back to the station, but when it became clear the distance they'd have to cross to safety alone would be perilous, I kept them with me.

We wandered the streets looking for other stray humans, our numbers increased to around forty, not including me. Some of the humans I'd found huddled behind the windows of their apartments, and I noticed them only as they looked out in terror as the world shifted and changed before their eyes. Sometimes I sensed humans, but not always. However, as the hours had passed, I'd been able to hone my senses to a sharper point. Certainly not as accurate as before the Shift began, but it was still helpful. It used to be a matter of using the air itself, but now it was the lines *between* the air I used—the cracks between the realms that created an invisible cobweb I could mentally navigate.

I wondered how Sasha was doing with her task of gathering humans into groups. Sasha had also opted for the city, while other Guardians had tried to land themselves in more rural areas. I imagined humans in suburban and rural areas would be in their homes, and I hoped they had the sense to stay there. While physical walls didn't stop Gateways from forming, they were more likely to form in open areas. But I feared the destruction would escalate as the Balance continued shifting. Soon, being indoors would be no safer than standing in the middle of the road.

Safety against the Tenebrian attacks was the primary goal. Having the humans' energy together could create a bubble of stability, which would help protect them from minor shifts, but it might also call Tenebrians to them.

However, nothing would protect them once the Shift was completed.

When three Lucidians I didn't know walked past, we shared a glance, telling each other all we needed to know without a word. They recognized my emotional imprint, noticed the group with me, and moved on to seek others in need of help.

But their appearance startled the already frightened group.

Convincing them to come with me had been tough, and convincing them to *stay* with me was an ongoing battle. If they thought they were being cornered or outnumbered, they'd scatter again and be at the mercy of Tenebrians.

"I saw more those things earlier," a young man, no older than seventeen, cried out. "They were chasing people and..." he swallowed. "... Laughing."

My lips pulled into a thin line. "Some of them can be dangerous. Were the laughing creatures orange or blue?"

"Orange, reddish..."

"The blue ones are here to help you. Like me." There was general murmuring amongst the group, and they fell farther behind me a few steps. I sighed and dropped my chin to my chest.

"How can you know that for sure?" a woman asked.

I stopped and turned to find the group of humans eight feet behind me, huddled together. "I'm doing the best I can to help. Things are happening beyond your understanding, and you must realize how difficult it would be for us to gain your trust." They stared at me warily, and I reached out a hand. "I promise I won't hurt you."

The humans eyed me, and a teenage girl made a move as though she were going to reach forward and take my hand, but an older gentleman, presumably her father, grabbed her shoulder and stopped her.

With a wave of my hand, I indicated the Guardians who had walked past earlier, the slight blue glow to their skin still visible as they moved down the city streets. "They could have hurt you, or chased you, but they didn't. They're looking for people who need help."

As the group continued to argue and mutter uncertainties, I contemplated attempting to shift into my human form. But I quickly dismissed the idea, recognizing it would make them more terrified than they already were.

The idea of a threat hiding beneath the skin of every human they encountered would do nothing to abate their fear.

There was silence for a moment, and some continued to look at me warily, but I relished the few who analyzed me with a newfound curiosity.

Eventually, a woman said quietly, "Maybe we just have to trust *someone.*"

"Listen, lady," the teenager's father began as he wrapped an arm around her shoulders. "No offense to this blue thing here, but with whatever the hell is going on, I think the only ones I'll trust are other people."

I arched a brow as he hunched his shoulders slightly after he'd finished speaking, as if he expected retaliation. "I won't hurt you," I responded, and was thankful for how his posture relaxed—a small sign there was hope the humans could trust me yet. I'd expected resistance, but it was frustrating having to explain myself repeatedly when there were so many other humans to consider.

There were so many to save, and not enough time.

"Okay." I flexed the tension from my fingers, but stopped when several of the group eyed my hands wearily. Guardians had no training for this, and it seemed such a glaring error not to prepare us for the chance this might happen, based on the hope it wouldn't. "I'm going to assume that all of you either don't live around here or can no longer access your homes?"

An elderly couple started weeping silently at this, and I pressed my lips together. I'd found them as their townhouse collapsed into one of the cracks in the earth that continued to spread. There were other murmurs around the group, which I accepted as affirmative.

"I need you to find a small café or a shop with not too many large open spaces."

"How do we know we can trust you?"

"Just *listen,*" I said, and the words came out louder and harsher than I'd intended. Immediately, regret bloomed in my chest when the humans flinched away from me. It became harder to keep a steady head. The mixture of being on Earth and the loss of the Balance messed with my being. It had only been hours—what would happen after days? I continued, "Find somewhere, and hide."

"Where are you going?"

My lip twitched as I looked at the woman who'd expressed a desire to have someone to trust. She was middle-aged and dressed formally, but she held the same flicker of fear in her eyes that was everywhere. "I'm going to get help."

A young man stepped forward. "I'll go with you."

I tilted my head and considered. Perhaps having a human would be to my advantage if they could convince other humans to trust me. But he may slow me down. "No," I answered finally.

"But—"

"No, you stay here." My words were forceful this time, dripped with influence, and a flash of white across my eyes that I couldn't contain. He stepped back, his brows knotted together as he raised his hands before him, but said nothing else.

The silence stretched out, and something tingled at the back of my throat until I finally realized what I *should* have said. As I opened my mouth to thank the young man for offering, a Gateway opened yards away and shook the ground, before it slammed shut again. When the orange light and black ink remnants stayed in the air, I stepped toward the group and started hustling them toward a line of shops.

A man lingered toward the back of the group as I guided them, and when I touched his shoulder, he turned his head toward me. "Are you okay?" I asked. I knew what the answer would be—*of course,* he *wasn't* okay, none of them were.

But my brow furrowed when he replied, "Okay."

Through the contact, I attempted a quick read on him. "Are you happy? Sad? Angry? Scared?"

"Okay."

I'd seen this in more than one human, and my concern had

increased with every case I'd encountered. He remained staring at me, and I took his hand and squeezed his fingers, but he didn't react.

Shock? Or something else?

When I searched his essence, what I found didn't make sense. I put it down to the Shift in the Balance—I knew it messed with my powers, maybe it messed with my ability to read as well.

I tried again, but the result was the same.

There was nothing.

I could feel nothing within him—no emotional imprint, and no emotions. He was empty, as though without the Balance, there was nothing for him to exist in harmony with.

Was this the fate of all humans?

I guided him toward another man to help him walk with them. "Go, now, please. Close the blinds and hide. And stay together."

There was hesitation, no doubt about taking instructions from me, but there were enough people in the group who went without further question, and the rest followed. I watched them go until they were inside a boutique café, had drawn the blinds down, and waited for the telltale click of a door lock before I turned and ran down the street.

They didn't quite trust me, and maybe they were so confused and frightened they were willing to cling to any sign of leadership they could find.

It wasn't the bond I'd been hoping for, but if it kept them safe, it was enough.

Chapter Five

Samael

When Dad looked at me, he asked with equal parts hope and shame, "Did you arrange to meet them somewhere?"

I pressed my lips together. "There wasn't the time, Dad, and we couldn't be sure we would even land where we wanted."

Dad dropped his head and pulled his arm tighter around Mother's waist. "I know, son, I'm sorry I didn't do more."

"You were worried about Mother."

His brows pulled together as he shook his head. "Yes, but so were you, and yet you still managed to keep your head straight enough to send your friends to Earth to help. Whereas I..." he trailed off, and the memory of the rage and pain which had radiated from him after he'd seen the vision of Mother in Tenebris seeped into my soul.

"No one is trained for this, Dad. We need to stay focused and find them ourselves." As Dad opened his mouth to answer, I held up my hand. "No more self-deprecating. Be sad-Dad on your own time." I glanced sideways to see the shadow of a grin on Dad's face, and returned the small smile before it dropped. After banding together, the others allowed me to draw on their power to locate my friends, and we'd found the general area, but would need to get closer before we tried again. However, despite Dad praising me for being able to keep my mind on my duty, I silenced him because it wasn't true, not really.

I edged closer to Dad and dropped my voice to a whisper, "I want to get to David."

Dad's jaw dropped as though he were about to protest, and I didn't need him to say anything to know what he was thinking. We had to find a way out of this, and Roger seemed to believe he had a plan, but we needed to find Sasha first and then get somewhere safe. My appreciation of Sasha's control of her power had only grown since I'd discovered she, too, was part human.

Perhaps that would help us when we needed it most.

I understood all the dangers and priorities, but I also couldn't leave David alone and in danger. While dragging a human around could be counterproductive, I knew Dad wouldn't argue the moment his eyes dropped to where Mother was curled up next to him. Her steps were inconsistent and slurred, as though every other step she needed to remind herself to keep moving. Or perhaps it was simply Dad who was dragging her forward. The way she leaned against him, her spine curved as she slumped. It was such a contrast to her usually confident posture.

It was like she had already given up.

Dad would do anything to protect her, as he would have done when he thought her human. He looked up, nodded at me, and gestured down the empty street with his free hand. "Lead the way."

As we continued to walk, John and Roger remained a few

paces behind me and my parents. I wasn't sure whether it was out of respect or for protection, but this was hardly the time to get to know anyone. Roger was my grandfather, and I supposed John was some sort of surrogate Uncle, but all of that would have to wait until we got out of this.

If we could get out of this.

"Where are we going?" Roger asked John.

"To find Samael's partner," John explained.

"A human?"

"Yes."

I didn't turn around, but I could feel Roger's eyes on my back as I led the group through the back streets and tried to avoid the chaos of the main areas. Roger took a few long paces and came to my other side. Dad offered him a glance, but he said nothing before he looked ahead and continued walking.

"You fell in love with a human," Roger offered.

It wasn't a question, but I answered anyway. "Yes." Roger released an amused huff, but he wasn't mocking me, more curious. "Like father, like son, right?" I said.

Roger returned my smile. "Guess it runs in the family."

I recalled what Cascus had revealed to Dad and me about using half-breeds to increase the Guardian population and wondered if Roger or John knew about it. There would be time to ask later, but for now, I focused on each step that took me closer to David.

The group halted as I held up a hand, and Roger's back stiffened. He stood beside me as we strained to hear running footsteps and the unmistakable screeching and chittering of the Guardian's native language. From where we stood, we watched as a small group of Tenebrians bolted across the nearby intersection, followed closely by a group of Lucidians.

One of them stopped, breathing heavily, and her piercing blue quills glittered in the sun. "Are you all right?" she shouted at us, her eyes large with concern.

I held my hands in front of me. I'd almost forgotten we were all in our human form. Raising an arm, I waved. "Sulus, it's me, Samael."

Sulus released a strangled sound between a choke and a cry of relief, and closed the distance between us. I stumbled back a step as she immediately threw her arms around my neck, and I buckled slightly under her, not prepared for the hug. Dad kicked my ankle until I returned the hold, and wrapped my arms around her lower back.

Hugging without the intention of sex was unusual for Guardians, and I'd not known Sulus to express such human-like affection before. She settled into my arms for a moment before she slowly pulled away. "I'm glad you're okay, but I've got to go. Since coming to Earth, these hours have been busy, and I don't feel it will settle any time soon."

I nodded. "Stay safe."

Sulus smiled and touched my arm, gently dragging her fingers down to my hand before she took it and squeezed. "You too." She moved to turn away, then turned back to face me and studied me intently. "You know, I always liked you. But..." Her smile took on a regretful quality as she added, "You have someone else, don't you?"

Emotion rushed into my chest, and I pressed my lips together to keep it inside. Though I didn't doubt, even with the state of the realms and our powers, Sulus would be able to sense it.

Gratitude for her speaking to me so openly.

Happiness for when I thought of David.

Guilt for not noticing sooner, and perhaps for her feeling she couldn't say anything in a world where emotional connection was still condemned.

But I loved David, and there was no one else I wanted to be with.

"Yes," I answered, and squeezed her hand back. "I'm sorry."

She continued smiling at me, her eyes glinting with sorrow and pride. "It's okay, don't be sorry. How were you to know? Guardians don't talk like that..." She paused, the moment heavy with regret. "I'm happy you have someone. You deserve to be loved." She dropped my hand and offered me a smile, heavier with meaning than before. "Keep each other safe," Sulus added, before she turned and ran off in the direction the others had gone.

My chest ached, and I placed a palm over my heart. "Hurts," I muttered.

"Emotions hurt, mate," John added quietly.

"I like the hurt," Cael said as he nudged his elbow into mine. "Reminds me of the good things."

Roger watched the interaction with his eyes slightly narrowed, but a whisper of a grin played on the corner of his mouth. "Well, things certainly have changed in Lucidis."

As we rounded the corner onto David's street, a surge of energy kicked into me as I sensed the edges of David's imprint, and I ran. The journey here had been slower than I'd hoped, as we'd stopped to help several straggling groups of humans and ushered them indoors. While I was thankful we hadn't directly encountered any Tenebrians, it did concern me about where they were and what they might be up to.

I had an idea of what they might be planning, and I scowled at the thought.

Waiting for night.

It sounded ridiculous in its simplicity, but it would work, wouldn't it? The fear the humans had as their world collapsed around them, people died, and strange creatures emerged from rips in the air itself, would only be multiplied tenfold at the idea that the night held monsters.

I hated the thought that had occurred to me, and I hated even more that it was likely to be true. They'd allow us an inch of hope, only to shatter it once the sun lowered and cast the city in darkness.

Jogging up the three small steps to David's door, I knocked rapidly a handful of times and shifted my weight from one foot to another as I waited. The moments passed, and I almost reached up to knock again when I felt David's presence behind the door and sensed his hesitation. Confusion and fear came off him in waves, and my stomach churned at the concoction of emotions.

The emotions we had sensed over and over on the way here.

Emotions that didn't help the delicate state of the Balance as it continued into the Shift.

"David, it's me," I yelled through the barrier between us. The door swung open a moment later, and David grabbed my shirt and embraced me tightly. I took the chance to flood David with calming influences, not considering or caring the drain it might have on me, and as David relaxed into my arms, I held back a sob.

David tensed in my arms, and I pulled back as he stared wide-eyed over my shoulder at the damage in the street. Large cracks crisscrossed across the road, and a light post was on a steep angle as it teetered on the edge of collapse. Most of the buildings were unscathed, though dust shook from the walls with every shake of the earth.

"Where's your roommate, David?" I asked gently, and when he didn't look at me, but continued to stare at the street, I cupped his cheek in my palm. His eyes met mine, and I swallowed back the emotion that welled in my throat at the fear in his eyes. "David," I said again, "Where's your roommate?"

"He's uh... he's..." David swallowed and seemed to take a moment to center himself. "He's at his grandparents' place. Out of town. Jackson is with him."

I nodded, thankful they were safe and hating the selfish thought that bubbled to the surface.

A human we don't need to look after while we look for a way out of this.

"I had no idea..." David shook his head as he surveyed the street. "It's so much worse than I thought."

"You haven't been outside?"

David's eyes met mine. "You told me to stay inside."

I choked back another wave of emotion, unable to find the words. *He trusted me.* Before I could speak, David's gaze had landed on the group of people waiting at the gate, and his brows pulled together. "Is your Mom okay?"

"No really, no."

"Is she injured? Can I help?"

"Listen, I'll explain everything—"

"Samael, what's going on?"

Pulling away from David, I grasped his hands and squeezed them gently when he didn't immediately look at me. "You need to come with us. We're going to try to fix this, but I need to know you're safe."

"Fix this? What? How do you know what's happeni—"

"I promise I'll explain everything when we're somewhere safe, but we must go."

David permitted me to pull him forward out of the house, and I paused as David patted his pockets to check for his keys before he pulled the door closed behind him and locked it. I held myself back from protesting. He needed this sense of normality. He'd need anything he could take to keep him grounded with what he was about to experience.

With the truths I had to tell him.

I could only keep David shielded so much, and things would worsen before they got better.

"My parents," David said, gripping my hand as we descended the path. "I need to get my parents."

My heart clenched, and I looked up to find Dad watching me as I glanced desperately between him and David. Dad seemed to follow my train of thought through my indecision, and his expression hardened as he decided for me.

"Samael, go with David and get his parents, then meet us at John's," he said, and my expression twisted.

"Are you sure?" I asked, and everything I didn't say hung in the air. I had a duty as a Guardian, but how much help would I be if the man I loved suffered?

But Dad understood, of course, he did.

Dad nodded and squeezed Mother next to him. "We'll find Sasha and meet you there as soon as you can." He turned to David and held out his hand. "Cael. I'm Samael's father. I wish we were meeting under different circumstances."

David took his hand, too stunned to shake it, and they stood clasping hands for a moment. "I don't even understand what these circumstances are."

"That's probably for the best. Now go."

Mother's eyes were fixed on me as Dad steered her away, and her face scrunched up as if she were about to cry. She mouthed *I love you,* and went with Dad.

"I love you too, Mom," I said, and watched as they walked away before David gave another insistent squeeze of my hand to bring me back to him.

I pivoted to face David, but before I could speak, David asked again, "Really, though, is she okay?"

"No, but we're working on it. She's not physically hurt, just overwhelmed, scared, and weak." David's brows drew together, and he looked like he was going to push the matter, so I continued before he could, "How far to your parents' place?"

"Walking? About forty minutes, I guess."

"Do you have a car?"

"No, and I doubt public transport is running."

Throwing a glance at the late afternoon sun as it prepared to set on the day, I pressed my lips together. The night would reveal all the secrets it held within its shadows. "We'd better get going, then. I don't think we'll want to be alone when it's dark."

David opened his mouth, probably asking *why,* but he decided he'd rather not know.

David darted through the compact yard toward his parents' front door, passing concrete planters lined with seasonal flowers, his shirt damp with patches of sweat. The afternoon had taken on an unseasonably warm feel, and it was uncomfortable. The air was grimy and stuck to my skin as we moved through it. David had mentioned a prickling sensation under his skin, and I don't think he believed me when I suggested it might be due to the strange weather.

I hated lying to him, but there would be a time to tell him everything, and this wasn't it.

On our way through the city, David had held my hand most of the way, and when I occasionally pulled him to the side and shoved him behind something, or tucked him behind my body, David said nothing. But as always, David watched me as though he were analyzing me, as if he could read my thoughts. He knew I was hiding something, but he also accepted this wasn't the time to talk about it. I did not explain my behavior, and concealing the truth cut almost as deep as lying.

As David stood on his parents' porch, the earth trembled under his feet, and he grabbed the door handle for support as he yelled, "Mom. Dad. Open the door!"

"David?"

David's shoulders dropped with relief at the sound of his mother's voice, distant from one of the back rooms. Her shoes scuffed on the wooden floors as she trotted down the hallway. As she reached the front door, another tremor shook the house, as there was an explosive force from the street. David was shoved forward into the house as the door unlatched, and I gripped the doorframe to steady myself. The wood of the frame cracked under my grip, and I glanced upward at the brick house, closing my eyes against the cascade of dust that fell from the outer wall. David straightened, hugged his mother, and ran his hands over her arms as if to check if she was hurt.

"David," I said as I stepped through the doorway. "Something is going to happen, I can feel it under my skin. We need to get out of here now."

David's mother looked over his shoulder at me and grabbed David's hand. "David..." she whispered, "... is he with you?"

"Mom, this is Samael. Samael, Evelyn." He cut her off before she could speak. "There's no time, Mom. I'll explain later. Where's Dad?"

She spun, her skirt flying around her ankles, and strode back down the hall. David and I followed and ducked every time there was a shudder, and dust dropped from the ceiling. Evelyn called out, "Ian? Ian, we're leaving."

"What?"

"We're leaving. David's taking us to safety."

As we rounded the corner into a second, wider hallway, David's father emerged in the doorway from a room at the far end. David and Ian stared at each other for what felt like an eternity, and every second stretched out as everything left unsaid passed between them. I cast my eyes downward for a moment. I'd never told David I'd witnessed the scene with his parents, how could I? But when I raised my eyes, David's father took me in before his gaze returned to David. His expression softened, and his shoulders slumped as he started twisting his hands in front of him.

"David, I—"

The quake and explosion occurred simultaneously, and threw David and his mother off their feet. I barely managed to steady myself, and my hand slid on the wall before I reached forward with desperation.

"*No!*"

A crack tore its way through the building David had called home, and separated David from his father. The floorboards split, sending splinters flying, and Evelyn screamed, covering her head with her arms as the cracks climbed the wall and spread across the ceiling like spiderwebs. There was a second explosion, and a Gateway materialized behind David's father, shattering the doorway and forcing him forward over the deep crack in the floor.

David and his father shared a moment of pained eye contact.

Then Ian was gone.

"Dad!" David cried, threw himself forward onto his stomach, and crawled to the edge of the fissure which ran through the house. He looked over the verge, and I came up behind him and dropped to my hands and knees, but there was nothing to see. Nothing but sheer blackness from an eternal depth running into the earth itself. "*Dad,*" David screamed into the void. There was no response, not even his echo came back to greet him. He tried again and again, and reached over the edge with one arm as I gripped the back of his collar and dragged him away from the precipice.

"Ian?"

We turned at the whisper of a voice, small and yet filled with all the pain of loss. Evelyn looked at David with wide eyes that swam with tears as the color drained from her face. Staring at the spot where her husband had disappeared, her fingers twitched as if she wanted to reach out, but wasn't sure what good it would do.

"I'm sorry," I said as I turned to David. "I'm so sorry, but we have to go."

"*Ian.*" The pain of Evelyn's cry drove a blade through my heart, and I flinched at the wave of energy that came from her. She lurched forward, and I caught her with an arm around her waist.

David continued to stare at the crack as a few additional rocks broke off and fell into the nothingness. There was another smaller shudder of the earth, enough to cause the cracks to spread farther across the ceiling, and threaten to pull the house down around us.

"David, we have to go." I tried to keep my voice gentle as Evelyn went limp in my arms, her eyes wide and unseeing. The air around us prickled my skin as the instability spread.

We needed to move.

Now.

I never wanted to influence David, but I had no choice.

"Let's *go,*" I said, the words smooth as silk as they spilled out into the air between us.

Finally, David looked at me, and I touched his back as David rolled and straightened his shoulders, wrapped an arm around his still-silent mother, and guided her toward the front door. I followed them, walking through a curtain of dust that glittered in the disturbed air. When Evelyn paused, I held back the intense urge to shove them both until they were out of the house.

"We have to go, Mom," David said.

As if my heart could take any more, it shattered at the break in David's voice. An uncomfortable sensation crept up my spine, as I felt like a monster for not allowing them the time they needed to grieve, or even fully accept what had happened.

As we turned down the hallway, David threw a look back at the hole in the ground where his father had been only moments before. It didn't escape me that it was the same place David had last seen him before he moved out after their argument.

"I love you, Dad," David whispered into the air as tears streamed down his cheeks. "We should've made things right when we had the chance."

Chapter Six

Esco

Broken Homes, Healed Hearts.

The stairs crumbled under my feet as I made my way up eight flights to the not-for-profit organization. I cursed in the ancient language when I slipped and my knee landed heavily on the crumbling concrete. With a glare, I faced upward, only two flights to go. It seemed a lot to risk my life to check out *this specific* office within this particular building, but the wave of sadness I'd picked up on as I'd walked on the street had forced me to sidestep around it as though it were a physical block.

So now I moved toward it, intent on rescuing whatever humans were there.

The building was a hazard, and as the Earth shook, dust fell from the walls, accompanied by the occasional pebble. Whoever these humans were, they were dedicated, but it was time to leave now. To distract myself from the crumbling of the walls around me, I bent to pick up a brochure on *Broken Homes, Healed Hearts,* and skimmed it. A charity which offered assistance to victims of domestic violence to escape their situations, and to make sure they didn't end up homeless, including protection for children and humans' animal companions. They'd also attempt to get those responsible for the violence to be held accountable, but that wasn't always possible. The priority was to protect the victims and offer them a future, which was a significant undertaking.

As I reached the office, I gripped the doorframe and pushed myself through the open doorway, expecting to see hordes of humans gathered in fear, or at the very least, flitting about in an attempt to tie up loose ends before they evacuated.

Instead, I faced a lone man sitting at his desk.

He stared out the window, looking without really seeing, and it took him several moments to notice my presence. When he did, a flicker of his brow was the only response he gave to what should have been alarming—a strange blue creature standing in his office. My brow pulled down. Was he also affected by the coming of the Shift, in that he no longer felt *anything?* But the wave of sadness I'd experienced... it had come from here.

A buzzing of a news reporter's voice sounded from his cell, and he locked it and placed it face down on the desk before he turned to me. He was handsome, middle-aged, though the lines around his eyes and brow portrayed more stress than perhaps he should have at his age. When he continued to stare at me in silence, I took a few steps into the office and froze when another quake shook the building.

"It's not safe here," I said as I held out a hand, thankful at the very least he didn't appear afraid of me. "We need to leave."

"I'm not sure what's worse, really," he said in a low tone as he indicated his cell. "Thinking this crazy shit is only local, or finding out it's happening everywhere else at the same time."

"Is there anyone else here?" I asked.

He shook his head. "No, just me. Everyone else is at a fundraiser. Well..." He lifted a shoulder with a sad smile. "*Were* there, I suppose. I imagine the event was cancelled and everyone tried to find safety."

"Unlucky," I said, and he shot me a startled look. Whoever this man was, I felt he needed to talk, and while this wasn't an ideal time, if I could get him talking, perhaps I could get him to follow me. "Unlucky you weren't at the event too, I mean."

He huffed. "I never do those events anyway. I prefer to stay behind the scenes." He put on a higher-pitched voice, "*But Ed, people will want to meet the man behind the work. You deserve to be recognized.*" He shook his head. "I don't, though. Thankfully, she'll never know why."

We both turned toward the window as the building across the street collapsed. Slowly at first, a few bricks fell from above our line of sight before the entire building came down. The ground shuddered menacingly with the promise of the same fate beneath our feet.

"Please," I put my hand out again and took another step closer to Ed. "Come with me."

I held in my sigh of relief as he stood, but instead of coming closer to me, he walked to the desk next to his and fired up a laptop. "I need to email some files to Celia. We have no backup outside of this office. After this is over, whatever *this* is, they'll need to rebuild the charity."

Before I could think of a response, Ed dropped himself into a seat and patted the chair next to him. "I don't know what the fuck you are, if you're a monster or an angel, or simply my imagination. But I don't want to leave this building."

"Ed—"

"What I *do* want, is for someone to listen to my sad bullshit story before I die. Will you do that for me?"

I glanced around at the walls, noting the cracks, but nodded stiffly before I sat next to the man. His smile was hollow, and he continued to copy and email files as he spoke. "Celia doesn't understand why I don't want people to know who I am. I have no interest in gaining credit for this work or being recognized in any way. I've invested everything I had—money and time, including selling my apartment to keep this charity afloat and make it what it is today, and it's the best thing I've ever done." He sighed. "Probably the *only* good thing I've ever done. To date, we've saved hundreds of vulnerable people, women and men alike."

"Sounds like you've done a lot of good."

He eyed me. "But how much good is needed to make up for the evil I've done?"

"Celia would want you to survive," I said.

"Celia, Celia, Celia." He sighed again as he clicked through another file. "Her name means heaven, but to me, it spells hell. Because she's everything I don't deserve. She's light, happiness, and laughter. She's a future with a wife, children, and a home. A future I can never allow myself to have. When she'd hear me coming into the office in the mornings, she would turn and smile at me, and the whole world would melt away." He chuckled. "Sounds so corny, but it's true. She wants me, she may even love me, but I can't let her in, or allow myself to be loved. Because Celia was the ultimate pain, the love I can't allow myself to have or *feel,* because she deserves better than who I am."

"What could you have done to deserve punishing yourself for so long?" The man in front of me—Ed—intrigued me.

Something about him poked at a spot in my chest I'd not paid much notice to before. I'd been aware of it at certain times in my life, but a Guardian's life has no room for emotional connections. I tilted my head as I watched him, and tried to force the effects of the Shift away from us so I could focus on his imprint. Sadness. So much sadness surrounded him, it blanketed him and thickened the deeper I probed. There was no light, simply a secret he guarded. "What are you trying to make up for?" I whispered as I pulled my senses away.

"There was a woman... decades ago now, as if time passing somehow makes it better." He paused and stared out the window again, before, as he cleared his throat, he seemed to regain himself. "What's worse is she wasn't the first. She didn't want me, and I would've forced her. I was perfectly willing to push her down into the filth of that alley and fuck her as she cried for me to stop. To feel the power and the rush that came with such an act, degrading her and getting turned on by her tears and struggle. I was stronger than her, bigger, fitter, and she would have had no chance." Ed gripped his stomach as if remembering it was enough to make it feel as though his body feel as though it was eating itself from the inside out. I leaned back in my chair as he talked, unable to correlate the sympathetic man in front of me with a man who would conduct such a violating and sick act. He patted his stomach. "This is what guilt feels like. I've mostly gotten used to it over the years, an ever-present feeling I couldn't shake, and didn't want to. I deserve the constant reminder."

I swallowed. I was no stranger to the dark acts humans were capable of, but the waning sympathy I felt for Ed clashed heavily inside me with my disgust for his past, and I struggled to control the conflicting feelings. Is this what it felt like to be human? It was confusing and painful.

Not sure if I wanted to know the answer or not, I asked anyway, "You said you'd done it before, what makes this woman different?"

"Because the next morning, she was dead." I flinched at the deadpan tone of his voice, the words delivered factually. "She was found in some warehouse outside the city. Tortured, murdered, and left there like something to be discarded, as some final insult to her." He glanced at me quickly before returning to his computer. "I didn't kill her if that's what you're thinking, but I discarded her that night, too. Whoever killed her knocked me out as I was attacking her, and took her from under me. I never reported it to the cops, not that I would've been much help anyway, but I was a coward in more ways than one." He ran his tongue around his cheeks, then grimaced, as if hating the taste of his truth. "When I found her in that bar, I should've put her in a cab and sent her home. I should've made sure she was safe. Instead, I dragged her somewhere dark, intending to violate her. If I hadn't, maybe she'd still be alive."

I stared at Ed, unsure of what to say.

"You don't need to say anything," he said, saving me from the pressure that built in my throat. "Did I deserve even the small moments of happiness I'd had since? What about all the things I'd done before then? I don't deserve any happiness. So, instead I threw myself into this, and hopefully some of the lives I helped heal and save will make up the tiniest bit for Ana's death."

A pang struck my chest, but before I could speak, Ed's hand shot out and gripped my arm. We watched together as, after a particularly rough rumble of the Earth, a web of cracks explored their way up the wall near his head and reached toward the ceiling.

His cell beeped, and Ed reached across to the other desk to grab and glance at it. "Celia," he said without prompting. "She wants to know if I'm safe." Ed shook his head. "I'm exactly where I'm meant to be." He turned to me. "Go."

"Ed, you can come with me. Think of Celia—"

"I *am* thinking of Celia, and Ana, and all the lives I ruined. I've had my time, I've done what I can to make things right. I'm staying."

"Please."

Why am I crying?

I swiped at my cheek as a tear fell, and I stared at it as I lifted my finger away from my face.

Ed smiled. "Go. Don't let me have your death on my conscience as well."

I swallowed. "Tell Celia you love her." His eyes widened, and it was the most emotion I'd seen from him. "Tell her," I repeated.

As the ceiling started to crumble and collapse, he sighed as though keeping himself alive was an unwanted effort and tapped out a text message to Celia. "It might not even get through," he muttered, "Cell towers are probably collapsing with the rest of the world."

I sucked in a breath as I read what he'd sent.

I always loved you, Celia, but I never deserved you.

Ed placed the phone down as it pinged in response, and stared at me until I began to back out of the office. I lifted my hand in one last attempt to save his life, and he responded simply with a shake of his head and a small smile.

The building began to crumble in earnest, and after I left the office, I bolted down the stairs. As I reached the road, I shook the dust from my quills and kept running, needing to be a safe distance from the building as it collapsed behind me.

Ed's imprint continued to resonate with sadness, but now also with relief.

Before it abruptly ended.

Chapter Seven

Cael

Ana's hand squeezed mine as I harnessed her powers with my own to track Sasha's imprint. It didn't take long to pinpoint her location, given we were closer than we had been earlier. However, finding her in the back streets while she was also on the move was another challenge. She may have even partially cloaked her imprint to keep herself safer from wandering Tenebrians, or perhaps was in her human form and kept herself hidden to avoid alarming the humans.

While I understood these motivations, I had to work to mask my frustration. Sasha had no way of knowing we were searching for her at that moment, and I knew she wasn't doing it on purpose. But every setback felt like a personal attack. Simply another thing stopping me from keeping my family safe, and it grated against me.

When I spotted her, I called out and left Ana with Roger and John as I rushed to help usher a group of people into a nearby building.

"I don't know what else to do," Sasha said as we returned to the others. "I tell them to stay in groups and stay inside, but what good will it do if this continues? The Gateways opening will only remain outside for so long, and how helpful will their combined emotions be if all they're feeling is fear?"

All good questions, none of which I had the answers to. Sasha didn't expect me to have the answers. These questions plagued us all. "Hopefully, it will keep them safe from the Tenebrians until we can get this under control," I said as I surveyed the empty streets. "Although the silence in itself is worrying. The Tenebrians aren't stupid, they'll start looking in buildings when they can't find humans outside."

"That's what I'm worried about, then they're as good as trapped." She sighed heavily and grabbed my wrist. "You were looking for me, so I'm guessing you have a plan? Please tell me you do. I feel so useless."

"We have ideas. We're heading back to John's to sort it out."

"Why my help?"

I hesitated. "Because you're my friend." It wasn't a lie. I cared deeply for Sasha.

Did she know of her mixed heritage? Doubtful.

The time to have those conversations would be later.

Sasha had always been powerful, and now I understood why.

"We were hoping you'd be with some others," I added.

Sasha shook her head. "Esco and I separated. We can try to find her if you want."

"Only if she's close," I said. "I don't want us to be out at night."

With Sasha's help, we were able to track down Esco. As we rounded a corner, she stumbled into view, the relief palpable on her face. She raised a hand and opened her mouth to speak, but Sasha held up her palm and ran to meet her.

As we came level, Esco brushed Sasha's hands away from her. "I'm weak. I need to recharge," Esco said, turning her hands over and studying them. "But you can't do it for me, I'll drain you. We need to do it together."

Pressing my lips together, I considered the options. We could recharge off each other, she was right, but preferably outdoors in case there was an energy surge. "We'll all have to wait until morning. We can't afford to be out when it gets dark."

"I'm not sure what difference the dark makes," Esco said as her brow furrowed. I didn't answer. My thoughts were tangled up with my encounters with Nathaniel—he was always at his most active at night. I wasn't sure if Tenebrians had a flair for the dramatic, if they genuinely preferred the nighttime, or if they had a deep understanding of the connection between human fear and darkness, and took advantage of that.

Esco continued, "Where are all the Tenebrians, anyway? I expected to see more of them."

"Working their way through the city, I suspect, either it's dumb luck we haven't run into them, or they're actively avoiding us because they can't be bothered fighting and just want to cause chaos with the humans," Sasha said.

Or they're waiting for the dark.

I wrapped my arm tighter around Ana's waist, and we continued moving.

A handful of blocks from John's home, I held my arm out and halted Ana and Roger's movement as the rest of the group fell in behind us.

"Can you feel that?" I whispered.

Ana peered over my outstretched arm. "They're coming."

Ana's monotone concerned me, and when I glanced down at

her, I couldn't see any of my concerns reflected in her eyes, only a stoic acceptance of the situation.

I wanted to reassure her, to tell her everything would be okay. "Ana..."

The Tenebrians advanced simultaneously, emerging from alleys and within buildings, six or more of them. They hadn't bothered to change into their human form, and they stood drawn to their full intimidating heights, their quills and scales quivering in anticipation.

"We were hoping for humans, but this is much better," one said.

Another laughed. "I thought they *were* humans. Their imprints are weak."

"Especially this one." They indicated Ana. "Isn't she the one they used to tip the Balance? So easily manipulated, a human with the powers of a Guardian. What a waste."

They laughed, and my hands curled into fists at my sides. Ana stirred next to me, but despite her lingering power, she was in no state to fight. "Walk away," I said, "and there won't be any trouble."

This was met with general laughter. "Foolish Lucidian, trouble is exactly what we're after."

Sasha slowly drew moonstone blades from her pockets and handed one to Esco. After the movement was caught in my peripheral vision, I glanced back at them, wishing I'd had the foresight to arm myself before I left Lucidis. Looking back at Ana, I realized the Elders might have been right about one thing—I was compromised when it came to her.

To me, my duties were coming second to her safety.

Everything came second to Ana.

A spike of panic hit my chest at all the things I *didn't* know. Roger's plan was at the forefront of my mind, a plan he hadn't fully disclosed to us yet. What if it didn't work? What if the plan came down to choosing between Ana and the Balance? I was already a traitor to my Guardian heritage, as I knew I'd take my chances with the new world as long as Ana was by my side. She had been so hard on herself for not being strong enough to stop the Shift once it began, but what if *I* wasn't strong enough to make the right choice if I needed to?

My group picked up on the change around me, misinterpreting the shift in my mood as a sign of preparation to fight, and each dropped into a defensive stance. This drew another bout of laughter from the Tenebrians, and one of them pointed at John.

"You're not supposed to take sides, Contact."

"I think all rules have gone out the window, mate, starting with what you lot did to the Balance."

"All we did was claim what was rightfully ours. Any worthy Guardian would see that. When—"

The Guardian jerked backward as a knife pierced his arm. I spun and watched as Esco returned to a standing position after having completed her throw. She shrugged. "The rules have gone out the window. We have a mission to complete, and he kept talking."

Sasha smirked, and my jaw dropped, unable to find the words to respond even if I wanted to. A stirring built up behind me, and I turned to locate the source. It began with a build-up of emotions that felt as though they had boiled over after being hidden and suppressed, growing to a point where they could no longer be contained.

Ana stared at the Tenebrians, expressionless.

The stirring didn't come from her.

As the Tenebrian stood and pulled the knife slowly from his arm, there was a howl of rage behind me. I spun as Roger charged toward the Tenebrian, and with a move that was both out of character and fast for his age, Roger snatched at the knife the Tenebrian held.

His hand curled around the red scales of the Tenebrian's throat. "You took her from me," he snarled out as he turned the blade, twisting it from the Tenebrian's grasp as he tried to fight him off, before Roger drove it into his neck.

The Guardian fell to his knees as Roger drove the knife in and forced him to the ground. The Tenebrian's rage faded into a smirk as he waited, staring defiantly at Roger, their hands still intertwined around the blade. As Roger stepped away, the Tenebrian looked at his hands, and the smile was wiped from his face as shock took over.

While the wound glowed from the moonstone and his image flickered, he wasn't transported to Tenebris.

He returned to his solid form and remained stubbornly on Earth.

Without the Gateways forming correctly and without their healing power, the Tenebrian wouldn't be returned to his homeland.

My gaze flickered between the Guardian as his blood leaked between his fingers, a deeper red than the orange tinge of the scales on his shoulders and chest, and Roger. Roger took another step back, realization setting in a moment before the words were spoken.

"You're dying," one of the other Guardians stated factually.

"But—" The Tenebrian collapsed forward and slapped a palm to the ground. He pulled the moonstone blade from his neck, but as the blood spurted from the wound, he realized his mistake too late. The others stepped to the side so the splatter of blood did not touch them and watched him with mingled curiosity and anger as he scrambled to stop the flow before he fell forward onto his face. He jerked once, then became still.

My comrades, the Tenebrians, and I stared at the fallen Guardian, but his body didn't disappear. Slowly, our gazes returned to each other. "Seems if we die on Earth now, we die for good," I muttered, the threat lingering between the words.

The Tenebrians glanced at each other, deciding their next move between them silently, before they strode away.

"We're just going to let them leave?" Sasha asked after a beat as she shoved my shoulder.

"We have to focus. If we keep running around dealing with smaller issues, we'll run out of time to fix the Balance."

"They're going to find people to hurt," Ana said. I looked at Ana as she spoke. She wasn't crying, but I almost would have preferred it if she were. Any emotion would have been preferable to the deadpan way with which she dealt with these situations.

"I'm sorry, Ana, we can't save them all. We need to get the plan together, and we need somewhere safe to do that."

Ana shrugged. "It doesn't matter. We're all going to die, anyway."

"Don't say that."

"Why?" Her look was defiant. "The Tenebrians won't stop. They're never going to stop. Look at all the things they did to try to tip the Balance. They have no boundaries, no control.

They're just going to keep hurting and killing and destroying, and even *if* you can fix the damage I did, they still won't stop."

"Ana..." Roger spoke up. "It wasn't your fault."

"How was it *not* my fault?"

I touched her wrist but let my hand drop when she jerked away. "You were used, Ana," I said.

She stared at me. "What do you mean?"

"Cascus used you. He was a traitor," I said, spilling the information I'd hoped not to burden Ana further with. "He intentionally made you angry about his insistence that you do not return to Earth, knowing you would one day. He lined up the Tenebrians to cause chaos, to create a dome of negativity, and identify the points of greatest impact. When he realized the extent of your powers and how he could use them, he told them to kidnap you and use you to shift the Balance."

"But..." Ana's brow pulled down as she rolled the information around in her mind. "It *was* me."

"You were manipulated on a mass scale. It wasn't your fault." My lip lifted into a snarl when she opened her mouth to argue, determined to blame herself for something outside her control as though any level of control of one's powers could withstand that level of manipulation and planning. "I'm sorry I didn't see it for what it was and protect you from it."

Ana's eyes darted between mine, back and forth as she searched for sincerity beyond my words, but as always, I spoke the truth. Her breathing rate, which had increased steadily since the Tenebrians showed up, now slowed, and the stiffness in her shoulders and joints evaporated as she slumped again. For a brief moment, I thought she had finally accepted this was outside her control, but the thing that flickered within her essence wasn't relief or acceptance—it was grief. "They'll never stop, Cael. What kind of world is that to save?" she whispered.

I stared at her—the essence of her had changed with a finality that terrified me. Ana had given up and closed herself off to the world. This was beyond the self-preservation she did after her mother died, and her walls were thicker than when I'd first met her. She'd created a world inside herself, and she planned to stay there.

"Ana..." I cleared my throat, my voice barely above a whisper as I leaned down to face her, "... we need you. *I* need you." We looked at each other for a long moment. Ana blinked hard and looked at the ground when the tears started to come, and as much as I hated to see her cry, the spark of emotion was something I could cling to. *Somewhere* she was in there, hurting and afraid, but she was there. Tears meant she still cared. Cared enough to hope, and felt fear that the hope may not be fulfilled. But it was *something.* I pulled her close to me and spoke to the group without turning. "We need to keep moving. It's not far now."

As we walked, Roger came up next to Ana. "I'm sorry I lost control."

She returned his gaze for a moment. "You don't need to apologize."

"No, it was foolish, I should never—"

"You should never have done a lot of things," Ana said with a slight huff. "But standing up for Mom is something you should always do."

Before he could respond, Ana moved away, and when Roger and I shared a glance, I wasn't sure he'd have known how to reply anyway.

When we reached John's home, Esco took Ana upstairs with John in the lead, while Roger, Sasha, and I stayed on the street.

"We need to protect this place," I said.

Roger stared up at the building, an old concrete water tower that had been converted into an apartment. Despite the designer's assurances, it ultimately proved unpopular and sold for significantly less than the planned market value due to the winding stairs and small floor space of the actual living area. But it was perfect for John, and he had been there since he took on the role of Contact for the Guardians.

Sasha nodded, her eyes wide. "I haven't done it with something so big before." Like me, Sasha had protected individual humans for a short time, or a single room, but never an entire building, and never with such an unstable environment.

I rubbed my hands together. "No, neither have I. But we have to try. We need a base to plan from and rest."

Holding hands, the three of us stood close to one side of the building's curve and allowed our joint energy to flow through us, leaving my and Sasha's fingertips as we touched the wall, still warm from the absorbed afternoon sun. The dust shifted from the old bricks as we forced positive energies into the building itself to stabilize the area, protect those within, and repel Tenebrians at the same time. Sasha's arm started to tremble with the effort, and I noticed her struggle as I glanced at her.

After a while, Sasha dropped her hand. "I can't do it anymore. I'm going to drain myself."

Following suit, I dropped Roger's hand, which tingled with the remnants of power. Roger had tried to let the power flow through him and not absorb it, but he, too, was drained, and his body's instinct was to restore his dwindling powers. I appreciated his effort to try to override his body's instinct.

"It'll have to do for now," I said as I rubbed my hands together. "Tomorrow, we'll have to look at finding a way to access Lucidis to recharge."

Sasha entered the building, dragging her feet, while Roger and I sat by the front door to wait for Samael. After a brief silence, Roger turned to me. "You don't trust me, do you?"

"I trust you."

Roger smiled. "Okay, you trust me because you felt my being. What I meant was, you don't like me?"

My lip twitched as I held back a snarl. "You hurt Ana." I glanced at Roger out of the corner of my eye. "She's *my Ana*."

"Once upon a time, she was my Ana."

"You left that behind when you left her and her mother."

"I deserved that." He sighed. "Cael, you must try to understand. I wanted her to live a human life, but every time she was near me for too long, it brought out the Guardian in her. There was no way around it, trust me. I tried everything, including hiding my essence. She was too sensitive to my presence."

"Maybe because she loved you."

"Perhaps. There are a lot of things about love I still don't understand, especially when it comes to humans and Guardians together." He eyed me for a moment before he faced the street again. We both stilled as in the distance a small group of Tenebrians flitted between two buildings, but they didn't even glance our way. "I know you see humanity for what it is, and I think you understand my actions more than you're willing to accept, because your feelings for Ana blind you." Roger smiled at me. "I'm not complaining, I am happy she has someone like you."

I was about to answer, probably to defend myself and claim I couldn't possibly understand his actions. But would I do the same? I'd already admitted to myself I'd let the world burn to protect Ana, would I, like Roger, let myself burn with it?

Without question.

Samael's imprint struck me in the chest, a tiny pinprick of recognition of my son, and I looked up to see him at the end of the street. Standing, Roger immediately followed suit, and we waited for Samael to reach us.

"I'll let Ana know that he's safe," Roger said after he glanced at my face and moved inside.

As Samael came level with me, I pulled him into a hug without hesitation. Samael was as drained as the rest of us, and we fed off each other's energies, enough to make us feel better, but not sufficient to make a real difference. True recharge would have to wait until tomorrow, we all needed sleep. Standing back, I nodded at David and held my hand out to the woman next to him, taller than Ana but petite in comparison to Samael's and even David's height. Even in her current state of distress—her dark hair falling from the clip where before it would have been held in an elegant style, her floral skirt and black top covered in dust, and her deep brown eyes which betrayed the sorrow hiding behind them—she still had an air of class about her.

David opened his mouth, but when he stood silent, his eyes not quite seeing me, Samael spoke for him, "This is Evelyn, David's mother."

I brushed my lips across the top of her hand, and she held my gaze as something that could have been amusement passed across her face. But then it was gone, and her sorrowful eyes were the only feature that betrayed emotion on an otherwise blank mask, halfway between shock and desperation to keep herself from breaking down.

Without words, I tilted my chin to indicate the space next to them where David's father should be. Samael shook his head as David looked at the ground, and my shoulders slumped. I did not need to ask what had happened—it was in the air around us, and although twisted and muted by the oncoming Shift, the loss was still thick between us.

Another loss that weighed heavily on the atmosphere and their shoulders.

Another push against the Balance.

"Come inside. We are safer here." I guided them inside, closed and locked the door quietly behind us, before following Samael up the stairs.

Chapter Eight

Samael

"So, you're not human?" David asked, with an uneasy glance at Esco.

I looked into David's eyes, admiring how he managed to be handsome even when his face was covered with angry red blotches. He had finally broken down earlier and retreated to John's bedroom, where he held a pillow to his face to muffle the sounds of his anguished crying. Evelyn sat on the couch, glancing at the door as silent tears streamed down her face, while Sasha patted her folded hands. I could tell that Sasha wanted to soothe the woman but was concerned about her power levels and had to resort to a more human level of comfort. David's pain seeped through the closed door, but I knew he needed some time.

David and I sat on the floor while Evelyn sat with her hands neatly folded in her lap and made small talk with Sasha and Esco when they tried to communicate with her, but she wasn't engaging, and I couldn't blame her. She'd screamed upon seeing Esco, and it had taken all of us to convince her she was not a threat. David, on the other hand, upon seeing Esco, had let his gaze slide to me.

As if he knew.

Looking into David's eyes, I wished I could lie to make things easier for him.

"No," I answered finally. "I'm not human."

David released a slow breath and made a sound of acknowledgment before he stared back at the gas fire as the flames flickered on a low setting behind the glass window. I'd tried my best to explain the existence of the Guardians, the Balance, our roles, and what was occurring.

But what was challenging to describe was even harder to accept.

"Can I see?"

David's words startled me out of my thoughts. "What?"

His eyes raked up and down my body. "Can I see you? The real you."

"Umm..." Glancing uneasily at Dad, I flexed and released my hands several times. I shouldn't, but I wanted to make David's acceptance of this easier, and if it helped, I was willing to try. David had seen me naked and had touched me in a way that no one else ever had. But none of that compared to how vulnerable and exposed I felt faced with the prospect of showing him my true form. Taking David's hand in mine, I glanced back at Dad again before I focused and forced the skin on my hand past its resistance to shift back into my Guardian form. David watched in awe as the skin on my hand changed, the smooth skin he knew so well, the skin he had touched and caressed, flickered over into glassy blue scales and long claws.

When David drew his hand away, my heart pounded against my ribcage as I sucked in a breath and held back the pain. I stopped forcing the change, my hand returned to my human form as David stared unblinkingly.

"Are you okay?" I whispered, feeling as though my already broken heart was torn further apart when David leaned away from me. It was an almost imperceptible movement, but the air changed around us as the space between us increased, and I couldn't pretend I didn't feel it.

"I need a minute to think about this." I nodded and stayed seated on the floor as David stood and made his way over to his mother. He took the spot on the couch that Sasha vacated at his approach and draped an arm around his mother as she leaned into him.

I didn't look up as Dad sat next to me.

"So," I said, licking my lips, my mouth dry. "He might not want me anymore." My voice cracked, and I wondered where the Guardian Dad had praised for having control over the situation had gone, because I didn't feel as though I had control over anything anymore. "It looks like you were right. Maybe he can't love me for who I really am."

When I finally managed to drag my gaze from the floor to Dad's face, he watched me with his lips pressed together in a thin line. He turned to stare at the fire, sighed, and squeezed my hand. "I didn't want to be right."

As I dropped myself heavily on the floor beside Sasha, she propped her elbow on the couch cushion by Roger's leg. Everyone had gathered in the living room after we'd settled in and had something to eat. Evelyn was asleep in John's bedroom, and David sat in a recliner chair in the corner. His eyes were closed, and he seemed to be sleeping, but I could feel he was tense and very much awake. David hadn't spoken to me since our discussion, and as hard as it was to keep my distance, I'd done my best to be respectful. I left him to sit in the recliner, where he pretended to sleep, with a slight furrow settled between his brows as he likely ran through a world of questions in his mind.

If he would let me, I could give him the answers to all his questions.

But I'm not sure they would ease his pain or concerns.

"So, what's the plan?" Sasha asked.

All eyes turned to Roger, and he cleared his throat. "Well..." He glanced at Mother. "I've been considering the position of half-breeds for years now. They contain a power that brings out the best in both the human and Guardian side. I think..." He hesitated again. "It's just an idea, but I think if we can get a few of them together, we can use them to restore the Balance."

"The way I was used?" Mother looked at him, her expression carefully blank.

"No, not at all. We explain the situation and teach them how to harness their power."

Dad's brows drew together. "That sounds time-consuming. How do we even begin to explain to them what's going on?"

"How do we *find* them is an even larger question?" Sasha added.

"Well." Roger cleared his throat again and tapped his fingertips together in his lap. "Actually, I have already found some."

“Who? How?” I suppressed a grin at the accusatory tone of Sasha’s question as she glared at him. She knew only the surface of the history between Roger and Mother, but had immediately and loyally taken Mother’s side. Sasha trusted Roger as much as she needed to, and no further.

“It’s what I’ve been doing for the past few decades. It hasn’t been easy, but I had a few good leads before my powers weakened. There was a lot of patience, a bit of chance, maybe I told some Guardians I came across I would expose them using moonstone...”

The stunned silence that followed this statement was punctuated only by Esco. “You *threatened* Guardians?”

“Look, I think you’re underestimating how widespread the disruptions from Tenebris have been over the years. Many Guardians were partially willing to help, but were hesitant because of the Elders’ denial. So, maybe I had to persuade some of them to help me track and locate.” He glanced around the room. “I could always feel Guardians when they were close to me, and sometimes I drew from their powers to recharge mine. Occasionally, I made contacts who helped several times, but we couldn’t keep in touch for long. I also had my secrets to protect.” Another sideways look at Mother. “Needless to say, it’s been a long journey, but I know a dozen or so half-breeds who could help. Together with Ana, it could be enough.”

“*If* we get it done before the Shift completes,” Esco said.

Roger nodded. “If we get it done in time.”

“Ana is unique,” Dad said, and Roger turned to him. “Her powers are as they are because she lived on Earth for decades as a human, and then in Lucidis as a Guardian. Other half-breeds won’t have the same power.”

"No, but they'll have more power than a full-blood Guardian."

Esco cleared her throat. "Exactly how many half-breeds are there? I thought Ana was..." She threw an apologetic look at Mother and patted her knee. "I mean no disrespect, Ana, but I thought you were one-of-a-kind."

"Guardians have been using humans to keep their numbers up for years," Dad said.

At the silence that followed, I added, "It's true, Cascus told us."

"How did you know there were others?" Again, Sasha's voice was laced with suspicion and edged with displeasure as he watched Roger.

John said, "After Roger and I met, it wasn't a huge leap to consider other Guardians may have also fallen for humans, or at the very least, been tangled with them enough to have a child."

Mother faced Roger. "How did you come up with this idea?" Her voice was quiet. I missed the commanding tone she usually took on, putting on a brave front even when she was out of her depth, but that part of her seemed to have been left in Tenebris.

"It was you."

"What did I do?"

"You didn't do anything in particular, just observations from when you were a child. Even then, the combination of human and Guardian gave you impressive power, especially when you were with your Bronte and me. Sometimes your power was overwhelming for a small child." He looked at John, and I followed his line of sight and noted the proud smile that adorned his face.

John smirked. "I remember, sometimes at school, the whole

class would cry if you were upset." He looked as though he was holding back the urge to smile. "The teacher wouldn't know what to do, and then she would cry too." John made a sound which seemed to be a suppressed laugh before he cleared his throat and waved his hand at Roger to continue.

"When I noticed Tenebrians increasing their activity two decades ago, it gave me the idea that perhaps the strength of joint parentage could be powerful in all the right ways. I doubled down on researching, locating, and making connections and contacts. They're mostly younger. Those who'd been on Earth for four or five decades, or more, tended to have effectively squashed their Guardian heritage, but the younger ones were still a powerhouse waiting to be freed. When..." he trailed off, looked hesitantly at Mother, then continued, "... and when I felt the Shift and felt you, it only cemented my suspicions of the power of half-breeds."

"And you simply *guessed* half-breeds existed based on your own experiences?" Sasha said.

Roger looked hard at her. "It's a funny thing. When you break the mold and see humanity for what it is, for its strength, you very quickly realize you weren't the only one. The Elders, past and present, were not as careful and clever as they thought. I felt in other Guardians what I felt in myself—those who broke the mold—and they were willing to help. With a rumor here and there, and time, I found some of the children they thought were hidden."

"So, how do we do this?" Esco asked, bringing the conversation back to the present.

"The hardest part is going to be controlling the Gateways to find them. They're unstable and unpredictable. It's going to take a lot of energy."

"So, first we need Lucidis," Dad said.

"Yes."

"But we need to bring them together on Earth," Dad added.

"I think that would be best since Earth is the center."

Dad let out a long breath and echoed my thoughts. "This isn't going to be easy."

Understatement. I kept the thought to myself.

"No, but it's the only plan we have."

I asked, "You said we'd need to train them to control their powers, right?" Roger nodded, and my brows furrowed. "That sort of training would take years, or months at the very least."

"Yes, but if we had a powerful force which could bring out their hidden powers..." Roger said.

Dad looked at Mother as she gaped at Roger, and he tucked his arm protectively around her. Roger approached Mother, kneeled before her, and took her hands. "Ana," he started. Mother closed her eyes as he tucked her hair behind her ear, but it immediately fell in front of her face again. "I know I'm asking a lot of you, but you could be the link which ties all the other half-breeds together. We could harness their powers."

Mother shook her head, and I frowned at the waves of pain that emanated from her.

Roger pressed his lips together, and my back stiffened. I wanted to grab the back of his shirt and yank him away from Mother. He was going to ask her something painful. He was going to hurt her. I looked at Dad, and he, too, was staring at Roger with a deep furrow etched between his brows. "Ana," Roger started again, "Do you think that if you had some time to recharge, you could..." He hesitated. "Focus enough to shift the Balance back?"

Mother's eyes filled with tears, and with a low growl, I gave in to my urge and grabbed Roger and pulled him away from her. "I don't know," Mother said, her voice a wavering whisper, "I don't even know what I did the first time." When she looked around the group and saw everyone watching her, her tears fell harder, leaving damp lines on her face that trailed down to her chin. Her lip trembled, and I grabbed her hand as the dark cloud around her broke.

She hadn't resigned to the end—she'd been hiding that she was on the precipice of falling apart.

Guilt dropped in my stomach like a lead weight for not shutting Roger up as Mother clutched her stomach and cried out, "I'm sorry, it was an accident. I didn't mean to do it."

Dad leaned over, pulled Mother toward him with one arm, and shushed gently as he held her, rocking slightly on instinct. Dad and I glared as Roger leaned back on his heels and dropped his hands to his lap. "Ana, I didn't mean..."

"Just leave her be." Dad's tone was firm, like that of a parent to a child.

Roger's eyes darkened. "Don't think you're the only one here who cares for her."

"I'm not," Dad announced, his expression and rage matching Roger's. "But you're the only one suggesting we use her."

"Surely you realize the stakes here, Cael. I had to ask, but I never intended to force her."

"I think we should all try to get some sleep." Sasha stood abruptly before Dad could reply, and I squeezed Mother's hands. "Someone should stand guard."

"I'll take the first watch," John said. "I only have the one bed, so everyone is just going to have to find somewhere to rest."

Roger looked at Mother. "I didn't mean to upset you, Ana, I'm sorry."

"I'm sorry I'm not stronger." She sniffled as Dad pulled her closer to him. "I'm lost and scared. There doesn't seem to be a point to any of this. You're asking for my help, but how can I do anything other than make it worse?"

"I know it feels like that." He held his arm out, and she took his hand momentarily, before she dropped the contact and clung to Dad. "But we'll figure it out together."

Chapter Nine

Ana

Cael and I found a private place to sleep in the only other separate room of the small apartment. There was barely enough space for us to lie on a thick quilt, but I liked it. Being in a close, enclosed space with Cael meant the room could fill with our energies, however dwindling they may be. This small space would become ours, even if only for one night before we returned to the anarchy outside. Initially, Cael had considered sleeping downstairs, but we all decided it was better to stay close together and could only hope that our group energy would be enough to stabilize the area and prolong the protection infused into the building.

From both quakes, Gateways, and wandering Tenebrians.

Darkness fell, and as predicted, chaos reigned outside more than before. The whoops and laughs of the Tenebrians as they darted around the crumbling streets were broken only by the screams of people and intermittent gunfire. I squeezed my eyes shut and could only hope some humans managed to kill a Tenebrian or two, at least enough for them to realize they weren't beyond death and there would be no healing Gateway to help them if they were wounded.

We lay next to each other, and as I flinched at another round of gunfire from outside, Cael tucked his arm around me so I could rest my cheek in the nook of his shoulder. He kissed my head, then rested there, breathing in my scent and essence.

"We have to bide our time, Ana," he whispered as he brushed his fingertips down my arm. "I know you want to help the people outside. But we need to conserve our energy."

"I know," I whispered back, and pressed a kiss to his chest. "Knowing there's a bigger picture doesn't make the sound of their suffering easier to handle."

"No, it doesn't," he admitted, and I knew even through the uneasy swirling of the Balance Shift, Cael could feel the humans' pain and fear as acutely as I could.

I didn't want to think about it anymore.

No matter how many times they told me it wasn't my fault, the fact remained I had played right into their hands. Cascus has goaded me into going to Earth, and neither he nor Vikt would have known of the true potential of my power if I hadn't taken the bait. Without me, forcing the Shift would have taken longer, and perhaps in that time, we'd have been able to rally some support and take more drastic action.

Or was that only wishful thinking?

Even the Elders who weren't traitors to their realm hadn't been aware or willing enough to acknowledge that something had been going on. Cordus may have, perhaps, but he was dead. My brow pulled together as for the first time, I considered perhaps his death hadn't been simply old age.

My chest felt hollow, and I sucked in a breath, desperate to be closer to Cael, and perhaps find some of the hope he held inside.

Tilting my face up, I brushed my lips against his. After the kiss, Cael moved to straighten his neck and lie back. I gently caressed his cheek, pulled him in for more, and moved my lips against his in the dark room. Tracing my hand down his body, I began to undo his jeans, and Cael wrapped his hand around my fingers, halting my movement. "What are you doing?"

"I want to be with you."

"Ana..." When he trailed off, I grasped the silence, kissed him again, and lifted one leg over his, intertwining our bodies. He broke the kiss and whispered, "Are you sure you're up for this?" The dark cloud was still about me, and the concern was apparent in his eyes. I'm sure he could feel it. Whether I wallowed in my pain or put up a wall to keep it all inside, Cael would be able to feel it.

"Cael..." I swallowed. "I need to be close to you, and maybe we can recharge each other in more ways than one."

He released his fingers from where he'd grasped my wrist, and slowly dragged his touch up my arm before they came to rest on my cheek as I deepened our kiss, and undid his pants. Cael moaned quietly against my lips when I grabbed him, and I shushed him gently as I closed my eyes and focused on the weight of his erect cock in my palm. Leaning forward, I kissed him again as he wrapped his arms around me. He didn't want to rush this, or to rush me, and was content to enjoy the feel of me next to him again.

But I needed more, and I needed it now.

Since being in Tenebris, my soul had become an empty shell, and I craved the closeness that only making love with my partner, with *my Cael,* could bring. Everything outside this apartment was broken. The world was being taken over by those determined to destroy it, and what was worth saving? If we were to rebuild, we would only be offering the world and humanity up to be destroyed again.

Squeezing my eyes shut for a moment, I then fluttered my eyelashes over Cael's cheek as I gripped his cock, and he groaned as I focused on blocking out the world outside, and imagined there was nothing beyond the four walls of this room. Nothing in the entire universe but us, and this moment. Rolling myself on top of Cael, I allowed myself to get lost in the kiss and the sensation of his tongue and lips across mine. Warm and inviting, soft and firm at the same time. His tongue played with mine, and he'd take control for a moment before he pulled back. Each time he retreated from me, I'd only close the space, and licked and nipped at his lips when he tried to break the kiss. As I lowered myself onto Cael's cock, he started to moan, and I clamped a hand over his mouth as I straddled him, and sunk until he was seated deep within me.

Fuck.

My body responded, even though my mind was still trying to protect itself, and I rocked where I sat as the delicious thickness of him filled me. Leaning forward, I pressed my breasts against his chest, feeling him through the fabric of our remaining clothes while we moved together, completely in sync with one another. Cael ran his hands down my back and over my ass, and pulled me onto him, before thrusting up hard. I bit on his shoulder to muffle the cry of pleasure as the slick drag of him inside me, amazing on Lucidis, was beyond ecstasy on Earth. I kept my face buried between his neck and shoulder and moved with him, meeting his every thrust upward with a tilt of my hips.

The air around us shifted and wavered as in our closeness we drew from each other, and fed off each other's essence, stronger together than we were apart.

Sitting up, I placed my palms on his chest and started bucking my hips against him. Cael bit into his forearm, and I clenched around him as the sight of his desperate clasp for control flared desire within me. He tilted his head back and stifled another groan as I rode him, lifting only to drop hard onto him. A change in angle, and I could bounce my hips, and ride him in earnest. His hands came down and fingers gripped my ass, and his eyes rolled back as he tried desperately to remain quiet. I'd lost hope, lost my connection with the world, and myself. But I wanted it back, and with him, it felt almost possible. Every sensation was amplified, and my fingernails dug into his chest as my peak rose.

"Ana, I'm going to... I can't—"

But I didn't stop, and his plea only made me ride him harder. I wanted to bring him to the peak I needed him to feel. Because even the orgasm which fluttered inside me warned me it wouldn't help, that the pleasure would be only momentary, and immediately after, I'd be back in the abyss. Cael's pleasure would amplify mine, and I inwardly cringed at the selfishness of the thought, but as much as I wanted to pleasure him, I wanted to feel it too.

I wanted to feel *something*.

Cael tried to hold back, but perhaps he'd forgotten how intense these sensations were on Earth and struggled to maintain control. The physical, combined with the emotional, was powerful and all-consuming.

"Ana, please—*fuck,*" he begged me, but I didn't slow down,

my desperation evident through my movements. Biting his arm again, Cael muffled his groan as he came, and his orgasm triggered mine, and I slowed my movement to draw out our pleasure as I hissed through my teeth. I continued to rock my hips in small, slow circles until Cael's head dropped back against the quilt and he panted. I closed my eyes and allowed the essence of his pleasure, which flowed around the room, to absorb into me.

Lifting myself from him, I lay down next to him again. Cael leaned against me, breathing heavily, and the hair around my face fluttered with every one of his outward breaths.

"I love you," he breathed the words out on a whisper.

"I love you, too."

But as he wrapped his arms around me and curled against me, and I felt his heartbeat slow and his breathing steady as his exhaustion finally caught up with him, I didn't feel the renewal I had hoped for. The hopelessness was a still hole inside me, expanding and filling me with a blackness I couldn't escape.

There was no spark of hope, no wave of love and affection that made me want to roll over and nuzzle into Cael's cheek.

I needed him, I *loved* him.

I *know* I did.

So why couldn't I feel it? I couldn't feel anything.

If I tried to search inside, I found nothing.

Not one damn thing.

John apologized as he placed an assortment of mismatched

bowls and cutlery on the small dining table, along with a few half-empty boxes of cereal, at least one of which was stale.

"Sorry, love," he mumbled, offering me one of the cereal boxes. "Wasn't expecting company."

I offered him a weak smile before serving myself something to eat. No one was complaining. Food was food, and we had more important things to focus on than the lack of our favorite breakfast.

"I tried opening a Gateway this morning."

Cael glared at Sasha. "When?"

"When I was finishing my watch, I thought I would try."

"And?"

"And not much. It felt like it was right there, just beyond my reach, but I couldn't see it."

"We're going to have to try together," said Esco.

Cael hummed out, "That's the plan."

We finished eating in silence. I certainly had nothing to offer in a conversation. I barely resisted the urge to cringe when I thought about opening my mouth and talking. Everything I could possibly say felt as though it would only burden everyone further, as if I hadn't done enough damage. Cael kept glancing at me and would offer a reassuring look, or perhaps squeeze my hand. I tried to smile in return, but every time it got weaker until it was barely a twitch of my lips.

After we'd eaten, we moved outside and stood in the empty street, blinking in the sunlight. David approached Samael. "What are you doing?"

Samael's eyebrows shot up as David asked, and he tried to mask his surprise and mingled relief. As far as I knew, David hadn't spoken to Samael since finding out the truth, and had barely *looked* at him. But here he was, initiating a conversation.

I looked at my chest as if I would see some physical evidence of a glimmer of hope.

Samael explained, "We're going to try to open a Gateway back to our home realm, to see if we can recharge our powers and find some help."

"Can I… um, watch?"

"Of course." Samael looked at David, and I reached out my senses, wondering what David must be thinking. But I couldn't find anything beyond the loss and confusion that clouded his being, and if I tried to go further, the sensations were muddled and confused.

Right, the Shift. As if I could forget.

David gently touched Samael's shoulder, then moved away and stood by the front door with Evelyn.

"Shall we try one at a time or…" Roger asked.

Cael pressed his lips together in a tight line, as if trying to brace himself when he couldn't know the outcome. "I think we should assume the worst, and all try together."

We moved closer to each other, shoulder to shoulder, and linked arms and intertwined fingers until we could feel our energies merging between us, forming a single energy force. I reached for John, but he shook his head with an unconvincing smile and lifted his shoulder. "Tenebrian," he said as he tapped his chest. "I don't want to confuse the energies of opening a Gateway."

"They open at the same time," I said.

John took a step back. "Everything had changed now, Ana, we don't know."

"Ready?" Cael asked before I could answer, and he looked

down the line. Everyone nodded, and he glanced directly at me when I didn't respond, and I gave him a single nod. We all faced forward, with one hand each facing outward, ready to touch the invisible wall that resided beyond the air. The channeling of our energies rippled the air around us, and we took a moment to sync up. I didn't have much experience working with other Guardians like this, and allowed my energy to be guided by Cael's as he stood next to me. I focused on my hands and fingers, and the fine hairs on my arms lifted as the air shimmered.

I glanced at John, and his mouth was agape. I doubted Tenebrians worked together like this, and that was probably for the best. Proof of what the Tenebrians could achieve when they worked together was all around us now in the decimation of the Balance. John stepped back, held out an arm, and guided David and Evelyn behind him, before retreating slowly.

"Ready?" Cael asked.

I brought myself back to the moment and felt the tingling of power in my fingertips.

"*Now,*" Cael said.

The reaction was instant.

Roger, Cael, and I were blown off our feet, and Samael, Sasha, and Esco barely managed to maintain their footing as the Gateway formed and expanded within the space of a nanosecond. The force of the creation sent a blinding white light over us, blanketing us with the influence of Lucidis and dissipating as it stretched out behind us. The remnants of the power hit John with enough force to make him step back against David, and his lip lifted into a snarl as no doubt his skin tingled from the energy of Lucidis. Not his home realm, but energy nonetheless. I held my forearm before my eyes, shielding myself against the light emanating from the open Gateway, which shimmered and remained in place. It was big enough to drive a moving van through.

As the Gateway settled and the light dimmed, my eyes narrowed at how the edges flickered and waivered. Ripples of blue and white swirled around the outside, only accentuating the undulating effect. In front of us, Lucidis was visible, as if the Gateway were simply a door opened into a garden. I didn't recognize this area of Lucidis—technically, it could be anywhere in the world. But I guessed it didn't matter. We needed it for its energy, which should be the same regardless of where in the realm we were.

Assuming Lucidis still could offer positive energies.

Under normal circumstances, unless directed otherwise, a Gateway would open in the same area of Lucidis as it was on Earth. But these were not normal circumstances.

Esco flexed her fingers. "That initial wave was incredible. I feel great."

"Me, too," said Sasha.

Cael stood, held out a hand to help me to my feet, and dusted off my shoulders before he turned to Roger. "We might not get many chances. Can you track the half-breeds from anywhere in Lucidis?"

"I can try."

"Then let's go."

"Wait." Cael and I turned to Esco as she said, "I'm staying."

"What?"

"I need to protect the humans, Cael. Someone has to protect them."

"Others are already helping on Earth, but we need your help

here."

"You can do it without me. I need to stay." While usually quiet in nature, Esco's tone made it clear there would be no argument. There was the smallest flicker of pride in me before it was smothered by concern. I was happy she was standing up for what she believed.

But what had she seen in the hours before we'd found her?

"I'm staying too."

Cael's jaw dropped as he pivoted on the spot. "Samael?"

"Samael, no," I said, and reached out to him.

Samael glanced at David as he took my hand. "I have protecting to do here, too."

My chest felt as though it had caved inward.

But why? This wasn't goodbye.

As far as you know, whispered a nasty voice in my head.

Samael pulled me into a hug and whispered reassurances as Cael went to protest, but was silenced when Sasha gently touched his shoulder. "It's not a terrible idea, Cael. Any good done on Earth will still help if we're trying to correct the Balance, and it'll help when we need to return to have a strong imprint to focus on."

She was right, and I sighed against Samael's chest. I'd be able to find his imprint to come back, I was more certain of that than I'd been of anything else since I'd pushed the Balance over the edge. No amount of wavering energy or imbalance would keep me from Samael, and having him here would be an anchor to get back to Earth. When I looked up, Samael nodded as he met my eyes, and I sniffed and squeezed him again before I let him go.

"Be safe," I whispered.

Cael shook his head, his eyes wild, before he turned. "John?"

John hesitated. "I don't even know if I can help."

My fingers twitched as I watched Samael take a step closer to David.

Maybe I was needed here too?

Cael's link to Earth would be stronger if Samael *and* I were to stay...

Cael reached out to me, and when I faltered, his face fell. "Ana, please, we need you."

My hesitation ate away at me internally, and continued to do so even as I took Cael's hand. "What if I only do more damage?" I asked. Voicing my fears made them feel real, and Cael wrapped an arm around my shoulders as I began to tremble.

"We'll be together, with Roger and Sasha, and we'll be able to balance each other out."

I watched his eyes, and although he said it with such certainty, Cael knew as well as I did he couldn't possibly promise that. None of us knew the full and lasting effects of the Shift coming into play. My lips parted, but I couldn't bring myself to ask the deepest fear that plagued me at that moment.

What if we can't make it back?

Samael was here—my *son*—and having us separated tugged at something in my chest. I placed a palm on my chest and frowned. It was as though I knew what I should be feeling, but when I felt it, it was only a semblance of the emotion it should be—a shadow of the feeling rather than the feeling itself.

As if reading my mind, Cael whispered, "Nothing will keep our family apart, Ana." And I bit my bottom lip as I nodded and followed him toward the Gateway.

Before we entered, I grabbed Samael's arm and pulled him

close to me. "Keep yourself safe, and keep that man of yours safe, too. I love you."

Samael kissed my forehead. "I love you, too, Mother."

Cael turned. "Leave the Gateway open. The influence from Lucidis can't hurt. Be safe."

"You too."

I watched as the group split against my better judgment. John, Samael, and Esco drifted back toward David and Evelyn, while Cael entered Lucidis with Roger, Sasha, and me by his side.

Chapter Ten

Heather

As an explosion rattled the building café, I huddled closer with the group of strangers as we sat together in a corner. We'd been hiding overnight, and I'd stumbled across this café to find it already had several people inside. They'd been led here by some *creature* and told they'd be safer if they stayed indoors and together. After being on the run since the quakes first started when I was grocery shopping, it was nice to feel like I had at least a hint of safety.

Even if it was only an illusion.

No one knew what was going on, and before the internet cut out late last night, the news had offered no answers. Reports of quakes and strange happenings across the globe, but no explanation and no instructions on where to hide or what to do. It was as though all at once the world decided to fall apart, and it was every person for themselves.

The café *had* been a suitable spot, but I wasn't sure how long we could remain inside the small space. These people had stayed in the café after being told to do so, because what other choice did they have but to trust its word?

I shielded my eyes as a blinding blue and white light tore through the wall, as in *through the wall*, cutting through it as though it wasn't even there, and shattered the front windows as it expanded.

"I think it's time to leave," I said, barely holding in my sarcasm, which I'd discovered yesterday was my coping mechanism. A series of nods and murmurs followed, before a woman screamed as a hand—blue, glass-like, and clawed—reached through the light. An intimidating, almost seven-foot figure followed it, and we cowered into each other as the creature stared at us with unblinking blue eyes. A young man watched the creature as it remained still, looking back at him. Its eyes were intriguingly human, but surrounded by an unfamiliar skin. A monster's skin.

The young man stood tentatively and edged toward the creature, waving his hand behind him as one of the women hissed, "What are you *doing?*"

He replied to her without turning, "Don't you remember what she said? We can trust the blue ones. She led us to safety, didn't she?" My eyes widened as he approached the creature. "Hello?"

It tilted its head, and after a pause, responded, "Hello."

Its voice was deep and grating, spoken as an unintentional stage whisper, and sent a wave of discomfort down my back, clawing at my spine. The young man trembled slightly but stood his ground. He was so close, too close, and shadowed by the creature's large frame.

The blue creature reached out its hand, holding it in the space between them, and after a moment's hesitation, the young man took it. The second they made contact, the creature tightened his grip on the man's hand, and he cried out as his fingers broke under the grip, and he struggled to wrench his arm away.

"Oh my God..." I whispered and clambered to get away from the creature. The group panicked as the man screamed, and while several went to help him, the creature ignored them as if they were no bother. A chair was broken over its back, and it barely flinched, and instead brushed the offending man away. As I edged my way along the wall, I sucked in a breath, not daring to take my eyes from the creature. When its gaze flickered to mine, my entire body crawled with sensation. Like the beast was the reaper himself. The man's screams were dying out, and he slumped, as though his energy was being sucked from him.

Was it doing something to him?

Oh fuck oh fuck. This can't be real.

When he started yanking his arm with sudden, jerky movements in a wild attempt to escape, most of the group panicked and fled the café into the street. I hovered uncertainly around the window, which looked into the café, and bit my fingernails.

"We have to help him," a woman cried.

"How?" I asked desperately.

Tell me. Tell me how and I'll help.

The more afraid the man grew, the more the creature laughed. The creature wrapped its clawed hand around the man's throat, effectively cutting off his screams as it squeezed.

"Ah..." It hummed. "The Tenebrians were right. Fear *does* feel good."

He broke the man's neck with a snap, and his lifeless body slumped to the floor with a hollow thud. The creature turned its gaze to me, and I ran.

My shoulder ached, but I dared not toss out my bag or any of its contents.

Initially, when I'd run, taking the canvas bag of groceries with me had been something I'd done without thinking, but since the canned food had fed myself and the group I was with last night, it seemed foolish to consider throwing it away now.

Although a dinner of canned peas and corn wasn't pleasant, no one complained, since no one else had anything else to offer. The café had already been cleared out.

A shudder ran down my spine despite the sun on my shoulders as I bit my lip. I hoped everyone from the café made it out alive. Closing my eyes, I tried to push away the image of the young man having his neck broken by the blue creature, but it remained insistently in the forefront of my mind.

What the fuck was going on?

Adjusting the bag on my shoulder again, I groaned as I stopped before turning a corner. I didn't even know where I was going, and instead, I found myself wandering aimlessly through the city streets. I guessed I hoped to come across another group of strangers to take me in. Peeking around the corner, I barely contained the squeak of surprise that escaped my lips at the group of people who surrounded my local supermarket, the one I'd been at only yesterday.

The supermarket was nothing more than a pile of rubble.

I approached as a man I didn't know scratched his head, and simply muttered, "Well, fuck."

Pressing my lips together, I asked him, "Were you there overnight?"

He nodded as he rubbed his temples. "Yeah, seemed like a good place to be, you know? Food and supplies and whatnot. Security doors, even. But it came down this morning."

"Now, what do we do?" a woman asked, looking at me.

I regarded her before scanning the area—the streets appeared empty. I didn't know these people, but I was now somehow considered part of their group simply by being in their proximity. Something touched me inside at the idea that a group of strangers would again take me in without question, but I didn't want to move from one building to another, and hole up until it wasn't safe anymore. "I think I'm going to try to get home," I said.

Maybe home wasn't safe anymore either, I didn't know, and I wouldn't know until I tried.

"Alone?"

I opened my mouth to answer, but paused when I heard it.

The sound.

The sound we'd heard all last night, the sound which kept us from having a decent rest, even with two people on constant lookout.

Screeching and excited chattering, which grated unpleasantly against my eardrums.

Last night, it had been distant and echoed throughout the streets and buildings.

Now, terrifyingly, it was so much closer.

Turning hesitantly, as though if I delayed the moment I saw them, it would delay having to deal with the situation, a group of the creatures came into view, skulking out from the side lanes and dotting the main street. There were two, then five, and their spikes trembled in a way that caused the morning sunlight to dance off the orange streaks. An effect that would have been beautiful if it hadn't made me feel as though my skin was crawling with insects. My eyes darted rapidly between them as, in turn, they each closed off any chance of escape.

As we were approached from all sides, the twenty or so people I found myself trapped with and I backed ourselves up against what was left of the building that had been their protection. When the ground trembled again, the creatures paid it no attention and laughed as we cowered in fear, madly looking for an escape.

"Look what we have here... some humans have emerged." The creature glanced at the collapsed building behind us before its menacing gaze fell directly onto me. My stomach crawled, a deeper and darker feeling than the blue creature had given me, and I felt as though I wanted to try to shrug out of my skin. "Pity about your hidey hole," it said with a flourish of a hand motion at the rubble. My brows furrowed, the creature had an accent which bordered on Irish, and a series of thoughts passed through my mind.

A creature with an accent?

Was he from another part of the world?

How did he get here?

But no thought was more prevalent than the one that pushed forward, and had repeated itself over and over for the past twenty-odd hours.

What the fuck *is going on?*

Another creature grunted, a monotone voice with no hint of any inflection. "Sick of talking."

There was a slight nod from the first one who spoke, and they burst into a sprint and rushed toward us. I screamed as two of them swept past either side of me, and a woman and a man shrieked as they were scooped up. My feet were fused to the ground, and I stood trembling, trying to force my body to act. Their speed was intimidating. If I tried to run, I'd never make it. My breaths came in heavy pants. I managed to turn around, and my eyes widened as a woman was snatched and pinned up against the remainder of the crumbling wall behind me by her throat. She struggled, and I released a sob I couldn't contain as chaos erupted around me—some creatures chased down those who tried to run, tackled them to the ground, and beat their heads against the road until they stopped struggling. If someone witnessed the attack and began screaming, the creatures would turn on them.

Fear exploded around me, as though I could feel the fear from everyone as well as myself, and when I opened my mouth to scream, no sound came, only a pathetic crackling whimper. A creature stepped in front of me, and I couldn't even bring myself to step back as I tilted my head to look up at it. Sharp teeth glinted in the sunlight as it grinned at me, and my fingers curled around the handle of my bag, which hung at my side.

It leant down, inhaled, and hummed, and I stood trembling as a small part of me recognized the low voice as female. "Poor, poor humans, hmmm? All this unexplained destruction, it must be so confusing for you." She practically purred as she curled a tendril of my hair around her finger, and I whimpered. "You felt safe in your hiding place overnight, didn't you? But eventually, every safe place you find is going to fall apart. The edges of your realm are disintegrating, and we're here to enjoy every bit of it. Every time you feel safe, it only means that when your illusion of safety collapses, your fear increases."

"You... you want us to be afraid?" I don't know what possessed me to try communicating with the creature. Perhaps I thought if I could keep her talking, I could get away somehow. But I flinched and squeezed my eyes shut every time there was a scream or a sound I could only assume was bones breaking around me.

The creature chuckled, and I knew there was no way I could outrun her, but I wouldn't go down without a fight either. With a grunt, I heaved my bag and swung it at the creature's head. She snarled as her jaw broke, and I also gagged at the sound of the bones popping out of place.

I might regret this.

Pivoting, I rushed at the creature, which still had the young woman pinned against the wall, and struck it with the bag. Having canned food within it certainly helped, and the creature screamed in rage as the bag struck between its shoulder blades, its body curving inward after the impact. When it turned on me, the other woman escaped. "Oh shit, oh shit, oh shit," I repeated as I swung the bag back and forth, and the creature raised its hands to cover its face as I struck repeatedly. Another creature grabbed the woman who escaped before she could help me, and it ripped at her clothes while she screamed before it laughed and threw her over its head and across the street, her body rolled limply as she hit the pavement.

"No," I cried out, and in my distraction, the creature wrenched the handbag from my hands and tossed it to the side, scattering the remaining dented cans across the road.

As the creature advanced on me, I stepped backward, and my

gaze flickered between its claws, fangs, and the unsettling look in its eyes. A fog of black passed across the whites of its eyes, and I couldn't have torn my gaze away if I tried. For every step I took back, it took one forward, and it seemed to be enjoying the slow approach and my increasing heart rate. When a can collided with the side of its head, it shrieked, and I flinched at the grating sound. The snarl it made when it bared its teeth at me would haunt my dreams.

If I get out of this alive.

Another can came flying, catching the creature in the face and breaking its nose. Dropping to the ground, I crawled along and found a place to hide within the rubble, squeezing myself between broken bits of wall and ignoring how the rough edges dug into my skin. Peeking out, the street had become flooded with more creatures, but these were the blue ones. The sunlight threw a light around them that made them appear as saviors at the dark moment, where I had almost accepted my impending death. The image of the blue creature killing the young man in the café came to the forefront of my mind again, and I tried to sink myself further into my hiding space as I watched the scene unfold. The blue creatures were equally as menacing and unpleasant in appearance as the red and orange ones.

But they were protecting the humans...

The enemy of my enemy is my friend, or so they say.

I could not survive against these creatures alone, or even with a group of people. They'd come in and decimated us as if we were nothing but playthings. Glancing around, I tried to see the extent of the damage without leaving my hiding place, and covered my mouth to hide my squeal when I saw one of the men lying dead, bent backward, eyes wide and unseeing.

Fuck, fuck, fuck.

A red creature spotted me, and as it approached me, it was tackled from the side by a blue creature. All at once, my hiding spot felt less like somewhere safe and more like a trap I was cornered in.

Fuck it.

Launching myself forward, I snatched one of the fallen cans and threw it as hard as I could, point-blank at an orange creature. A loud crack sounded when it collided with its jaw, and as it turned on me, another of the blue ones grabbed its arms from behind and forced it to its knees. When it grabbed the orange creature's head, I gasped and looked away. I didn't need to watch it to know what had happened when I heard the sickening crunch of bone and the thud of a fallen body.

"Oh, God." My intention to help was quickly replaced with thoughts of escape, but my attention was drawn to two of the younger people from the group, barely teenagers, huddled by the collapsed building. Sprinting toward them when the ground trembled again, I gritted my teeth, ignored the twist of my ankle, and tackled them to the side as further collapse sent heavy rubble tumbling to the place they'd been. I lay panting on the ground, and groaned as I pushed myself to sit. The young girl winced and grabbed her side, using her other hand to help me to my feet. She nodded curtly to me, her lips pressed into a fine line, and she tried to hold back tears.

Turning, the remaining orange creatures were fleeing, and the blue creatures rounded up the few surviving humans. Most had been either killed or had run early, and I could only hope they'd escaped the slaughter. Brushing myself off, I tutted at the tear in my pants and shook my head when I realized it was silly to care about it. But I *did* care, and I hated that I cared. With a limping stride, I tried to gather as much pride as possible to convene with the other survivors. My step faltered when there was another tremble in the earth, and I stilled until it passed. A crack formed between my feet, and I froze on the spot in indecision when another tremor came.

Do something, Heather. Move, move!

The crack widened, and my lip trembled.

Move!

Why was my response to fear so unpredictable? One moment I'm hurling myself into danger and attacking a monster with a can of beetroot, then the next I'm cowering in fear and unable to move.

A particularly harsh quake almost knocked me from my feet, but as I braced myself for the fall, I grunted when the wind was knocked from me. I tumbled, protected somehow from injury, and when I landed on my back and looked up, on instinct, I hammered my fists against the blue creature that had grabbed me. With a snarl, it snatched my wrists and held me still, and I stopped when his incredible coloring—deep blue streaked with pure white—made me suck in a breath.

I tried to yank my hands from his grip, and he snarled at me, deep and low, before he tilted his head toward where I'd been standing to make me understand. "You would have been killed."

My eyes widened as I rolled my head to the side and watched where the crack had turned into a sinkhole, which expanded and swallowed the supermarket and half the building next to it. The creature still held me, and I turned my gaze back to him to study his hands. Large and clawed, and a stark contrast to my delicate wrists and hands, adorned with gold bracelets and manicured nails, which were now beginning to split and chip. When I slid my hands from his, slowly and decisively, he didn't resist.

"Don't hurt me," I whispered.

His brow furrowed. "I am not going to hurt you."

I swallowed. "The other creatures did."

"Tenebrians. Orange and red. They are not us."

"No." I shook my head as fear gripped my chest again. The adrenaline was wearing off, and my ankle, leg, and ribs throbbed. "Earlier. It was a blue one."

His eyes widened. "It hurt you?"

"Not me. A young man, it kill—" I stopped and rolled my head to the side again as he snarled above me.

"I will not hurt you," he said again, and I nodded, wanting to believe him.

"Thank you for saving me," I whispered.

He grunted. "You are welcome, human."

The disdain in his tone at that last word wasn't lost on me, and he looked at me curiously as I frowned at him. "Please get off me," I said, half expecting him to laugh in my face and refuse. I released a sigh when he rolled off me and stood, and after I winced as I tried to stand, he held a hand out to assist me.

"Those humans you saved, did you know them?" he asked.

"No."

He tilted his head. "You could have been hurt."

"So could they. They needed help."

He stared at me momentarily, and I watched him watch me, leaning away from him on instinct. Was he planning an attack, or trying to read my mind? His jaw was tight with concentration, but his eyes were a strange mix of curiosity and intense anger. "Why are you afraid of me?" he asked.

"I don't know what you are." My breath hitched as he loomed over me, and I stepped back.

"I saved you."

"Yes, I know." I paused and eyed him carefully. "Thank you."

"I was not asking for your gratitude."

He continued to watch me, and I tried to control my fear of him, telling myself over and over that if he wanted to hurt me, he would've done so already. None of the red creatures, nor the blue one from this morning, had pretended to save us only to hurt us. It seemed they were from two opposing sides, either here to attack and inflict pain immediately, or they were here to rescue us.

"You are trying to control your fear," he said.

"I... you can tell that?"

"I am pleased. You have learnt I will not hurt you." With a nod, he turned on his heel and started to walk away.

I raised a hand and called after him, "Wait, where are you going?"

"To save more humans."

"But..." I glanced around. The other blue creatures had left when the remaining orange had fled, and had taken the few surviving humans from the massacre with them. I guess they saw me with the tall blue creature and decided I was in good hands. Was he meant to look out for me? "You're just going to leave me here? Alone?"

He stopped, turned, and stared into the distance, where I could see the shapes of the others leaving. "The group went that way." He pointed before dropping his arm. "Move quickly, and you will catch up with them."

The fabric of my top twisted as I curled it between my fingers, and glanced between the blue creature who'd saved me, and the retreating forms of the others. My desire to return home had been stamped into nothing, and all I knew now was that I desperately didn't want to be alone.

The longer I hesitated, the farther the group moved away, and even crossing that distance alone exploded butterflies of fear in my stomach. When I turned back to the creature, he watched me curiously, a small furrow on his brow as my indecision plagued me.

"But..." All my previous confidence had evaporated, and it was as if there were now a tether between this particular creature and me. I couldn't have explained it if I tried. Perhaps because of the boldness of his coloring, he appeared more predatory than the others. But he'd also communicated to me when some barely spoke at all.

And when I asked him to get off me, he did, despite the heat that passed between us at the contact.

Shaking my head, my entire body started to tremble as I sucked my bottom lip into my mouth. Once again, I found myself frozen to the spot, unable to decide, let alone find the strength to move. I jumped when the creature laid a hand on my shoulder, not having heard him approach, and I looked hopefully up at him.

Make my decision for me. I can't even think right now.

Could he read my mind? Earlier he'd seemed to be able to sense exactly what I'd been thinking without me having to say it, and despite knowing whatever was happening was occurring across the globe, despite knowing even in this very city there were likely hundreds, or thousands of people who needed help too, all I could think were two words.

Save me.

The creature dropped his hand from my shoulder, and my skin warmed where the contact had been. I lifted a hand and touched where he'd touched me, wondering if he'd *done* something. I didn't know the powers these creatures might hold. When I looked up, he was gazing down at me with an unreadable look, and I felt safe with him. He glanced up long enough to watch the rest of the group disappear around a distant corner, then he said, "You can come and help me find other hiding humans. We need to get them all together."

"Wh-why?" I whispered.

"Bringing their energies into one place will help protect them."

I didn't understand, but I nodded anyway. "I'm Heather."

His eyebrow arched and lip curved, and it almost looked like amusement. "Ferox."

Ferox started walking, and I followed, lengthening my stride to keep up with him. Occasionally, I glanced sideways at him as we walked, but he didn't speak, nor acknowledged me much beyond a small glance.

Not much could be said for his social graces, but at least I felt safer.

Chapter Eleven

Cael

The man moved through the shaky Gateway with grace, his long legs stepping through and hands held out to his sides as if he could grip the Gateway and use it to keep himself steady.

"So, this is Lucidis, huh?" he asked before he jumped slightly when the Gateway snapped shut behind him.

Bending forward at the waist, I planted my hands on my knees and took a few deep breaths. Lucidis's energy shimmered around me, but it was difficult to latch onto. Certainly, being here was more charging than being on Earth, but it wasn't the same as before the Shift began. Glancing over at Ana, she had her eyes closed and her head tilted up, while Sasha had resorted to kneeling to plant her palms directly against the soil, trying to absorb all the energy she could.

"Cael, Ana, Sasha—this is Floyd."

"Hi." Floyd lifted a hand in an awkward wave.

With another deep breath, I straightened and clasped his outstretched hand. His dark eyes widened as I prepared to take a read on him, and I arched a brow as his concentration increased before he tried to do the same to me. Lending him some of my energy, I assisted him in reading my essence, and his eyes widened as he felt my being. He appeared to be in his late thirties—it was difficult to tell precisely, and he was tall, lean, and tanned. As a Guardian, he was inexperienced. It was as though I was being read by a child Guardian.

But when I felt his essence in turn, I broke the contact.

Inside him was a churning similar to that in Ana. Not as powerful, not by a long shot, but the same combination of Guardian and human, and the same battle where the two halves tried to merge and fight each other simultaneously.

Dare I hope Roger's plan might work?

When I'd broken the contact, Floyd continued to stare at me. "Are you a Guardian?"

"Yes. Cael." Floyd looked around him, transfixed, and I inwardly cringed. "Don't look too hard. Lucidis is usually much more glorious than this." My gaze followed his, and while Floyd appeared enamored with the realm, I couldn't help but note how it appeared dull and washed out. The lines were blurred, the plant life had lost its color, and like on Earth, intermittent quakes occurred, and Gateways opened and closed randomly.

We'd attempted several times to capture an open Gateway and redirect it, as Samael and I'd done to find Ana, but to no avail. Our first attempt had been to reach the United Kingdom. Roger's idea was that we should get those farthest away first, and I agreed. However, it had proven useless, and the man we'd been trying to reach couldn't be located.

None of us speculated out loud that he might be dead.

Locating Floyd in Canada had been easier, but by no stretch of the imagination a simple task. The energy had ebbed from my body as we'd struggled to hold the Gateway open so Roger could shift its location. Sweat beaded on Sasha's forehead as she planted her bare feet harder against the soil to draw from the realm and force out the energy from her fingertips.

We had one, and now we needed to do it again.

My attention was drawn to Floyd again as he asked, "It's happening, isn't it? The thing you told me about with the Balance."

Roger's face was unreadable. "Yes, and we don't have much time to make it right."

"I-I don't know what I can do."

I grasped his shoulder. "Your presence is all we need right now."

"Floyd, look at me." Floyd turned to face Roger as he continued, "We've got to find some more of the half breeds, but they're all across the world. Reaching them is difficult, and the Gateways are hard to maintain." Roger's gaze flickered quickly to me. "This might be uncomfortable, but we must use your energy."

"No," I said, and Floyd looked at me, his eyebrows raised. "It's too soon, you could drain him entirely."

"We need all the energy we can get."

"Not at the expense of his well-being, Roger." I held up a finger when he opened his mouth, effectively silencing him. "Don't you dare tell me I don't understand what's at stake here. We *all* understand what's on the line, but you must stop putting it before everyone's lives."

"You have no idea what decisions I've had to make."

"Yes, we do," Ana mumbled, and my chest ached. Roger looked at her as though she'd run a stake through his heart, and he dropped his chin to his chest.

"Okay. Floyd, lie on the grass, try to feel the realm, and get as much energy as possible."

"Alright." Floyd walked, aware of four pairs of eyes on his back, before he awkwardly sat a few feet away and glanced at us, offered a half-smile, lay on his back, and closed his eyes.

I waited a beat before turning to Roger and intentionally placed myself between him and Ana. "Who's next?"

"Emma, she's in the United Kingdom too."

"We tried there."

Roger's eyes narrowed. "And we'll try again."

Before I could answer, Sasha's hand was on my arm. "Come on, we knew this wouldn't be easy."

"I don't like using her like this," I pushed out through gritted teeth, knowing Roger was close enough to hear, but wishing he wasn't.

Sasha glanced at Ana, who still had her eyes closed, but her brow was furrowed. "Neither do I, but you understand why, right?"

"Of course, I do," I snapped.

"I'm ready." Ana came up to my side and looked up at me. I stared into the deep brown of her eyes, wishing she would reflect some of my emotion at me. But she was still mostly a blank slate, and while cracks would appear in her armor now and then, and I'd glimpse the Ana I knew, she'd only shut down the walls harder and stronger than before.

The only time she opened up was when we needed her power to draw from, and it was starting to feel like we were using her as a battery.

"Ana, you need a break."

"We'll get Emma, then we'll break." When I kept staring at

her, she offered me a hollow smile. "I promise."

With a grunt, I took her hand and linked my other arm with Sasha's. Sasha took Roger's hand, and we concentrated on the space together, forcing open a Gateway. It was small and shimmered unconvincingly before it shrank until it was no bigger than a golf ball. Ana forced some energy into me through our physical touch, and I scowled as I took what she offered and stabilized the Gateway with Sasha. Roger was the only one familiar with Emma's imprint, so the job of shifting the location of the Gateway was on him. Keeping it open and steady, while still allowing for movement across the globe, was tricky under normal circumstances, and was even more challenging now.

Ana dropped to a knee, and I almost broke contact with Sasha.

"No," Ana whispered, and pain radiated through my body as I watched the ache on her face, her brows pulled together, and her jaw tense as she struggled to keep it together. Her fear dripped through our connection, and my eyes widened as I realized what she was doing.

She was giving enough to help us and make the Gateway happen, but she was holding back.

Ana was afraid that if she let go entirely, she'd be dangerous.

Forcing herself to maintain such control was draining her more than the Gateway would have if she had allowed her full power to come through. But what if she was right? What if she unleashed, and the Gateway collapsed or exploded?

I bit the inside of my cheek and winced at the torture she must be going through, not simply with the push-and-pull of energies, but the internal struggle she faced every moment. She closed off to protect herself, but mainly because she thought we needed protection from her.

Oh, Ana.

"Almost there," Roger called, "*Emma.*"

Opening my eyes as the Gateway stopped shifting and settled within a bedroom, I watched as a young brunette girl sat bolt upright on her bed. "Roger?" Her brows pulled together. "Why does your voice sound all distorted and weird? Is this what a Porthole sounds like?" Emma ducked her head as if she were struggling to hear.

"Emma?"

She frowned and tapped at her ear as if she could clear the static.

"Emma, come through."

"What?"

She squealed when she finally saw us, and her gaze travelled from me to Sasha before it settled on Roger. "Emma, come through. I'll explain when we're all together."

When the Gateway appeared to crack at the top, Emma held up her hands, and my eyes widened as I realized she was trying to stabilize it from her end. "Am I even helping at all?" she cried out. "It feels like I'm doing nothing." She waved her hands about before she dropped them to the mattress. "Oh my God, it's happening, isn't it?"

Roger leaned through and held out his hand. As Emma reached for him, the Gateway grew, and her eyes widened as it expanded to the size of her bedroom. "Um, is it supposed to do that?"

"No." Roger unceremoniously grabbed Emma's shoulders and yanked her forward.

"Hey," she cried as she snatched at his wrists. "I need to tell my parents where I'm going."

"Sorry, Emma. There's no time. The Gateways are unstable." He glanced uneasily at Ana, and I glared at him, hoping he could finally see the strain this was on her. As he tugged Emma through the Gateway, it collapsed, and Ana dropped both hands to the ground. Emma turned as her bedroom window exploded, and glass shattered across her bed before the image disappeared.

"Oh my God, Roger, my parents are going to think I was kidnapped or something." Emma grabbed her hair, and her brunette waves stuck out between her fingers.

"I'm sorry, Emma. We'll make all that right later, but we have bigger things to worry about now."

Emma turned slowly in a circle. "How is this possible? You can access the whole world from here?"

Floyd stood and approached as Roger answered, "Yes. Emma, this is Floyd, from Canada."

Emma shook his hand. "Um, Emma. Emma from Britain." She laughed awkwardly.

Floyd smiled back. "This is weird for me, too, Emma."

They held hands for a moment, and small energy waves passed between them as they attempted to get a read on each other. They were both inexperienced, but something sparked when they touched, and my eyebrows shot up as Roger glanced at me, a glimmer of hope in his eyes that we were moving in the right direction. A flicker of temptation fluttered to life within me to get Ana to clasp hands with Floyd and Emma, but experimenting with their power could wait.

"Cael," I said, and held out my hand.

Emma dropped the contact with Floyd and turned to me.

"Emma." She took my hand, and immediately, I felt the Guardian half within her. Much like Floyd, it was newly battling with the human half, having been relatively recently brought to the surface and not having been exposed to the influences it required to flourish. While Lucidis felt as though it were dying, it could still be drawn from if I focused. With a grimace, I filtered what I could from the air and channeled it into Emma, and her eyes shot up to mine as she felt the change. When her palm started to glow a slight blue, she gasped and yanked her hand away.

"Sorry." She awkwardly wrung her fingers together. "I'm just not used to all of this."

"It's okay. I know it's a lot. Unfortunately, we don't have the time to ease you into it, and there will be a certain element of experimentation."

Her eyes narrowed. "Experimentation, how?"

Sasha added, "Nothing nefarious, we simply need to see how you react to different influences. Lucidis, Guardians, other half-breeds." Her eyes too flickered to Ana, and I closed my eyes for a moment to squash down the anger that bubbled in my stomach. Ana was needed to help restore the Balance, but treating her as though she were a tool was no better than what the Tenebrians did.

But how could I consider the possibilities, and protect her at the same time?

"So, you need us half-breeds?" Emma asked.

"We'll explain everything once we have you gathered," Roger said as he held his hand out to Sasha. "While our strength seems to grow with the more of us who are together, so does the instability of the world."

Sasha held her hand to me, and I stared at it before glaring at Roger. "No. We need to rest."

I could almost see the internal debate within Roger, and I prepared myself to fight my point with him. As a Guardian, I was stronger than he was. If it came down to it, I would do what was necessary to ensure Ana had a break.

Roger was mistaken if he thought he was the only one battling between duty and love. It appeared that since he'd spent so much of his life preparing for an eventuality the Elders didn't seem to consider, he'd lost some of the empathy he'd found when he'd fallen in love with Ana's mother. His loyalty to his duty was still strong, and while I respected that, I wouldn't allow it to be at the expense of Ana's well-being.

"I'm okay, Cael," Ana said as she stood.

"You promised." There was almost amusement in her expression at my statement, and my anger withered as I looked at her. "Please, rest."

Sasha dropped Roger's hand. "I think we could all use a rest to recharge."

Roger sighed, nodded, and sat on the ground. We all followed suit, and in the silence that ensued, Sasha nudged Emma with her elbow. "Tell us how you found out about your mixed heritage."

Ana sat beside me, leaned her head on my shoulder, and I wrapped an arm around her. Her small sigh of contentment was enough for me to cling to. She was okay, or would be, eventually. The smallest signs she was still there were gifts, and I clung to each one. She hadn't stopped blaming herself, and I didn't think she would, no matter what we did or said. Coupled with the control she was enforcing on herself, it's a wonder she didn't crumble to the ground and refuse to get up.

Once again, she'd proven stronger than I think even she was aware.

"Roger found me three years ago," Emma started, and glanced at Roger as if asking for permission to continue. He nodded, and she continued, "He contacted me asking what I knew about my birth parents—I was adopted, see? I thought he would tell me *he* was my father, but he claimed he could help me learn about my heritage. We met in a public place, and when he told me..." Emma blew out a breath, her cheeks puffed up

Floyd chuckled. "I know what you mean. I didn't know if I should listen or run away."

"Obviously, it was difficult to accept what he was saying, but then he touched my hand and it was like... floodgates opened or something. I could sense the people around me, and the emotions of those at the café overwhelmed me, leaving me with a jumble of confused feelings. Everything all at once. It was a lot, and right before I thought my skin would burst apart, he took his hand away."

"You were angry," Roger added.

"Damn right I was angry. You'd contacted me under false pretenses, and then told me not only that other realms existed, but that my father was *of* one of these other realms. My birth mother, of course, would have had no idea, a one-night-stand resulting in a child she didn't want, I don't hold that against her."

"But you were adopted out?" Floyd asked.

"Yep. I love my parents, and they *are* my parents as far as I'm concerned. You weren't?"

Floyd shook his head as he brushed his hands over the grass.

"Nope, Mom raised me as a single mother."

"You never asked about your dad?"

"Of course, I did, but she said they were together only a week or two, and when he left, she never found him again." He lifted a shoulder.

"When did Roger find you?"

"About twelve years ago."

"Did you practice your powers?" Emma asked him.

Floyd grimaced. "Not really. Wishing I had, though."

"I did. Well, I tried at least." Emma looked at Roger. "Roger told me there were half-breeds all across the world, hundreds, maybe thousands, and most people wouldn't give him the time of day. He was finding as many as he could, although it had taken him years to refine his technique for finding us, for recognizing the imprint of a half-breed."

"Did he tell you why he was looking?" I asked.

Emma nodded. "Yes. He said partially because he had a half-breed daughter himself, and thought there must've been other Guardians who fell in love, but it was only when he dug deeper did he suspect some breeding program." She shuddered. "So, I assumed at some point a male Guardian would come for me, try to get me pregnant, then take the child."

I snarled, but said nothing. That was the plan as Cascus had described it. But did they simply hope the women would want to give up their children, or did they take them regardless?

Floyd stilled before he looked up. "You don't think... *I've* gotten a Guardian pregnant along the way somewhere?"

"I dunno, Floyd, how many unprotected one-night stands have you had?"

"Enough," he answered flatly.

"It's possible," Roger answered.

Floyd's brows furrowed as he returned to brushing his fingers through the grass.

"Emma..." She looked up as I spoke. "You said Roger's reason for finding you was only *partially* because he had a daughter. Did he tell you why else?"

I could feel Roger's eyes on me, and Emma glanced between us before she answered. "He said one day he might need us and that it may not happen in my lifetime, but he'd noticed patterns that led him to suspect the event would occur sooner rather than later. He told me to practice what he'd taught me, just in case."

"What event?"

Emma looked uncomfortable, as if she'd told a secret she wasn't meant to, and Roger said, "I haven't hidden anything from you, Cael."

"What event, Emma?" I pushed.

"The Shift of the Balance."

My gaze settled on Roger, and he held my look steadily. "You suspected what the Tenebrians were doing this entire time, didn't you?"

"I had my suspicions, yes." When I didn't answer and pulled Ana closer to my side, Roger added, "I can feel your anger."

"I'm not angry at you, Roger, I'm angry at myself for not seeing it sooner."

Glancing down at Ana, I found her looking up at me with those heartbreaking eyes. I tried to force a smile, an apology for everything she had been through, things that may not have happened had I realized sooner. The corner of her lip twitched in her attempt to return the gesture, but it was all she managed.

Squeezing her by my side, we connected our essences through the contact.

She was still my Ana, but inside, the light of hope was gone.

Ana reached forward, grabbed my other hand, and stared at our intertwined fingers. The flow of energy between us increased, and my brow furrowed. I tried to block the energy, but couldn't stop her from recharging me. Ana could more effectively draw energy from Lucidis, and she was sharing it with me.

"You're more than this, Ana," I whispered as I leaned over and buried my face in her hair. The energy flow skipped as she gasped, and her jaw muscles tightened as she held in her emotion. "I promise, when this is all over, you'll never feel used again."

"Love you," she muttered, so quietly I thought I'd imagined it for a moment.

"I love you, too." I kissed the top of her head, and when I looked up, Roger was standing and helped Sasha to her feet.

"Ready?" he said, and while he looked at me, I knew he was asking Ana.

Ana nodded, and we stood together.

Roger flexed his fingers as he sighed heavily. "Alright. Next stop, Mumbai."

Chapter Twelve

Heather

Leaning against a building, I allowed myself to sink slowly, ignoring how the bricks snagged at my hair, and slumped against the wall. Ferox and I had been walking for hours and had found two more small groups of people. I was glad to be able to help, but I was tired. The people were quicker to trust Ferox because of my presence. Ferox had herded them all toward the city center, where they were trying to gather as many people as possible to keep them safe.

A moment of hesitation had snagged me, and I almost considered going with one of the groups of people. But I felt safer with Ferox than I did wandering the city alone or even with other people who didn't know what was going on either. Previous experience had shown me that safety in numbers didn't necessarily help.

I could tell Ferox found peoples' lack of trust frustrating. "I have spent my entire life protecting them," he muttered angrily after the first group hustled away from us, and he'd turned on his heel with a huff. I pressed my lips together as I followed him. He'd explained to me briefly what Guardians were and their purpose, and I can only imagine how frustrating it must have been to try to help more, only to have them respond with fear at the sight of him.

Beyond that, it almost seemed as though the fact that he was frustrated was in itself a frustration to him. Whenever he'd shown any signs of emotion—usually anger or impatience—he'd swipe away at the air around him, as if feelings were something which came from outside him, rather than inside.

Hugging my arms around myself against the chill of the dark and the anxiety of what lay within it, I settled in for a long night. Ferox sat beside me and offered me some food he had collected along the way. "Tomorrow, we'll head west."

"Am I helping?"

Ferox looked at me. Even sitting down, he was an impressive figure, intimidating due to his height and build, as well as the bold colors that made up his scales. "Yes, you are helping. The humans do not trust me."

There was a bubbling of frustration in his voice. "Does it upset you? That they don't trust you?"

He laughed, harsh and cold, a grumble through his sharp teeth. "I am not upset. That is a human weakness."

"But you're angry?"

He rounded on me, and I shrank against the wall. "I have done nothing but protect humans my entire life, and they treat me like a monster. I could kill them all so easily, but I choose to help instead. This should be enough." He glared at me as though what all people thought was somehow my fault, and my eyes widened under the intensity of his gaze. Ferox huffed. "I would change my appearance, but..."

"Wait, what? You can do that?"

He turned, staring resolutely back at the alley wall before us. "I should be able to appear human, but I cannot. Something in the air..." He didn't appear to be talking to me now, but was talking to himself. "Something with the changes, I cannot shift anymore. I am stuck in this form."

I took in his appearance and wondered if I should say something about *this form* not being so bad after all, once I'd gotten past the initial shock of him. I'd watched him often throughout the day as he moved through the city. He had distinct muscle definition beneath his daunting outer skin, but I hadn't had a chance to have a good look at his face until now. His eyes, while a striking ice blue, were underlined by a ring of deep blue, almost like eyeliner, which made him appear as though he were constantly ready for war. Although he continually denied having feelings about anything, there was rage within him, and it was clearer than ever when I could take a moment to look into his eyes.

I wouldn't go as far as to say he was hurt—angry, but hurt.

"I'm sorry they don't trust you. People are afraid."

"We are all afraid."

Ferox's back stiffened after the words had left his mouth, and as a shudder ran down my spine, my fingers twitched with the urge to hold his hand and to comfort him. I've never been particularly good at reading people, and my attempts at doing so often led me astray, resulting in being misled or hurt. But even to me, it was clear he didn't intend to voice his fears or anger, and as I tilted my head, I watched him while he worked through his thoughts. This Guardian was a strange creature, obviously capable of feeling but apparently deemed emotions beneath him. Were all Guardians like him?

He had known about the different realms his entire life, and that his home was only one of three. He'd known there were humans, and two types of Guardians.

And yet he was still afraid of what was happening.

If *he* was afraid, then what chance did I have?

I folded my arms over my chest, as though hugging myself would help abate the fear which seemed to crawl through the very air, and not simply originate from inside me.

Maybe he was on to something when he tried to swipe the air away.

I wasn't sure I was ready to know, but I still asked, "What exactly is happening?"

Ferox shifted uncomfortably against the wall as he glanced around the corner intermittently. He'd chosen a place that hid us from a view of the street but offered enough escape options if needed. He sighed, and while it sounded more like a grunt, it was definitely a sigh.

He was troubled, this Guardian man.

Saving the world was an insurmountable burden, I imagined.

"There's the Balance between the three realms, in constant motion due to all the human emotions, positive and negative, pushing it one way and the other. This is normal. We are the Guardians of the Balance between the realms." He looked at me as if to make sure I was following him. I raised my eyebrows and indicated that he should keep talking, and he cleared his throat. "The Balance has begun what is called the Shift, which means it has been pushed too far in one direction. The realms will merge, and Earth as you know it will continue to crumble. My home, too, is being destroyed."

"What can we do?"

He shrugged. "Not much. Band together, strength in numbers. Humans and Guardians may simply need to learn to survive together in what is left of the world." His upper lip creased at the thought, and I pressed my lips together in a thin line.

"I'll try not to take that personally," I muttered.

Ferox glanced at me. "Personally?"

"Your obvious distaste for humans." He blinked, but otherwise remained expressionless. A mixture of emotions plagued me when he continued to stare at me in silence. A spark of anger clashed with my uncertainty and fear, and a hint of amusement pushed against it all. "Do you hate us?" I swallowed, hating how my voice broke at the question. What was going on with my feelings? They were all over the place. My earlier inability to control myself in a high-stress situation, I had put down to terror and adrenaline, but I seemed to flip back and forth between different things. I cleared my throat. "For what we did to the Balance, I mean. You seem to... not like humans."

"The Balance shifting is not your fault," Ferox said blankly.

"But, you still don't seem to like us."

"Humans are weak."

My eyebrows raised, and Ferox's lip twisted. Would it be too much to hope he'd realize he'd said something harsh? He'd been blunt all day, but now and then I caught him as though he were considering his words.

"Humans..." he rolled the word around his mouth while he thought. "Humans *feel.*"

"So do you."

Anger flared in his eyes. "I do not feel."

I scoffed, and he snarled. Perhaps I shouldn't be so blasé with taunting this creature I knew little about, but I *did* know he wouldn't hurt me. He'd had more than enough opportunity to, and instead had been protective, and ushered me away or hid me behind his body when there was immediate danger. "Liar. You feel. I can see anger in you right now."

He huffed air through his nose and slumped roughly against the wall. After a moment, his expression cleared, and he sighed again. "Earth must be affecting me."

"Maybe that's not such a bad thing," I said.

Ferox narrowed his eyes at me. "Explain."

"Explain why you think feeling is a weakness."

"Humans lack control. They *react* to things immediately."

"Ah, so you *can* feel, you *choose* not to."

"Guardians do not feel."

"More lies." Ferox snarled again at my response, and I shook my head. "Okay, let's call a truce before this argument escalates. Obviously, I don't know enough about Guardians to make an educated call, but I guess what I meant about it not being a bad thing was..." I smacked my lips as I relaxed against the wall and tried to find the words. "Life is hard, and sometimes shitty things happen." I squeezed my eyes shut. All too recently, I'd broken my own rule and taken home a man I'd just met, because I thought we had a connection, and he'd used and rejected me in the harshest way.

Back to me being terrible at reading people.

It was my turn to sigh. "Life is hard, but I can't imagine not being able to feel the good things too. Something exciting might happen, and then I feel *nothing*? That would suck the big one."

"The big what?"

I laughed. “See? You don’t get to feel how funny that was.”

Ferox had turned his head to the side and continued to stare at me. “You are strange, Heather.”

“I’m human, maybe we’re all strange to you.”

His lip twitched. “Perhaps. But I like you.”

“You do?”

“Yes.”

Maybe I imagined the flicker his eyes did up and down my body, maybe I didn’t, but the shudder which ran through me wasn’t one of fear or disgust.

I cleared my throat. “So, this is it then? The end of the world. There’s no going back?” The question successfully distracted me from the confusing jumble of emotions and my abrupt, acute awareness of Ferox’s proximity, as well as the muscles of his arms. However, the turn in conversation also reminded me of the destruction so far, and my initial thought had been that I’d never again have my comfortable lifestyle. My clothes, my home, and my shoes. Small things, like being able to buy groceries rather than foraging, or something similar. Looking at my outstretched legs, I internally scolded myself for these thoughts. People were dying, and more important things were happening right now than the loss of my creature comforts.

Did the fact that I was aware how selfish it was to think that make it okay? Did my secondary thought, correcting the original train of thought, wipe the slate clean? It had been so easy to focus on the superficial things, because I’d had nothing else to worry about. Yet in a matter of hours, the entire world had been turned upside-down, and I’d been forced to face the reality of not only my own and other people’s imminent deaths, but that I had nothing to show for who I was beyond some nice *things.*

Who was I beyond that?

Ferox shook his head. "I do not think there is a way to go back." He watched as I absorbed his words, my chest feeling hollowed out and sunken.

Ferox remained silent, and I rested my head on his shoulder. "What are you thinking?" I whispered, as exhaustion began to take hold of me.

"I was thinking I protected humans, because they needed protection." He remained still with me, leaning against him. "You are small and fragile, and I will do my best to keep you safe."

I didn't know if he was talking about humans in general or me specifically, so after I stifled a yawn, I mumbled, "Thank you."

"I do not know how many we will be able to save when the Balance finally lets go of the thin thread it is holding on to, but I will do everything I can to help."

"You're a good man, Ferox."

"Get some sleep," he said as his body stiffened. "We need to get moving early."

I nodded and sighed as I relaxed against Ferox, wishing for a dreamless sleep.

When I awoke, the sun had not yet risen, but the sky held a pinkish warmth that indicated daybreak wasn't far away. The air was cool and crisp against my legs, the breeze easily breaking through the fabric where it was torn, but I was warm and content, and in my half-asleep state, I didn't feel like moving yet. Wanting to stay comfortable for as long as possible and given what awaited us beyond this moment, I closed my eyes again. With a dramatic sigh, I fluttered my eyes open and looked up at Ferox to find I was nestled in the nook of his arm and shoulder, and his large arm was wrapped around me. No wonder I was warm and cozy. As I watched, Ferox opened his eyes and glanced down at me. We stared at each other silently for a moment, which seemed to draw out into minutes.

When his shoulder twitched under me, I sat up so he could slide his arm out from behind me.

His brow furrowed. "We were embracing."

Rubbing my arms, the sting of the morning chill was more prominent without the closeness of Ferox. "I guess we were."

"Did we have sex?"

My back straightened, and I tried to keep my face passive and remind myself Ferox wasn't human, and perhaps his customs weren't the same. But from the deepening frown on his face, he'd noticed my shock at the suggestion. "No, we didn't."

He looked at the spot I had been leaning. "So, why were we embracing?"

"For comfort, I suppose. To feel safe and not alone."

"This is something humans do?"

"Sometimes," I said, and brushed my fingers through the knots in my hair for something to do. "Sometimes we cuddle when we care about someone... or we're sad or scared or happy," I added as an afterthought.

"Sad or scared or happy?" His lip twitched—it was almost a smile, and I narrowed my eyes at him.

I'd been judged on my looks my entire life, and no matter what I did, it never seemed enough. If I wore expensive brand-name clothing, people would think I was vain and only cared about money. If I wore generic clothes, people would call me a slob. There was no middle ground, and I could do nothing to stop being judged. Consequently, I allowed myself to buy the clothing *I* wanted, letting my love of fashion and desire for quality drive what I chose to wear, and disregarding everyone else's opinions and thoughts.

At least, I *pretended* not to care what anyone thought.

They had taught me a harsh lesson—how to judge others on their appearance as I had been judged—and it was a difficult habit to break.

But being judged purely for being a human being? That was a new one.

Ferox watched me for a moment before he stood abruptly, leaving me kneeling on the ground at his feet, in awe of his gigantic stature. Standing hastily, I brushed the grime from myself as best I could. "I'm sorry. I must look a mess."

He looked me up and down, his eyes lingering on where my dress pants cinched at my waist, then at the small tear in my top above one of the buttonholes, exposing a hint of breast. The corner of his mouth turned up. "You look good."

Another chill ran up my spine, and it had nothing to do with the morning air and everything to do with the seductive and suggestive nature of his tone. As if he could sense the effect he'd had on me, his smile broadened, and he continued to grin as he turned to stride toward the street. Shaking my head to clear my mind, I followed him.

How could I even *think* of Ferox that way? I noticed his body and his eyes and wondered how his hands would feel on my body or how his scales would feel under my fingers.

Not only was he practically a stranger—he wasn't even *human.*

Chapter Thirteen

Heather

The few small groups of people we'd found in the past couple of hours had been ushered toward the city center. Thankfully, I was wearing flats instead of heels when the apocalypse struck. But they were hardly designed for hiking, and the ache in my feet was exacerbated with each step.

But Ferox had work to do, and I wanted to help.

I wanted to do *something*.

As we entered an area dotted with small restaurants, nerves sprang up in my stomach, and I swallowed against them. Whether Ferox had been skirting around certain areas, or if I was imagining it, I wasn't sure. But I'd heard the screams of terror as they'd echoed throughout the streets as we walked, the sound bouncing around the buildings and making pinpointing it difficult. My fingers twisted together as I followed behind Ferox, my eyes darting from side to side, looking at every nook and shadow, and simply waiting for one or more of those red Guardians to leap and attack. Ferox could track people using some sense I couldn't figure out, which I'd resolved to ask him about at some point when we stopped for a rest. I'd tried to talk to him as we walked, but it seemed that too much probing and personal questions set him on edge, and while he'd been chatty enough this morning, catching him in the mood to talk was something I was still figuring out.

Movement caught my eye, but when my head whipped around, it was simply a large crow flying from a rooftop, and I sighed out my relief. If I never reencountered another red Guardian, I'd be happy. I watched Ferox walk ahead of me, leading the way purposefully, and I couldn't help but think that he was intentionally keeping me from areas where I might not be safe.

Well, *more* unsafe. I didn't think anywhere was particularly safe at the moment.

But it begged the question, could he potentially be avoiding places where survivors might be hiding, to keep *me* safe? Grimacing, I shook the thought from my mind. Ferox had greater things to worry about than my safety alone, and despite the hints that he found me physically attractive, he wouldn't abandon his duty for one human.

"Are you hungry?"

I turned at his voice, and smiled as I placed a hand on my stomach. *Was* I hungry? I couldn't even be sure. The churning in my stomach from anxiety and concern hadn't stopped since the first earthquake, but had at least reduced to a simmer since Ferox found me.

He followed the movement of my hand and nodded once as though that were confirmation enough, and squinted as he scoured the area of abandoned cafes.

"Are you hungry?" I asked.

"Often. But I can ignore it."

A laugh tumbled from my lips before I could help it, and Ferox's gaze darted to my face. "Sorry," I said as I stifled my laugh behind my hand. "Just *often* was an odd response." I looked him up and down. I'd *almost* gotten used to looking at him without my gaze drifting to his crotch. He'd been naked since the moment I'd first seen him, and seemed completely unbothered by it, so I tried to be too. "But I had this mental image of you at a banquet table stuffing your face. You're a big guy, I bet you eat a lot."

His arms and chest flexed, and my cheeks flamed when I realized he was doing it intentionally. There was a glint in his eye as he looked down at me again, and a twitch of his lip was the only giveaway when a breathy giggle left me.

What was *happening to me?* He wasn't *human.*

As though I needed to keep reminding myself.

But he didn't treat me like a trophy, and he listened when I talked. It was odd. Despite his occasional comments about humans being weak and his apparent disdain for us, he never treated me as though I were anything less than worthy of his company.

"Come," he said, and grabbed my wrist as he dragged me toward a café. "I smell bread."

"How—" it wasn't until we'd breached the café entrance that the smell hit me, too, and I breathed it in gratefully. The smell of fresh bread was delectable, though I doubted it was that fresh anymore. The scent still lingered from the back room of the café. How Ferox had smelt it from across the street was beyond me, and I pressed my arms to my sides as abruptly I became aware of the sweat which clung to my skin.

Did *I* stink to him?

Ferox was already vaulting himself over the counter, and I scrambled to follow as he pushed open the swing door to reveal the bakery out back. I got caught up checking out the photos on the wall—no doubt family members of those who worked at or owned the place, and my heart stung. Was it difficult for them to abandon this café? Had it been in their family for generations?

Once again, I found myself looking down at my clothes. Every passing moment forced me to reassess who I'd been, and who I was, and while I never considered myself particularly shallow, I wondered how I'd come across to others.

Could I have tried harder?

I wasn't a *snob,* at least, I didn't think so. But is that how I was seen? While I supposed it shouldn't matter what others thought of me, the idea that nobody had really *seen me* in years stung. Not the real me, not the me that lies below the layers of expensive clothes, jewelry, and makeup.

How much of that was my fault for not trying harder to connect?

I loved my creature comforts, but perhaps I'd put them on a pedestal higher than anything else.

Is the end of the world the best time to assess myself like this?

Roused from my musings by Ferox's appearance behind me, I jumped as he laid a hand on my shoulder. When I turned, his eyebrow was arched, and he handed me a sourdough roll. "Eat."

"Thank you." I accepted the roll. "What about you?"

He held up another and bit into it as I nodded. When I continued to stare at Ferox, his brows furrowed as he swallowed. "What is wrong?"

"You're um..." I smirked and brushed at his shoulder. "You're covered in flour."

Ferox lifted an arm and gazed expressionless at the powder coating on his scales. I cried out when he shook his entire body like a dog, lifting his scales and the sharper quills on his back as he shook.

"Whoa," I whispered, my jaw hanging open as Ferox's scales shifted flat against his skin again. I hadn't realized how prominent they were until they were all raised. He stared at me, and I couldn't read his expression. It was as though he was searching my face for something. "Can I..." I placed my bread on a counter and lifted my other hand. "Can I touch them?"

He stilled. "Yes."

Ferox was tense as I moved forward, and gently, I placed a hand on his arm over the scales. They were hard, like individual pieces of armor, but as I brushed my fingers over them, they smoothed out together, creating almost a seamless transition from one to the other. Ferox's shoulders relaxed slightly, until boldly I reached up and ran my fingertip over a quill protruding from his upper back.

"Careful," he hissed the word out, and my gaze flickered to his eyes before I traced the quill to the very tip, and carefully tested it. It was sharp, and when I sucked in a breath, Ferox moved so quickly my head spun. With an arm around my waist, he clutched my hand in his and inspected the tip of my finger. "Did I cut you?"

"No," I breathed the word out.

The closeness of our bodies was impossible to ignore, and slowly his gaze dragged up my arm, over my chest and neck as he seemed to realize it too.

"What's happening?" I whispered, although I couldn't be sure I had spoken the words aloud. I was drawn to this being, and although I continued to remind myself he wasn't human, as though the evidence wasn't staring me in the face every time I looked at him, all I saw was *him.* Eyes full of soul, and confusion, yet a strength I longed for. I felt his attitude was simply a façade, and while it was unlike me to want to dig beneath the surface, with Ferox, I wanted to.

Ferox didn't answer my question, though I suspected there was no answer, and his gaze flickered as he seemed to look back and forth between my eyes.

"Eat," he said finally, as his arm slipped from around me. "Then we will continue to search."

I nodded and picked up the bread with shaking fingers, unable to get the sensation of Ferox's skin out of my mind.

Ferox pointed to a restaurant. "There is a group in there, a large group."

"Shall I go in first?" Usually, that had been the plan, but this time Ferox hesitated.

"There are too many of them, and humans are unpredictable. If they are scared, you might get hurt."

"I can defend myself."

He looked at me with a grin. "But you don't have your bag with the hard tins."

I laughed, then tilted my head when I realized I didn't know how to respond to Ferox making a joke. "Just stay behind me a bit, then. Let them see me first." And without waiting for an answer, I led the way into the restaurant.

It was darker inside, and the only light came from the windows caked with dust from the partially collapsed buildings. "Hello?" I called out as I took careful steps forward. "Is anyone in here? I've come to take you to safety."

A handful of men appeared from the shadows around the tables, and when I glanced past their shoulders and legs, the terrified eyes of women, children, and younger men, perhaps up to thirty people in total, peered back at me. My eyebrows flickered upward. I was impressed they'd managed to gather so many and keep them together. From what I'd seen and what Ferox had told me, larger groups tended to attract the attention of the other Guardians without Ferox's kind to protect them.

"Who are you?" one spoke. His voice was gruff, and he held a leg from a broken chair in one hand and rested it across his other palm like a club.

Holding my hands up in surrender, I said, "My name is Heather." My lip twitched as I resisted the urge to say *I come in peace.* It probably wasn't an appropriate time for an icebreaker. "People are gathering together in the city center, and I've come to take you there."

"You alone?"

At this, Ferox stepped into the sunlight, which lay across the floor in strips, and peeked between the gaps in the wood the people had used to cover the windows. "She is not alone."

The response was immediate, and one of the men grabbed my arm and shuffled me to the side as all the men's postures changed. They had been tense before, but now they were poised to attack.

"You're one of them," he cried.

Shaking my arm free from his grip, I stepped forward and

used myself as a barrier between the men and Ferox. "No, wait, please. He's with me, and he's here to protect you." The words came out in a rush, and I moved my hands in small pushing motions as if I could hold them back by will alone. I didn't want them to attack, partially because I feared Ferox could be hurt, and partially because I feared what Ferox could do to them.

He scoffed. "Not likely. We saw one of those chasing people down the street."

"The same color as me?" Ferox asked.

"I don't give a shit what *color* they were, they looked like you, *creature*."

Ferox's eyes narrowed. "I am here to help."

The man snorted. "I know what I saw, and I saw you weird creatures hurting innocent people. I'm as sure about what I saw as I'm sure we're not going anywhere with one of your kind."

"Please..." I pleaded and stepped forward again. It took a moment for me to catch the eye contact of the man speaking, his gaze pinned sharply on Ferox as his fingers gripped the makeshift club he held. "We are trying to bring everyone together safely." Releasing a slow breath, I struggled not to let the fear that crept up my spine show. When the man's arm twitched, I barely stopped myself from flinching. The irony that the ones I was most afraid of in that moment were my fellow humans wasn't lost on me. "I'm with him, and he's been protecting me. Some of the creatures are good, and some aren't. If he wanted to hurt me, he's had plenty of chances, but I promise he's been protecting me and wants to help you too."

"How do we know you're not one of them? Maybe they're shapeshifters or something."

My lips pressed together. "I don't think—"

A cry of surprise left my lips as a man leaped forward and sliced at me with a kitchen knife. Holding my arm in front of my face, the blade had made a clean cut across my forearm. I jumped back and gripped my arm as blood started to flow. "Son of a bitch!"

One of the older men rounded on the one with a knife. "What the fuck did you do that for?"

The first man stuttered, "Th-They're aliens. Maybe their blood is green or something."

"Does that look like a goddamn alien to you?" He pointed at me as I wrapped the base of my top around the wound and held it in place to stem the gradual flow of blood.

"I just—"

But Ferox was on him, and with his roar of rage, my pain spiked in time with the throbbing of my wound, as his anger seemed to penetrate my senses. Again, I found myself frozen to the spot, still unsure exactly how the Guardian's apparent powers worked, and tried to force my mind to *act.* Ferox crossed the room in two swooping strides, grabbed the man by the throat, and lifted him from his feet. One of the other men broke his makeshift club over Ferox's back and looked in horror at the splintered wood remaining in his hands as Ferox's rage-filled eyes, flashing white, glared at him.

"*No,*" I screamed as Ferox reached for the second man with his free hand and forced my way between the group. "*No,* don't fight."

The men retreated, their eyes suspicious and pinned on me, but Ferox still held a man by his throat, and his eyes bulged as he scrambled against Ferox's clawed hand. Placing a palm on his arm, I smoothed down the raised scales as I stared intently at

Ferox. Slowly and deliberately, his pupils slid to my face. "Let him go..." I whispered, as I brushed down some more scales, "... he's frightened."

Ferox growled, and the sound ended in a chirrup-like screech as he lowered the man and stepped back, dropping him unceremoniously to the floor.

"Please." I turned back to the man who seemed to be in charge. "We can't be fighting against each other. We're trying to help."

His gaze shifted between my blood-stained top and my face. He stared at me for a moment, and his eyes darted nervously between me and Ferox before he nodded stiffly. "Okay. But we're taking weapons." He lifted his chin at the other men, who immediately retreated to gather the rest of the group. The man Ferox had attacked stumbled to his feet, rubbed his neck, and coughed. He looked at me, and almost slipped as he backed away from me as though I would reach out and attack him myself. My brows drew together until I glanced behind me. Ferox's shadow covered me as he stood over me protectively, his scaled arms crossed over his broad chest. The man looked at Ferox in terror, then back at me, before he muttered, "I'm sorry."

"I understand," I said.

Ferox may have been rougher than required as the group gathered, and he ushered the men out of the building. He directed them to the city center and told them to hurry. They listened without question, and one of the women glanced back at me with sad eyes, pressing her lips together in what would have been a smile on any other day, but today it was a grimace of acceptance.

"Are you okay?" Ferox asked without looking at me as he

watched them retreat.

Lifting the fabric from my arm, I dabbed at the wound. "Yes, it's stopped bleeding. I don't think it was that deep."

"I do not understand humans," he said. "Why attack each other?"

"They're frightened."

"That is weak. Things are changing, and weakness will not survive. They need to learn."

"We're trying our best." I frowned at him. "That's why we must protect the weak, not hurt them..." I paused as I narrowed my eyes at Ferox. "I'm quite weak. You know that, right?"

He glanced down at me with a glint of triumph in his eyes. "Yes, but you have me."

Chapter Fourteen

Vikt

Should I be above seeking out and tormenting humans? Perhaps. But we'd worked for this for decades, and plans were coming to fruition. I may as well enjoy myself in these final days before the Shift is completed, as when it was done I'd need to fight and claim my rightful place as leader.

A nursing home near a hospital had been mostly abandoned, and I'm sure the staff had evacuated as many of the residents as they could. But as the building started to collapse and Guardians started appearing in greater numbers, they'd made the difficult decision to leave with the occupants who couldn't walk for themselves.

This left those bedridden within the buildings alone and frightened. My lips curled into a grin as I thought of the staff. They'd hate themselves forevermore for having to make the decision, but it had been a case of attempting to save the many instead of dying for the sake of a few. They'd be forced to carry the burden of their actions with them, and as I breathed in, I could almost feel the lingering desperation and self-loathing that permeated the air.

There was no fog anymore, not like how it used to be possible to build it. Instead, the air was a potent and toxic mix of fear and negativity, and the overwhelming presence of terror consumed any pockets of positive energy, snuffing them out of existence.

The building was old, and as the quakes and explosions had increased, the structure had deteriorated quickly. But I could feel a few lingering presences inside, thick with fear, and I wanted to take their last moments and make it worse.

As I approached, a staff member fled the building, and practically blinded by tears, she didn't even see me. Laughing, I watched as three Tenebrians chased after her as she ran screaming from the building, and they grabbed and slashed at her clothes as she fled. I entered, and almost slipped on a puddle of blood from a member of staff who'd been crushed by falling debris.

Coming into the first occupied room, an elderly lady lay in bed. She had her head turned and was watching the chaos unfold out the window, and I wondered how much she was actually seeing and how much of her mind was left.

As she rolled her head toward the door of her room, her eyes widened, and her oxygen mask became foggy as her breathing increased with her heart rate.

She stuttered as her hands gripped helplessly at the bed sheets. "Are you the devil?" she gasped.

A wide smile adorned my face. "Yes."

He wasn't difficult to find, even though he hid in his human form. A spark of indignation flared in me as I watched the elderly man shuffle down the almost empty street. I'd been unable to shift between my human and natural forms, and while I knew the only reason he *could* was because he was an Elder and held more power than I did, it didn't mean it wasn't irritating. I wanted to gain people's trust as a human, only to turn on them as a Guardian.

Not having the Lucidians over my shoulder attempting to correct every small shift I made was exhilarating. There were groups of them around the city, as there were groups of us. But they were so focused on trying to protect the humans, they couldn't keep track of all of us at once.

The elderly man neared a group of around a dozen wandering humans, and I slipped into the shadows to watch it play out. He could have the fun I couldn't, and I wanted to witness it at least once.

"Are you sure we're better off moving around rather than bunkering down?" A woman with dark hair twisted her hands in front of her.

"If we're in one place, we're open to attack, or a building collapsing on us. This way we've managed to avoid most of those... whatever the fuck they are."

The woman scoffed. "Mostly? You have a short memory, then."

He rounded on her as the group came to a halt. "If they had've run when I said run, they would've been fine."

"Those creatures were waiting for us. Maybe they can smell our sweat or something. But they were *waiting.*"

"It was bad luck, and nothing more."

She poked a finger at his chest. "We lost six people to them.

Six people." Several of the group sniffled, and she continued. "We thought you knew what you were doing, and you've been leading us in circles."

"If you want to leave, then *leave.*"

Her gaze was drawn to the old man, and she stopped to watch him shuffle along for a moment before she approached. "Do you need help?" When he didn't respond, she raised her voice. "Are you okay? How have you survived outside alone? Did you lose someone?"

The old man raised his eyes to hers, his form hunched over. His face remained blank as his eyes scanned the street and took in the people who stood behind her.

His face crinkled into a vacant smile. "I'm all alone. I seem to be lost."

I grinned. He called *us* dramatic, and here he was playing the role.

He was no better than us Tenebrians, wanting to play with our food first.

The woman pressed her lips together and held out her hand. He reached out toward her, and as his fingers closed around hers, she smiled kindly at him, her bright teeth and lips stained with the remnants of ruby lipstick, now smudged. My grin widened as the old man tightened his grip on her hand, and her smile faltered as his eyes glazed over with a smoky white before they slid back into the blue they were before. His grin widened and took on a sinister edge as he gripped her hand until I'm sure the bones were rubbing together. She panicked when she tried to yank her hand away and found she couldn't.

"Let me go," she said as calmly as she could manage, though her voice wavered. When he didn't, she cried out, "Let me *go!*"

A man and a woman from the group ran to help her and tried to pry the old man's fingers off her hand as she pulled, but he remained sturdy even as they tugged against him. The sound of her fragile bones breaking under his grip mingled with her screams, as one by one he snapped her fingers. The old man's hand glowed blue, and the people paused in their struggles as the woman sobbed and almost collapsed to the ground. As his fingers revealed claws that weren't there before, his skin started to ripple and flicker. Scales and spikes were exposed and tore through his clothes as he drew to his full height, unfolding and stretching, and allowed his quills to shred the remainder of his clothes from his body as they fell to the ground as rags.

"He's one of them!" a man screamed as he desperately tried to pry the now sobbing woman from his grip. As Cascus started to lift the woman by her destroyed hand, the others grabbed at her, but she was easily yanked from their grip. She kicked out, but had given up trying to work at his fingers, which gripped around her hand like a vice.

Cascus raised a hand to her throat and crushed her windpipe slowly, each finger taking its turn to tighten around her neck. Her screams turned to splutters, before all sound was cut off. "The weak won't survive," he growled out, and her eyes widened in fear moments before, and with a jerk of his wrist, Cascus broke her neck and dropped her to the ground.

"Run!"

The group fled, and a handful stopped to help those who stumbled in their panic while Cascus stood and watched them go with a sneer on his lips.

He wouldn't pursue them, but it was fun messing with them.

With a bark of laughter, I emerged from my hiding place, and

Cascus lifted his gaze lazily to mine. "Thought I sensed you."

"You enjoy it as much as we do. All this time acting as though we were beneath you."

He snarled. "You *are* beneath me."

Ignoring this, I said, "The Shift continues."

I followed Cascus as he stalked his way through the streets. "Something is wrong."

"What do you mean?"

"Cael and Samael, they will try to correct the Shift."

I scoffed. "They cannot."

"But they will *try*. I want to find them." His brow furrowed. "But I cannot find Cael."

"The Shift is affecting our senses—"

"For *weaker* Guardians, yes, but I can sense Samael, but not Cael."

"They will be togeth—"

"I am going to him now."

Falling into step with Cascus, we walked in silence for a while. He mostly ignored the chaos that reigned around us, whereas I indulged my curiosity and breathed in deeper whenever a hint of fear tickled my nose.

"I thought they'd be dead," I said, careful not to look at Cascus as I felt his gaze slide to me.

"I chose to save my own life."

Nodding, I held back my smirk, though I didn't doubt Cascus could sense my derision. It sounded like he'd been a coward, and at the reveal of his treachery against his kind and their duty, he'd fled rather than tie up the loose ends. It's not as though he didn't have the power to kill them. It was sheer cowardice and nothing more. "What if they have told others of your involvement?"

This was met with another sideways glance from him, and I didn't need to turn to feel the heat from his anger pounding against me. I didn't need his help anymore, so I no longer needed to treat him like a precious crystal to be held aloft. When an abrupt burst of anger almost threw me off my step, I reminded myself he was still many times more powerful than I, and perhaps goading him wasn't the best idea.

"Who would believe him?" he asked, and I grunted in response. "Regardless," Cascus continued, "we cannot allow them even to attempt to stop what has been started. Despite having little to no chance of succeeding, good deeds and positive energies can disrupt the change enough to delay it by a few hours or even a day or two, if they are lucky. The sooner the transition truly begins, the better."

With a rough shove, harder than necessary to get me to comply, Cascus pushed me behind a car as he spotted Samael. Humans surrounded him, and we kept our distance.

"What's the next step in the Shift?" I whispered.

Cascus grunted his displeasure at my continued questions. "Why do you ask?"

"I want to know what signs to look out for that the Shift is continuing as planned."

"I... do not know." I couldn't mask my surprise, and Cascus's distaste at having to admit it was evident. "I am unsure of the effects it will have. The knowledge wasn't passed down from Elder to Elder."

"Perhaps they assumed it would never happen again."

He snarled. "Perhaps."

So Cascus's cowardice was fueled by questions he didn't

know the answers to. Would Samael become more powerful because of his mixed heritage? Did the same rules apply to him that seemed to affect other Guardians, and would his senses be escalated or dulled?

Would he become a threat like Ana?

Cascus focused on centralizing all his powers so his essence was not evident, and when I felt the change in him, I did the same.

I scoffed. "I should have known they'd choose a base as mundane as the home of the Earth contact." I sought out John and noted the two humans with them, David was one, of course, because Samael had a soft spot for that particular human. The woman I didn't know.

If this was anything to judge their plan by, we had nothing to fear.

"Where is Cael?" I asked.

Cascus didn't respond, and that was a reply within itself. He didn't know and couldn't sense him any more than I could.

Cael was nowhere near here.

They went inside, and we waited.

As a Gateway opened near John's building, I barely stopped myself from crying out in surprise as Ana tumbled through it, tucking and rolling on the street. She stayed on the asphalt for a short while, curled up in a ball and quivering like the pathetic human that she was. When she stood, she wiped her face with one arm as she pounded on the door to John's building and called to Samael.

Samael opened the door as she was still knocking. "Mother." He pulled her against him in a crushing hug before he held her at arm's length and studied her face. "Where is Dad? What about the plan? Where are the half-breeds? Are they coming?"

Ana shook her head and grabbed Samael's arms, pulling herself back into his embrace. A spike of fear flared from Cascus, and my gaze was drawn to him.

Half-breeds? *More* of them?

For a moment, I was concerned that Ana would sense the fear from Cascus, but it seemed she was cloaked in waves of her own despair and couldn't see or sense anything beyond herself. Samael ushered her upstairs and closed the door behind them.

I turned fully to Cascus. "Explain."

His teeth were gritted. "They intended to use half-breeds to reverse the damage done by Anahera."

"*What* half-breeds? How many are there?"

He continued to stare ahead and muttered to himself, "How did they find them?"

When he said nothing more, I pressed, "Are you going to kill them this time, or are you going to run away again?" As I grabbed his arm, he whipped around with speed that surprised me, and I yelped as I was flipped onto my back and my head collided with the pavement.

My vision swam briefly as he stood over me. "Leave and do what you wish, I will wait here."

"I will wait."

He planted a foot on my chest, and I sucked in a ragged breath as he applied pressure. "Leave. The others will show themselves eventually, and Ana is mine."

Chapter Fifteen

Ana

Surrounded by the small group of half-breeds, I stood on shaky legs. My strength had been drained and recharged several times, and despite not feeling weak, my body was showing all the signs that it needed rest. A long rest. It had taken us considerable time to gather them all together, and holding the Gateways open was particularly draining. Every location had taken hours, and after each addition to our group, we needed to recharge in a realm with depleting powers.

It was a delicate line to tread, and I was over it.

The half-breeds were like me in so many ways, but different in more ways than I could count. They were planned and planted on Earth to create mixed children so they could assist with maintaining the Balance. It was insulting for humans to be used in such a way—to increase the Guardian numbers and draw from the combination of their powers as though we were not simply *tools* to control and maintain the Balance, but there to be used for breeding as well.

But me, I was an accident, a result of—so I was told—love and commitment. Glancing at my father, I bit my lip. I still had misgivings about what he'd told me, but I could feel no ill intent in him, and I found I wanted to have him back in my life as desperately as he fought to try to right the Balance.

Would I be willing to forgive him for leaving all those decades ago, so I could have a chance of having him back, and maybe rebuild some of the relationship we had lost? Was there anything he could do to make it up to me?

Did he *need* to? I understood his reasons, even if it wasn't the decision I thought I would make.

Occasionally throughout the day, I'd probe the air around him, seeking an element of a lie, or anything I could latch on to justify my mistrust. But there was nothing, and after all his time on Earth, he wouldn't be able to mask himself *that* well. His intentions seemed pure, even though he went about things the wrong way, or perhaps came across as harsher than needed.

What if I *did* find something? Would I dance around proclaiming I'd been right all along?

Maybe. Wouldn't put it past me.

Roger would meet my eyes when I did these scans and seemed to open up further, allowing me to feel who he was. But every time I felt nothing but the truth, and it matched up with the things he'd said, and afterward I'd sink inside myself again, and search for another excuse not to face the challenges that surrounded us.

Because I simply didn't feel I had the strength to do what they were asking of me.

I held back, knowing Cael could feel it, not because I feared my power, but because I feared I didn't have the control over it that everyone expected of me. What if they asked me to unleash and put the Balance right again, and instead, I destroyed whatever tether it was holding on to?

What if I killed us all?

The thought opened up a black hole inside me, and gratefully, I slipped inside it.

Scanning the faces around me, I saw that they, too, had been forced into a situation where they not only had to learn together but also trust each other because there was no other option.

Emma, an unwanted child from the United Kingdom, had been put up for adoption by her birth mother, who had fallen pregnant after a one-night stand. She was bright and artistic, and while I felt in another world, another time, we may have been friends, I kept my distance from her and the other half-breeds. She looked at me as though I had all the answers and had it all figured out because I had a certain level of control over my ability to read others.

But in this situation, with the world coming down around us, I was as lost as everyone else.

Floyd, older than the others and raised by a single mother, was concerned about any one-night stands he'd had over the years. Had he been an unwilling victim in creating children who would be born and raised in Lucidis? He learned from Cael that the Guardians could decide if they got pregnant or not, having almost absolute control over their bodies. But it would be as simple as her lying about being on birth control. Although he should have known better than to forgo protection just because someone *told* him it was okay. He should have considered a plethora of reasons, but he was young and foolish at the time, as many were. Floyd rubbed his hands over his smooth face every time he thought about it, and he looked younger than he was, even when in the throes of worry. He felt responsible and used simultaneously, and it was eating him up inside when he should be concentrating on the task at hand.

Arin, one of the group's youngest members, was someone Roger had only recently found through his contacts. He was born in Mumbai and raised by his mother and stepfather, whom he had always considered his true father. While he was aware from a young age that Veer was not his genetic parent, Arin had had no intention of trying to find his birth father, as they were a family exactly as they were. When Roger contacted him through social media, Arin initially brushed him off, but curiosity got the better of him. He could never have dreamed up such a thing as being part supernatural being, and he had battled with denial for months. That is, until he tried the focusing techniques Roger taught him and found that he could read people's emotions with such clarity, he might as well have been able to read their thoughts.

Grace, also from the United Kingdom and raised by a single mother, was a strong and resilient individual. She had taken up kickboxing as a teenager and was now in her mid-thirties, teaching multiple classes. When asked by Roger, she recalled several men who had attempted to lure her into bed for one-night stands. One had tried to force her to do so, which resulted in him having a broken arm and her running toward the nearest police station. She had no way of knowing if that was a Guardian or not. I would've preferred to think they wouldn't resort to force if the half-breed would not copulate willingly, but unfortunately it was entirely possible.

"There's one more I'd like to find," Roger said as we rested.

"Where are they?"

"Here." My eyebrows shot up, before I narrowed my eyes at

him. "In your home city."

"That's impossible."

He stared at me. "Is it? Why?"

I shook my head. "I don't know, it just feels... wrong they'd be so close."

"Her name is Regina, and I doubt you've ever met. If you had, especially before you knew Cael and what you were, you would likely have formed an immediate and unbreakable bond, much like you had with Cael."

I shook my head again and stared at the ground. No, Cael and I were something else entirely. Guardians didn't fall in love easily. When they did, they fell hard and strong and would unlikely love another being for the rest of their lives, even if their desired partner didn't return their feelings. This Regina may have been a friend, maybe even someone I could've felt an unexplained kinship with, but she would be nothing like Cael, and I resented the implication that it was so simple.

When I looked up, Cael held my gaze, the corner of his lip lifted into a thin smile, as if he knew exactly what I'd been thinking.

"We'll get Regina when we return to Earth, and she'll have to learn from the others as quickly as she's able."

There was a certain aura of pride that surrounded Roger as he stood. He'd spent decades tracking and gathering these half-breeds, and as they introduced themselves, shook hands, and compared powers, it was nice to watch them reveling in the feeling of a kindred spirit for a difference they could never explain to anyone. It was like a family Roger had gathered himself, and I could see his protective gaze as he watched them all.

The same look he had when he looked at me.

Moving closer to Roger, some things were plaguing me, and while we took a moment to recharge, this was as good of a time as any to question him about the half-breeds.

Indicating the group, I said, "If this is something Lucidians were doing for generations, and there were hundreds, maybe thousands of half-breeds dotted around the world. How is it that you were only able to find five?"

"I found many more than that."

I sighed. "Fine. How is it only five would help?"

"Do you remember when Cael first told you what he was?" Roger asked.

I stared at him. "Yes, of course."

"Do you remember how you felt?"

"I get what you're saying. It's unbelievable." I lifted a shoulder. "The entire thing was just unreal, like something from a movie."

"Now imagine that same scenario, but it's a stranger approaching you, sometimes from a great distance." My brows pulled together, and I stood silently as I considered this. "Locating the half-breeds was only part of the battle, the other part was getting them to trust and believe me. I did find hundreds and risked my safety during some of those conversations, as some would even turn violent. They were not *all* good people, and even fewer were trusting enough to let me get close enough to show them the true depth of their powers."

"I guess that makes sense."

A flicker of a smile passed across Roger's face, and when my brows pulled together and my lips pouted at his expression, he chuckled. "You used to look at me like that as a teenager."

I released a humorless laugh. "I didn't like you."

Roger was silent. He didn't need to ask why. By that point in my life, he'd begun to pull away and disappear for longer and longer periods. He pressed his lips together and waited for me to look at him. "I never wanted to hurt you, Ana, and I know it will take time for you to trust me."

My eyes darted across his face, searching him again. I'm sure he could feel my essence as I reached out across the space between us to probe and feel, always seeking the truth. But as always, the truth was on the surface. Relenting, my power dropped like a blade had run through the air. Roger's expression twisted, as though he missed the connection as soon as it was broken.

Cael was looking at the group that surrounded us, and I allowed myself to take in the wonder of what Roger had achieved. He'd confessed he'd used my emotional imprint as a base, and it gave him something to focus on. He'd acted on nothing but that, suspicion there were others like him, and rumors, and had found these wonders.

Half-breeds.

At least, I thought they were wonderful. I doubted all Guardians would feel the same.

Cael cleared his throat, drawing everyone's attention. "I'm sorry, I'd like to give you more time to get acquainted, but time is a precious commodity, and I can't give you the time you deserve." He looked down at me as if silently asking for my permission. I pressed my lips together in an imitation of a smile. We both knew what needed to be done, and the role I played in it, but I feared Cael blamed himself for everything that had happened. He was trying to shoulder the blame that fell on me, and it should remain there. His sideways glances and querying looks before speaking to the group were his way of giving power back to me. But I didn't want it. I wanted someone else to take control, because I didn't know how much control I had left in me.

Cael cleared his throat again. "I'll keep this brief, as I'm sure most of you know the basics. There is a Balance between the positive and negative forces in the world, and it's been tipped. This is what is causing all the destruction you have witnessed." There was a scattering of nodding, so Cael continued, "Those creatures you've seen are Guardians in their true form. Some are trying to help, others are enjoying the chaos while the Balance continues to shift toward a point of no return."

"How are we supposed to help?" Grace asked. She stood in a pose that indicated she was ready for anything that might come her way. But doubt shimmered in her eyes when the dim sunlight hit them, as if the light revealed a truth she was trying to hide.

"We believe there is power within the half-breeds, the ability to harness both the human and Guardian side. We want to work together, bring our powers and yours together in one force, and shift the Balance back."

"We don't even really understand what this *Balance* is. Being told about it is one thing, but I've never felt or experienced it. So, how are we supposed to correct it?"

Sasha looked at Floyd as he spoke. He'd asked the question with no malice and without Grace's defensive tone. "We will be there to guide your powers. You only need to focus your energies and give us something to draw from. We don't have time to train you how to control your powers, so we're going to ask you to unleash them, and we'll control them."

"Unleash them..." Floyd mumbled, and I pressed my lips together again as I looked at the ground. I understand their hesitation. In theory, it was so easy. But Guardians had a lifetime to learn to control their powers, and were born into a world where it was second nature. Now they were expected to do the same within a matter of hours. I glanced up to see Sasha as she continued to watch Floyd before her gaze travelled around the group, each of them distracted by a similar whirlwind of thoughts running through their heads.

As Cael opened his mouth to speak, Floyd interrupted, "Before I left, my Ma was acting strangely."

"How so?"

"She's old, I know that, but it's like she wasn't feeling anything at all."

Cael and Sasha shared a sideways glance. "That could be an effect of the Balance tipping, draining the emotions from humans with it as it shifts."

"*Could* be? You mean you don't know?"

"This is new territory for all of us."

Floyd and the others stared at Cael, as Emma mumbled, "Well, that's comforting." She hugged her arms around herself. "If this is all a game of chance, and no one really knows what will happen..." She twisted her hands together. "I think I'd rather be home with my family, for... You know? Our final hours."

"Emma." She looked up at Roger as he came next to her. "Please. With your help, we can fix this, and your family won't have only a few hours left."

"God. I want to believe you." Emma rubbed her face. "Fine. Fine. Let's do this."

Cael said, "We'll spend some more time here and teach you all to focus and draw from the power of this place."

What remains of the power of Lucidis. I didn't say it out loud.

Cael looked at me, and I almost smiled. He seemed always to know what I was thinking. "Ana is as powerful as she is because as a half-breed she was born and raised on Earth, then lived for some time in Lucidis. The joint influences from the realms and her heritage make her power the formidable force it is. We do not have that amount of time with you, but we will do our best."

"And so if we all use our half-breed power, and focus our energies or whatever, that'll bring the Balance back into line, and everything will be okay?" Grace asked.

"Yes," Cael said.

My eyes widened slightly as I whipped my head around, and I held Cael with a hard stare. Cael watched me with so much going on behind the deep blue of his irises. He'd answered with such certainty, and I wanted to rebut him. We didn't *know* for sure what was going to happen.

But these people put themselves on the line to help us and sacrificed being with their loved ones to be here. They deserved some hope at least, and I'm glad Cael could give it to them, even if I couldn't.

"It'll all be okay, will it?" I whispered.

He placed a hand on my arm. "Yes, it will all be okay. We will work together."

As I glanced at the group, all eyes were on me. Then, I looked back at Cael, and tears I refused to release burned behind my eyes. I felt useless enough without crying as well. "I thought Guardians didn't lie," I whispered.

When Cael opened and closed his mouth without a word,

the cavern inside me opened further. The black hole which had been inside my chest threatening to take over since I'd pushed the Balance over the edge shuddered, and sucked me into its depths. Were we destined to live this cycle over and over again? If we managed to repair the damage I'd done, what then? "And the Tenebrians," I said as Cael's eyes pleaded with me, "They will accept their fate and stop all the harm they're causing?"

"I... Ana..."

His hesitation was all the confirmation I needed. "They'll never stop." My voice dropped below a whisper, and when I looked down, the ground beneath my feet faded in and out for a moment, the green grass becoming translucent before it returned. Would the realm simply fall out from under our feet?

The world was ending.

"Don't you see it, Cael? *They'll never stop.*" I whispered urgently to him, and he leaned down to face me, cupping my face in his palms. I leaned into the touch before I shook my head. I needed Cael to understand. Surely, they all saw it too? Roger and Sasha. Surely, they knew this was all futile. "Humans will always be killed, always be tools, and always be used for their pleasure. Tenebris will always be a negative force unleashed upon the world, and they'll *never stop.*"

The air of Lucidis ceased to feel welcoming in that moment, and it crushed around me, as whatever remaining energies of the realm licked at my skin. I needed to get out of here, and my chest rose and fell rapidly as my breathing increased.

If I stayed here, I would do more damage than help.

I was powerful, my influence was formidable when I was upset, that had been proven time and time again, right? Whatever hope Cael, Roger, and Sasha held didn't extend to me. I couldn't feel it, couldn't find it within me. If there *really* were hope, there wouldn't be hope within *anyone* if I stayed here to taint them.

I stepped back from the group and looked at them all in turn. "I'm sorry..." I turned to Cael and shook my head as my hands clenched into fists at my sides. "I can't be here."

Ignoring Cael's protests, I squeezed my eyes shut and focused on the feeling of Earth and Samael. He was the only one I could cling to and ground me. Everyone here expected something of me that I couldn't deliver. Disregarding Cael's questions, I shrugged his hand off my shoulder, and felt for Samael's presence, seeking his familiar imprint until he was right beyond the veil of air in front of my fingers. With absolute confidence that it would work, I held out my arms and drew on Lucidis's power.

"Ana," Cael shouted as he reached for me.

"I can't do this," I cried as the Gateway flickered open. "If I stay, I'll only do more damage. I'll infect you all, don't you see?" With a blast that rocked the ground, a Gateway exploded in front of me, and I stepped through as Cael grabbed for me. The Gateway snapped shut behind me, and I took a deep breath of Earth air.

Chapter Sixteen

Esco

The town hall was almost geographically located precisely in the city's center, save for urban sprawl, which had slightly shifted its central position. It consisted of several buildings in a horseshoe design that surrounded a courtyard leading to the town hall's main entrance. The courtyard was the chosen location for gathering the city's people. From the limited communication we had managed, Guardians worldwide were doing the same—gathering humans in one spot in each city, and trying to keep them as positive as possible to slow the tipping of the Balance.

But as the destruction amplified, the humans became increasingly unsettled.

We could protect them from the Tenebrians, but we couldn't control the shudders that rocked the Earth or the Gateways that opened and closed with explosive force. Although gathering humans together decreased the likelihood of Gateways opening nearby, as time went on and instability increased, we'd not be able to protect the area forever.

We also couldn't protect the humans from themselves and

the swirling fear and incomprehension that churned inside them. It was difficult to keep them positive when we couldn't coherently explain what was happening and why, and I'm also certain some humans felt we were holding them hostage.

On my way toward the town hall with my most recent group of rescues, I'd decided to walk these humans directly there, given the large number of children within the group. I shooed them away, less than two blocks from the center, as my eyes widened.

"Go, go." I urged them forward with my hands, and the humans shuffled along. They nervously glanced behind them, disturbed by my sudden upset.

A two-story-high Gateway to Tenebris had formed and crossed the middle of the street. Several Lucidians were stationed near the entrance, assumedly to prevent humans from wandering too close and being affected by the negative forces that leaked from the Gateway.

My brow furrowed as I approached one of the Lucidians. I didn't recognize them, assuming they were from another community. However, given the uncontrollable Gateways, perhaps they'd landed here from across the country. "Why haven't you closed it?"

Her lip lifted in irritation as she growled. "You think we have not tried?" She waved her hand behind her. "It will not close, and we do not have the energy to spare to keep trying."

I stared at the Gateway, looking into the depths of Tenebris. I'd never been into the realm and hoped never to go. However, as the realms merged, this was likely to continue. A deep breath caught in my chest as the breeze around me swirled with the thin Tenebris air, and a shudder ran down my spine.

I wondered if we were fighting a losing battle.

We may be able to slow the tip of Balance, but then what? What if Cael and Ana couldn't succeed? Were we wasting our time when we should be preparing for the inevitable?

Gritting my teeth so hard my jaw ached, I nodded at the Lucidian and turned on my heel as I desperately tried to push the negative thoughts from my mind. The further I moved from the Gateway, the easier it was for me to shift them. But they were never entirely gone, the thoughts lingering within me, a reminder that perhaps all was indeed lost, no matter what we did.

"I am a *Guardian,"* I whispered to myself, the words coming out almost as a hiss. "I have a duty to uphold. I will not give up."

Ana had made me see that humans were more precious than simply controlling the Balance, though I had never told her. How would I find the words to say to her such a thing? Though I suspected she knew. I considered her a friend. My steps slowed and lost purpose when I realized perhaps I hadn't told her *that* either.

I *hoped* she knew.

The sideways glances she would give me, when her lips would curve into a smirk after she made me laugh, perhaps those were clues. The loud way in which she protested when we talked about humans as though they were tools. I meant nothing by it, it was simply how Guardians were, but I hadn't considered how it would appear to the humans until Ana. She didn't stand up to everyone in the community, only to a small group, and I considered myself lucky to be part of that group.

It meant she was comfortable around me, and explained why I'd been relaxed enough to laugh at her silly words.

Unlike Ana's loud and unapologetic laughter, my laughter

was quiet and subtle.

But I don't remember laughing before I met her.

Monia stood near one of the courtyard's corner entrances and greeted the humans as they came through. Her energy passed almost effortlessly as she distributed small amounts of calming influences to those who needed them most.

"Monia," I said as I came to her side.

"Esco." Monia reached out a hand and brushed her fingers down my arm. I watched the gesture with curiosity, and when I met her eyes, it almost appeared as though she, too, didn't quite know why she had made physical contact as a way of greeting. "Are you injured?"

Lifting my arms, I swept my gaze over my body. "I do not think so. Do you see a wound?"

"No, I asked as I was attacked, and wanted to make sure you were okay."

My brow furrowed. "You were attacked? By whom?"

She paused to clasp the hand of a human who was visibly trembling with fear, and when his tremors eased and he moved past her to join the crowd, she turned back to me. "A group of humans on the outskirts of the city. I attempted to get them here, and they responded with violence."

"Monia..." My gaze travelled over her body, and I noted the rough scrapes and smudges of blood on her scales. "Why?"

"They are frightened, Esco. I do not hold it against them." Her lip curved into almost a smile. "One of them was quite sarcastic. Thankfully, knowing Ana, I recognized it for what it was and did not say the wrong thing."

"Yet they still attacked." She flinched when I grabbed her elbow to lift her arm and inspect a wound. "What did they do this with?"

"Chains," she replied, and I sucked in a breath.

"You are okay?"

"I will heal." Before I could say anything more, a tall, willowy Lucidian approached. She was beautiful, her eyes an aquamarine blue, the same blue as the tips of her quills. A pang of jealousy shot through me, and I hissed at the reaction, drawing a glance from Monia before she turned back to the stranger.

She said something in a language neither of us understood, and I stared at her as Monia shook her head. "We do not understand you."

The beautiful Guardian's shoulders dropped as she looked resigned. She then looked around as if searching for a way to communicate with us before she held her hand out. Her every move was graceful, and Monia took her offered hand as she said. "Clarus."

"Monia." She touched a hand to her chest, and Clarus nodded and grinned before she turned to me.

"Esco," I said.

"Encantada," she muttered, and I smiled, unsure what to say. At least we'd covered the first hurdle. Monia and Clarus still held hands, and Monia's fingers tensed slightly as she squeezed her hand. I felt the energy transfer between them as they attempted to communicate without words. Hopefully, she could convey the essence of the protection we hoped to cast around the area. Clarus looked up from their joint hands and nodded again before she moved away and walked around the border of the courtyard. We watched her go, and without turning to face me, she said, "If Gateways are connecting points between realms thousands of miles away... perhaps the Balance is shifting faster than we thought."

For a few hours, I helped Monia greet and direct humans led here by Guardians, or those who had come across the gathering of their own accord. My fingers tingled with each passing minute, and I shifted my weight between my feet. The large number of humans created a clash of essences and energies I wasn't used to, and coupled with the shifting powers of the realms, which seemed to seep through the air itself. I wanted to leave.

As I opened my mouth to tell Monia I had to go, a group of eleven humans showed up and looked around the courtyard as they rubbed their arms in discomfort. We approached them, trying to keep our steps small and our gaits non-threatening. We had taken note of every encounter with humans and tried our best to adjust our behavior to make them more comfortable. "Welcome," Monia said as she stopped near the ground. "You are safe here."

They came to an abrupt halt, stopping several yards shy of her, eyes wide.

"I am Monia." She stepped forward. "We are here to protect you."

My brows furrowed as the humans backed away from Monia, and Monia dropped into a defensive stance when they continued to back up until they stood side by side with a Tenebrian. He placed his orange-clawed hands on two of their shoulders, and his long fingers draped over their small frames. My eyes darted between Monia and the Tenebrian, and I wondered if I could move fast enough to get the humans to safety before he injured them. But he was so close, and his long face peered at Monia from where he stood amongst the humans. He could kill at least three of them before I got close enough to him to retaliate.

Monia didn't move, and the moments stretched out in silence between us. One of the women glanced at me, and when I reached out to her, she squealed and ducked behind the Tenebrian.

Other Lucidians nearby watched unmovingly and waited for a hint of command from Monia that it was time to attack as she stared down the Tenebrian.

The Tenebrian leaned forward and spoke to the humans in a whisper that would have been gentle if it were not threaded with the harsh tone of his natural voice. "It is okay. These are good. Not all blue Guardians want to hurt you."

Monia tried to hide her shock, and I suppressed a spark of anger that flared in my chest.

He dropped his hands from the shoulders of the humans and nudged them with a touch so gentle it made my resolve stumble over itself as I tried to get a reading on the Tenebrian. He was powerful, guarded, and yet almost nurturing to the humans, and nodded with encouragement as they looked back at him, still afraid of us. The humans fearfully scooted past Monia and the other Lucidians before they lost themselves in the group of people in the courtyard.

"Lucidians do *not* harm humans," Monia hissed out at the Tenebrian.

"So you say..." The Tenebrian drawled, "... but those humans witnessed a Lucidian attacking their friends."

"That is not possible."

He shrugged. "Ask them yourselves. I found them wandering and led them here. If they were afraid of Tenebrians, would they have come willingly with me?" He didn't wait for an answer. "I am Vena." He looked like he was considering holding his hand for a handshake, but thought better of it. Touching a Tenebrian could be torture if they directed energy into us, and I wondered if it were the same for him to make contact with a Lucidian. "If I, as a Tenebrian, am here helping humans, it stands to reason there are Lucidians who may not be on your side."

Monia watched him cautiously before returning to her full height and dropping her arms from their defensive stance. "How can I trust you?"

Vena glanced around. "I have had ample opportunity to hurt you or those humans, but I brought them here instead. I understand what you are doing, centering the energies, and it might help, but I do not know if it will be enough to stop the Shift."

I approached Monia. "So, we cannot know who is on our side or not? We have to wait to see if they attack us first?"

Vena looked around. "It could be more complex than that. Consider that some already within these walls may be working against you."

Monia shook her head. "These are mostly members of our community. I know them. Those who are not, I have read, and sensed no ill intent."

"Very well, but stay alert. The lines between your realm and mine have faded and grayed into obscurity. All that remains is those who want the Balance to tip, and those who do not."

As he turned to leave, Monia asked, "Where are you going?"

"To save more humans." He cocked an eyebrow at her.

"Have you considered you may be able to help more in your human form?"

"Have you—"

"I am stronger in my Guardian form as a protector." Monia cut him off.

Vena stared at her. "Have you…" He paused while waiting for another interruption, "… tried shifting into your human form?"

Monia hesitated. "No."

"I think you will find if you try, you cannot."

When Monia's spine stiffened, I stepped in. "He's right, Monia, I too cannot change."

Vena nodded. "The Shift has affected us all, and changing forms is draining and difficult, bordering on impossible." He looked around, recognizing some of the beings present must be Guardians in their human form, mingling with the crowd. "I am afraid we might be stuck in our current forms until this is over. If it ever is."

"Cael will find a way to fix it." The certainty of my words shocked me for a moment before I took a deep breath and drew myself up. If the Guardians were to lose hope, too, all would be lost. We could not give up.

"Cael?"

Monia tilted her chin up with pride and a hint of defense. "My son and his partner, Anahera."

Vena smiled. It wasn't a pleasant look on him, and it did nothing to soften his harsh features. "You have every right to be proud. He is a fine being. As for Anahera, I believe she might be the key to all of this."

Neither Monia nor I asked how he knew of them, as though there was a silent agreement that these sorts of things could be discussed later if and when the time presented itself.

Vena turned to leave again. "Keep doing what you are doing here, and be on the lookout for all Guardians, not only Tenebrians. Let us hope Cael and Ana find a way to save us all."

We watched him leave, and I turned to find one of the women who came here with him also watching him go. When she met my eyes, she ducked back into the crowd.

"There is much to be done. I must go too."

Monia held my eye contact, as though she understood why I needed to leave. Closing my eyes against the torrent of worthlessness which washed through me, I opened them to find Monia still staring at me. "This area is draining," I said, and my gaze darted between her and the crowd before I continued, "Do you wish to go find survivors, and I will stay here?"

Monia's lip twitched. "I will stay. You go." I wanted to be strong enough to argue, to insist she give herself a break from the energies gathered here. But with shame, I realized I was too weak, and before I could reply, Monia added, "It is okay, Esco. I want to stay."

We stared at each other for a moment longer, and again, words I couldn't bring myself to say lingered on the edge of my tongue.

I'm asking because I care about you, not because I believe you are not strong enough.

But instead, I said, "I will be back soon." And walked away.

Physically entering every building was not only too time-consuming, and I risked my safety each time as the tremors shook the ground. As I wandered the streets, I scanned each building, seeking the signs of human life. A twinge at the back of my neck reminded me that some humans had had their emotional imprint interrupted and may not be locatable through senses alone. But I would be useless to anyone dead, and this method had already found me two families quite close to the city center. So, as I ventured outward, I stuck to it. I had escorted both families to the gathering of humans myself, becoming more aware with each group that their combined fear could potentially gain the interest of wandering Tenebrians. It was better to keep them in small groups and make multiple trips. I'd seen Tenebrians on the prowl as they searched for lost humans on the streets or in hiding that they could draw out and torture. I didn't engage them as I was on my own. My goal was to save humans, and nothing else. Taking on a group of Tenebrians would only drain my remaining energy.

Most buildings had been vacated already, but as I stopped on the pavement and craned my neck to look up at the building in front of me, the heartbeat of life echoed from inside. After a quick visual assessment of the building's structure, I moved inside.

The building mainly appeared abandoned, and several apartments at the rear had collapsed. Perhaps whoever was inside didn't realize the building could potentially crumble and thought home was the safest place for them.

I wished it were.

As I climbed the stairs, I checked each floor with a sweep of my senses before I moved on to the next. Sometimes, lingering fear could create a blind spot, and I'd wander into apartments only to find them empty. But there was life here, and I allowed the sense to pull me toward it.

Reaching the fourth floor, the air shifted around me as though sucking in a breath, and whispers penetrated my mind before I knocked on the door of the nearest apartment. The abrupt silence behind the thin plank of wood was as much of a giveaway to the presence of humans as the quiet talking had been a moment before.

"Hello?" I said gently, and put my face near the door so I didn't need to shout. I was more aware than ever that our natural voices were alarming to humans. One woman had told me it was grating, so I tried to dull it as much as I could. "There is a safe space in the town hall, and people are gathering. I've come to take you there."

There was still silence, then incredibly slowly, the sound of metal on metal clicked as locks were turned. The door opened a crack, and a small chain was visible across the open space. I considered the chain with a glance, having seen many of them since I'd been out gathering people. I suspected they would be easy to break, but if it helped them feel safe, I wanted the humans to have that extra protection, even if it was simply in their minds. It would achieve nothing if I were to slam my palm on the door and prove the chains were no more than a flimsy illusion of protection.

A woman with bright red hair stared at me through the crack.

The eye I could see was wide and fearful, something else I was seeing a lot of. No matter how often those fearful eyes fell upon me, it didn't lessen the pang in my chest. The humans were innocent victims, no more aware of the reason for the Shift than the Balance's existence in the first place. Not for the first time, I wished I'd been able to slip into my human form, then they wouldn't be so afraid of me.

"I'm Esco, what is your name?" The woman's lip trembled, and her gaze roamed my body. I tried to smile, but my sharp teeth alarmed her, and as she moved to close the door, I placed my foot in the way. I cringed, immediately regretful of the necessary action. "I'm sorry. Please don't be scared. I want to help you..." I let the sentence drift off, hoping she would fill the void with her name.

"Lynn," she whispered.

"Lynn," I repeated her name, and reached inward for a hint of my power to ease a gentle influence into my voice and let it travel through the air between us. Every time it felt like cheating, as though I should be able to gain the trust of the beings I had spent a lifetime protecting, but they couldn't help their fear. Besides, time was of the essence. What choice did I have? "Could you open the door, please?"

Lynn stared at me for a beat before she glanced at someone behind her, and after some urgent whispers, the door closed gently, and the chain rattled as it was removed. There was another pause, and I wondered if she had changed her mind, but then the door opened, and I entered the apartment. A second woman sat on a couch, her jet-black hair cut into a neat bob which brushed against her shoulders, and she had her arm draped over the shoulders of a child who shared her skin tone and hair color. I guessed the child was around her first decade, but which side of ten her age was, I couldn't tell. Lynn stood back from me, moved closer to the couch, and stood protectively between me and her family.

"Hello," I said, and resisted the urge to attempt another smile. "I am Esco. I'm here to help."

"This is Penny, and our daughter, Louise."

Nodding at them, I watched as Penny slowly gathered Louise toward her. "I'm here to take you somewhere with other people. It's not safe here." They stared at me before Penny glanced at Lynn, almost as if she were asking her, without words, why she had even opened the door for me. Lynn's eyes held no answers, for she wouldn't be able to explain the sense of calm that had blanketed her and allowed her to realize I could be trusted.

"My appearance alarms you, and for that I am sorry." I shifted uncomfortably as I brushed down the scales on my arm, wishing again I could appear human to them. "This building is collapsing, and two apartments at the back are already gone. It is not safe here."

Penny's eyes widened. "We heard something... we thought it was a different building."

"Please, we do not have much time."

Slowly at first, before the comfort of having a task and a destination allowed their movements to become more fluid, the two women and their child moved around the apartment. They gathered their jackets and changed Louise's shoes as she watched me with wide, curious eyes.

"Do we need to bring food?"

"Yes, if you have any, but not too much. We do not want to be slowed down."

I didn't know the supply situation at the city center, but more couldn't hurt. Lynn hurried to the kitchen and stuffed a backpack with a few packets and bottles that crinkled against each other. She flung the bag over her shoulder and took Penny's hand, Penny already holding on to Louise. "We're ready," Lynn said.

With my hand on the doorknob, I paused. The humans stood as though prepared for battle, and maybe they weren't wrong to feel that way. "If I say run, you run. If I say hide, you hide. No questions, no hesitation, okay?" I pressed my lips together in a thin line at how their eyes widened, but they nodded their acknowledgment and followed me out of the apartment and down the stairs.

"Cover the child's eyes," I said, and Lynn did as I asked as they tailed me past the destroyed apartment. While we could see no people, the blood stains indicated someone had been crushed. Lynn gasped and turned away, and Penny squeezed her hand.

As we turned the corner of the stairwell, where one wall had been blown out completely, movement caught my eye, and my arm shot out as Penny moved toward the motion.

"Wait," Penny said, and carefully shifted my arm from in front of her body.

Lynn pulled Louise closer to her, her hand still over the child's eyes, before she hissed out, *"Careful."*

Penny made her way toward the rubble, and I followed a few steps behind as she moved to a man who lay amongst the bricks, his spine was twisted at an unnatural angle, bone visible, and his arms were bent. His legs couldn't be seen, crushed beneath where the building had crumbled, and the concrete and bricks had begun to absorb the blood as it stained them a dirty red.

My fingers twitched. I hadn't felt him as I'd walked past, and I scoured his essence now and found only the smallest lingering spike of fear.

He was so close to death.

The man parted his lips to speak when he saw Penny, but only coughed a mouthful of blood over himself and the floor. Penny kneeled beside him as she took his hand and stroked his hair with the other. "Shh," she whispered gently, her voice comforting, and I let it wash over me, as though I were being soothed along with the man who suffered before us. "It's okay, help is on the way. You're going to be alright."

My brow furrowed, but I said nothing as his eyes glazed over, before relief flooded his face. He seemed unaware of the extent of his injuries, and I imagine shock had taken care of any pain, but he was frightened. Penny continued to whisper to him, telling him it would be okay and that he was safe. She shushed and hummed gently through the silences as a tear rolled down his cheek. Within minutes, his eyelids drooped, and he lightly squeezed Penny's fingers before he released a rattling breath and let her hand go.

He was gone.

Whoever he had been departed his physical body in front of us, and left Penny holding his hand as though any lingering warmth was a promise of life yet to live. Penny closed his eyes and remained kneeling with her head bowed. Her shoulders shook for a moment before she sucked in a deep breath, stood, and rolled her shoulders. Rubbing her hands over her face, she turned back to us.

Louise started to whimper, her lip trembling as Lynn continued to cup her hand over her eyes. Lynn shot me a shocked look when I placed a hand on Louise's shoulder. But I held her eye contact and eased calming influences into her daughter. When Lynn felt Louise relax, her brows pulled together as she stared at my hand, which still rested on the child's shoulder. When her gaze rose to mine, I did not explain and returned her stare. What could I say?

We made our way onto the street, and Lynn trembled as she took in the state of the building that had been their home. The reality that it could have come crashing down on them at any moment left anything she could have said choked and stuck in her throat. Lynn guided Louise ahead of us after I'd indicated the direction, and Penny fell into step next to me, with her arms wrapped around her chest.

I bent to whisper to her, "Why did you say those things?"

"What things?"

"You told that man everything was going to be okay, but he was dying. You told him someone was coming to help, but no one was." I huffed out a breath as I searched for the words, but when I found no other way to express what I wanted to ask, I settled for saying, "You lied." Penny watched me, and for a moment, there was a flare of anger in her expression. But it passed as she studied my face. "I mean no disrespect," I hurried to add. "I simply desire to understand."

Penny sighed. "He needed comfort, and that's what I gave him. Do you understand comfort?"

"I try to." My lip twisted as I relived my experiences and tried to locate one where someone had *comforted* me by lying. I couldn't think of any, and I immediately thought of Ana. She would explain this to me with a laugh, but I didn't expect the same from Penny. Sorrow ebbed and flowed around her being.

She grieved for a man she didn't know. After a moment, I said quietly, "Did it hurt to lie?"

The ripples of pain from Penny shifted as I asked the question, and when Penny closed her eyes as if willing herself to remain in control, I already knew the answer.

"Yes, it hurt. But it wasn't about how *I* felt. I couldn't save him, but I could comfort him in those moments. I could make sure he didn't die alone and scared. Everyone deserves that." Her words seeped into my skin, and Penny watched me process. After a beat, she asked, "Why are you helping us?"

"I protect humans."

I'd been asked this question many times over, and I tried to think of the best way to answer it each time. I could tell her I was a Guardian, but she wouldn't understand. Humans would ask what I was the Guardian of, and then I would need to explain about the Balance. It was too much for them when they had already dealt with a lot.

"I care," I added, hoping she could understand without me trying to explain what I felt, when until recently I didn't think I *could* feel. "I care about humans. We are here, and you are in trouble, and we can help."

Penny looked at me for a moment longer before she nodded and watched Lynn and Louise as they walked ahead of us. "Am I ever going to understand what's happening?"

I searched the essence and felt the thin tether she was holding onto in her distressed state.

"Maybe one day. But not now. Let me get you to safety first."

She nodded again and moved ahead to walk with her family, and I allowed them to. Watching them and our surroundings was easier when they were in front of me. I didn't tell them I was constantly scanning the streets and corners for threats, and let them walk silently. Louise sniffed occasionally, and Lynn's arm would tighten around her.

But I watched Penny with interest.

Just when I thought I understood humans, they taught me something new.

Chapter Seventeen

Ferox

"It's almost a romantic setting, isn't it?"

I looked at my human, Heather, and watched her gaze wander the street. Her eyes widened slightly, and the afternoon sun glinted off all the shades of brown in her irises. I followed her gaze. The sunlight dappled through the blossoming trees, creating a cascade of colors. My chest twisted as it reminded me of home. I'd never thought of Lucidis as *romantic* before, but I supposed from a human's perspective, it would be.

I had taken too long to answer, and Heather was looking at me with a slight smile curving her lips.

"I mean it would be romantic, if you know... the world wasn't falling apart."

I nodded stiffly, and discomfort curled in my stomach. Sometimes, I didn't know how to respond to what Heather said, and feelings of inadequacy twisted my gut. These were not feelings I was accustomed to, nor were I accustomed to feelings in general. There was another emotion I experienced when I looked at Heather, one I was sure I recognized, despite not having experienced it before.

How she'd touched me so delicately in the café was hard to shift from my mind.

Heather chuckled to herself as we continued to walk. Groups of humans in the city were becoming increasingly scarce, as they were either already in the city center or had evacuated the area entirely, putting distance between them and the tall buildings that threatened their safety simply by being present.

Heather hummed quietly. "Should we make our way to the outer suburbs? Grab a car and head out, then walk from there?"

"Do you have a car?"

Her cheeks flamed. "No. I live in the city and rely on public transport. My place doesn't even have a car park."

"I do not know how to drive."

"Hmm, I suppose you wouldn't know how to hot-wire a car either."

"Unlikely."

Heather laughed, and I smiled, even though I didn't understand the joke. "It would be a worthwhile venture, yes. Let's explore some new areas in the city to ensure as many pockets of humans are cleared as possible. Once we're done with the city, I will take you to the center and gather some other Guardians to accompany me to the suburbs."

I felt the shift in the air around Heather before she spoke. "Don't you want me with you? Haven't I been helpful?"

"Yes. But you will be safer there."

"Will I? I think I'm safer with you."

Pride surged through my chest, and I resisted the urge to pat my skin to temper how my scales flickered with the emotion. I didn't understand what was happening. Situations where I could look in from the outside as a passive observer were no longer possible, and I reacted with emotions. Each new one stirred in a different part of my body. Tingles of fear ran down my spine, pride swelled in my chest, and concern and upset churned in my stomach.

And my hands. They twitched when I looked at Heather, and I realized that though I ached to touch her, it was more than simply wanting a pleasurable release.

Stopping mid-step, I turned toward Heather. This human seemed to care for me for reasons I couldn't understand. I couldn't imagine being near me having been particularly pleasurable for her, yet she continued to be playful, smile, and talk to me even when I offered little response.

I was trying, though, perhaps she could feel I was trying.

Something in her made me want to try.

I'd watched Ana and Cael and knew their story, but Cael had submitted to human emotions while they were both in human form, and Ana only later discovered the truth about him.

I didn't think much of Ana in the beginning. She was a human trying to fit into a world of stronger beings. I treated her poorly, and eventually kept my distance. But I watched her, not for any particular desire, more the way some Guardians watched human interactions curiously, as if we could decipher their meaning and intent. Ana touched Cael when it wasn't necessary, and when there appeared to be no intent of intercourse. She simply... *touched* him—a brush of her fingers down his arm, the hand holding, hugs.

It was how Heather was to me.

But ours was different from their meeting.

Heather knew what I was from the beginning, yet she still cared and interacted with me. She touched me as though we were companions and not only conducting a duty together, the brushes of her fingers down my arm, or the way she grabbed for me when she lost her footing. Once, her hand lingered in mine for some moments before she dropped the contact.

Feeling her essence through the connection was incredible. She was beautiful. It was as though I could see humans on a different level through her, and all her weak emotions, hopes, and fears built into someone... perfect.

The time we'd spent together seemed to be forging a bond based on mutual respect and humor that I was still developing. She would tilt her head and look at me as though I were endearing myself to her.

"I have a job to do," I said.

"And I can help you."

"Heather—" My words were abruptly cut off as Heather screamed and launched herself toward me, her fingers gripping my arm. She yanked *hard, a*nd the surprise of the act made me stumble more than her strength. But I was thankful it had. As I tripped, an ax whirled past my head, and I felt the whistle of it through the air against my ear.

Heather stumbled and fell in her effort to bring me out of harm's way, but I regained my footing quickly and turned to see a Tenebrian sneering at me as he held another ax at the ready. On the edge of my peripheral vision, Heather scooted back across the road.

"Hide," I hissed out through my teeth.

"But—"

"*Hide.*" Heather's eyes widened at the harsh edge to my tone, dotted with the chatter of a language she wouldn't recognize. Desperation clawed at the inside of my chest to see her to safety, and the weight lifted slightly as she scrambled to her feet, kept low, ran toward the pathway, and ducked behind a tree.

"Get out of here," I growled out, turning back to the other Guardian.

"What's that you've got there? A little pet?"

I bared my teeth at the intruder. "Go, so I am not forced to hurt you."

He laughed and paused a beat before he charged at me. I bent and spun, scooped the fallen ax from the ground, and lifted it above my head in time to meet the assault of the Tenebrian as he brought another ax down.

"With the Balance shifting..." The Tenebrian panted, continuing to swing at me as I backed away and deflected each hit. "... if we die, we die for good. The Gateways won't heal us, did you know that?"

I barely managed to keep my face neutral as this information sank in. However, the Tenebrian's sneer told me he already knew what I wasn't saying, able to read the slight shift in the air I hadn't been able to control. He chuckled darkly as he aimed another swing at me. This one knocked the ax from my hands, and the ringing of metal scraping on asphalt sounded like defeat. Stumbling, I fell to the ground and could only watch as the Tenebrian advanced.

I hope Heather ran to safety.

"I think I'll find your pet after I kill you..." He sneered again, and my blood boiled as he licked his lips. "And fuck her in your blood as it stains the street."

I wanted to be angry, and wished the emotion had continued growing until I was forced to act. But instead, a deep sickness in the pit of my stomach at his words churned, as images of

Heather screaming as she was dragged away filled my mind.

Heather.

As the Tenebrian raised his ax, his spine stiffened, a shrill cry pierced the air, and a chilling crunch followed. My eyes widened as the Tenebrian stood frozen above me, his arms still lifted above his head. The ax he was holding dropped from his slackening grip, and I rolled to the side as he fell forward and landed with an empty thud, an ax buried in the base of his skull. My gaze shifted upward to Heather as she stood over the body, her breaths coming in heavy, aching motions. Shoving myself to my feet, I closed the gap between us as her breathing became increasingly unstable. I stopped right before physical contact, my hands twitching at my sides. When she sobbed and reached for me, I pulled her into a tight embrace, and her shoulders shook with the effort of controlling the emotions within her. Heather clung to me and ran her hands down my back as my quills flattened at her touch after having been raised during the attack.

"Oh my God, I killed him," she cried.

"You had to." She went to pull away, but I hugged her tighter against me. She didn't need to see the body, or the pool of blood which continued to seep out from around the wound. "You had to, it was him or me."

I held her until her essence shifted slightly, the change happening a minuscule moment before her heart rate slowed as she calmed.

As her breathing returned to normal, my spine stiffened against her hands as she continued to stroke my back. I mimicked her movements and ran my fingers down her back in comfort as I held her against me. Her body curved so elegantly against mine, this small being who needed my protection, yet had protected me. The push of her breasts against my stomach had my chest clenching, as need for her rose.

Heather's breath hitched, and I stilled.

She shifted awkwardly before I cursed and shoved her away from me. As she stumbled slightly, I turned my back to her and cursed again.

I'd become aroused at her touch. I was erect.

The Shift made reading her essence difficult, and without the physical contact and my back turned, uncertainty washed over me. Whether mine or hers, I couldn't tell. I heard a small gasp behind me, gritted my teeth, and closed my eyes. I took control of my body and brought myself back into line before I turned, snatched her hand, and roughly pulled her down the street and away from the body of the fallen Tenebrian. My discomfort distracted me enough almost to ignore the way she stumbled as she trotted to keep up with me.

She didn't speak, and neither did I as my thoughts whirled. Heather had protected me and put herself in danger in doing so. Then, she touched me tenderly and continued after she had calmed. The purpose of the initial touch was to seek comfort, so why did she keep touching me, unless...

No.

Shaking my head, a muscle in my jaw ticked, and I eased my grip on Heather's hand when she squeaked quietly. I'd seen how she'd looked at me in the time we'd been together. Despite how I'd proven myself, sometimes her eyes still held an element of uncertainty at my physical form. She was still a human—weak and susceptible—and despite my physical urges, it would be wrong to take advantage of her vulnerability.

She would never see me as anything other than a monster.

Perhaps she would have wanted me if I'd come here in my human form. Maybe her lips would have sought mine, and she'd have climbed onto my lap that first night and ridden my cock rather than only cuddled against me to seek warmth.

The silence was broken only by the echo of Heather's shoes on the pavement and my uneven breathing. With a huff, she tugged on my hand until I stopped walking. Gripping my arms, she turned me to face her, but I focused on a point beyond her head and didn't look directly in her eyes. Afraid I would see the uncertainty again, or how her gaze brushed over my body, as if to remind herself of what I was. Feelings stirred inside me again, and I clenched my jaw so hard I thought my teeth might crack.

I hated the feelings. I resented them.

Even more so because she would never feel them, too.

Heather reached up and touched my face, and on instinct, my hand shot up and gripped her wrist. She gasped, and I loosened my grip immediately. I didn't want to hurt her. With determination, Heather pressed her lips together and stretched her fingers until I relented and eased my hold enough for her to cup my cheek.

What does this mean?

"I am not injured," I said, still unable to meet her eyes.

"Why are you pulling away from me?" she asked.

"Why are you touching me?" When I finally met her gaze, I was immediately lost in the stunning brown of her irises. I loved brown eyes, especially hers—deep and endless, a smooth transition from one shade to another. Light and dark perfectly combined as she peered into my soul.

Slowly, she slid her hand from my grip, and my eyes followed the movement as her fingers ran down my chest. She paused near my scales, but as she ran her fingers over them, they smoothed against my skin. She paused on my taut stomach, and I met her gaze again.

"I feel a bond with you," she whispered.

"You are susceptible to your emotions."

A smile brushed across her lips, then was gone, and she looked into my eyes again. Her palm was still planted against my abdomen, inches from the V-line of my muscles. "Maybe..." she said, "... but I think you are too."

My brows pulled together, and I wanted to tell her she was wrong.

But Guardians don't lie.

Lifting my hand to her waist, I found the crevice of her hip bone under my little finger and caressed the spot. When she started moving her hips, a gentle gyration against my hand, my gaze darted to her eyes again. Her lids were dipped with heat and desire, and my fingers twitched against the warmth of her skin.

I'm not like you.

"I would..." I started, my voice fracturing as her hand moved lower. "I want to... but I can't change form..."

She shushed gently. "I don't want you to change. I want to be with you as you."

Lies.

But her eyes held no deceit, and her essence was clear. She wanted me, and I wanted her. I'd never been with a human in my natural form before, and the sparkling blue of my skin in the light against the sun-kissed warm tone of hers made my cock stiffen.

"Heather..."

“Please,” she whispered as her fingers curled against me.

It was all the affirmation I needed, and I leaned forward, grasped at her hair, and pulled her lips against mine. She submitted immediately, opened her mouth to me, and allowed my tongue access to explore her. The moan that dropped from her lips when I broke the kiss to trace my tongue down her delicate neck almost broke me, and I growled against her skin.

When she dropped her hands lower, grabbed my cock and rubbed me, my knees almost buckled. Chatter of my native language fell from my lips as I pushed against her eager hands—I was barely holding on to my control. As the air shifted around us, we abandoned our previous hesitations and took each other entirely. Everything that was her was there to take, everything that made Heather who she was. I greedily sucked her essence, wanting to keep the feel of her under my skin forever. I absorbed all of it and let it fill me. In turn, I released myself enough to allow her to bring out all the emotions I had been trying to keep dormant.

I’d heard the talk in Lucidis about how Guardians were changing and how some were *feeling* within themselves. But not me. Never me.

Why would I succumb to such a human weakness?

But Heather... *Heather.*

When she touched me, and after how she’d risked herself to protect me, it all came together. The jumbled puzzle pieces, many of which I’d denied or didn’t know existed, all fell into place. All the emotions I didn’t even know how to begin handling rose in my throat and escaped as an earthy moan as my teeth grazed the soft skin on her collarbone. Heather gasped and moaned in return, and I shuddered under the touch of her hands.

Grunting, I picked her up and cradled her in my arms as she continued to kiss me, nipping at my neck and mewing at me with sounds which tested my remaining willpower. Striding to a small parkland area on the side of the street, I laid Heather on the grass under a tree. When I moved to kneel next to her side, she sat up and stopped my motion by placing her palms on my thighs. Her mouth was so close to my cock, and it twitched in response to the warmth of her breath.

"You don't have to..." I muttered, and was unable to contain my moan as she smiled up at me before she took me in her mouth. My clawed fingers gripped her shoulders, and I fought with myself to contain my strength as she worked her mouth on me so deliciously. Tiny gasps and hums escaped her lips each time she reached the head of my cock, before she'd move down again and every inch her lips dragged down my shaft was exquisite torture. My fingers clenched, and she gasped as I gripped her shoulders harder than I'd intended. Regret seeped into me at the peeping sound she made from the pain of my hold, and I forced my fingers to release. I was on the edge of losing it, and when I could no longer control the thrusting of my hips, when I reached a place where I was more animal than not, I pulled from her mouth and shoved her to the ground. My weight fell on top of her, and Heather giggled in delight before she moaned as I rubbed my length between her legs. With one hand on the back of her head and the other on her hip, I held her gently for a moment and pressed my lips to hers like a lover would, moving against her as she melted into my touch.

Yanking at her pants, the distinct ping of the button hitting a tree barely penetrated my consciousness as I tugged at them until they relinquished to me and I could pull them down. Heather shifted her legs to help, pulled off her underwear, and threw them to the side as I was on her again. As she spread her legs for me, I lined my cock up, and groaned as her slick wetness coated the head. Pressing my mouth to hers, I entered her pussy. She was wet and waiting for me, and enveloped me with warmth and a willingness so sweet that it almost overwhelmed me.

I moved inside her with short, controlled thrusts as she writhed underneath me, each shift of my hips pushing me another inch farther inside. Heather's eyes snapped open as my hips became flush with hers, and she watched my face. Heather lifted a hand and smoothed her fingers along my tense jaw, and I realized I'd been gritting my teeth with the effort of keeping myself under control. She tilted her head, and my eyes softened when I met hers.

"It's okay," she whispered. "I won't break."

"Heather..." I didn't want to hurt her, and everything I didn't have the words to say was communicated through the hitch in my voice as her pussy squeezed my cock.

"Fuck me, Ferox."

With a moan that bordered on a howl, I unleashed on her. Heather gripped my back and shoulders, her nails raking up and down my scales as she pulled my body closer as I pounded into her. She wanted more, she wanted *all* of me, and I controlled myself only enough not to injure her. Heather cried out with each thrust, each one hitting the perfect angle within her until her legs began to tremble and her fingers spasmed.

Rolling onto my back, I gripped Heather around her waist and pulled her with me until she straddled me, my cock never pulling out from her pussy. Holding her eye contact, I gripped her spread thighs and thrust up into her with a jerk of my hips. She cried out and placed her hands on my chest, before she met my movements with equal enthusiasm. Reaching down I pinched and rubbed her clit, and groaned as her cries shifted in pitch.

Her hair fell across her face, and she whipped a hand back to flick it over her head before she looked at me, and held my eye contact for as long as she could. My lips curled into a smirk as I worked my fingers against her, and her eyes screwed shut as she moaned as her climax hit. I kept stimulating her until the trembling of her legs stopped and her cries turned into exhausted gasps. Drawing my hand away, I held her on top of me and pushed up into her, faster and harder, so every thrust made our bodies meet as I became fully enveloped within her. Groaning, I finished with a menacing growl as I came inside her, and her pussy pulsed around me.

Heather collapsed on top of me and rested her chin on my shoulder. I huffed loudly as her hair covered my face, and she chuckled, apologized, and brushed it out of the way. Snaking my arms around her, I allowed my body to soften while rocking gently against her.

Heather shifted against me as my cum leaked down the inside of her thigh. "Ferox..."

"Don't." I squeezed her against me. "Do not say anything."

There was another break in my voice, and I winced at the show of weakness, but said nothing further, and squeezed her slightly in my arms. There was nothing she could say that would tell me anything I didn't already know, and I wasn't ready for the words. This close, I could feel everything she felt, and the echoes of her orgasm had made mine so intense, I felt a burning at the back of my eyes that I wasn't familiar with.

But when I expected to feel her regret or fear swirling around us, instead, the air was heavy with the essence of her relaxation. Heather sighed as she melted against me, and I felt her more clearly than I'd ever read anyone. Even with the shifting of the Balance and the world falling apart around us, I knew her now, better than I'd known anyone, better than I knew myself.

I was experiencing things I'd denied I was ever capable of feeling.

Heather didn't need to speak to tell me what she was feeling, because I was feeling it too.

Our exhaustion had caught up with us, and Heather fell asleep in my arms, with my slumber not far behind. The parkland's trees and bushes hid us from the street's view, and as I squeezed my arms around Heather until she hummed in her sleep, I felt secure enough to sleep myself.

When I awoke, Heather was curled up against my side, her face pressed against my ribs. Every huff of her breath tickled my scales, and I stared at her for a moment before shifting my gaze upward. Sunlight still dappled through the tree's branches, so we couldn't have been asleep long. When Heather rolled over, I slid my arm out from underneath her and stood.

It didn't take long for me to find what I was looking for.

"Ferox?"

Heather's voice was small as she called to me through the trees. She hadn't moved, that much I could tell, and I turned and walked back to where I'd left her. She gasped as I stood on a twig, and the snap startled her.

"Sorry," I said as I entered the small space where she sat, her hand pressed over her heart.

Heather swiped her hair over her head and out of her face again and watched me approach. As I sat next to her, she looked down and slowly pulled her pants back on. Her skin was imprinted with the small indents from grass and stones, and a growl escaped my throat at her exposed flesh. Heather's gaze darted to mine, and she smirked at me before buttoning her pants up, flicking a finger at the missing button.

"I thought you'd left me," she said quietly, looking up at me.

"I would not leave you." Heather settled next to me, and I thrust my fist at her. "Here."

Heather's brow pulled together even as she held her hand out, and I dropped a pebble into her palm and watched as she turned it over in her fingers. It was smooth as though it had been in a river for generations, and tumbled around in the water, eroding any harsh edges. The silky grey of the color was broken only by the off-red dappling pattern.

It told a story, I thought.

"What's this for?" she asked, still turning it over in her fingers.

My back stiffened. "Do you not like it?" I stared straight ahead, or up into the tree branches, or anywhere but at her directly, as awkwardness crept into my being.

Finally, I was able to move my gaze to her face and found her smiling at me. "I like it. It's pretty."

"It is visually appealing." I nodded stiffly. "It is a gift."

Heather stared at me until I held her gaze for more than a few moments, and my shoulders relaxed as she continued to smile at me. Her eyes were bright, but my face remained impassive.

"Thank you, Ferox. It's lovely." She pressed her lips to the pebble and then kissed my cheek. "I love it."

Heather pocketed the stone carefully, and I looked away again and allowed myself to smile.

Chapter Eighteen

Samael

My arm tingled with unshed power as I hooked it around Mother, where she sat next to me on the couch. She'd burst through a Gateway and barely said a word since. I'd taken the time to explain to her what we had been up to—scouring the local area for survivors. But I'd insisted that David and his mother stay here while John and I ventured out, and it was difficult not to return regularly to check on them.

How long would the protections on the building last? If it was even doing anything at all.

David would have my essence all over him, and even with the Shift in progress, an experienced Guardian could pick up on that.

He'd be bait to a Tenebrian.

Guilt swirled in my stomach. I'd been unable to help as much as I wanted to, and David may be in more danger than he otherwise would have been if he hadn't met me. Or more specifically, if I hadn't found him.

But then again, he might also be dead.

Closing my eyes for a moment, I squeezed Mother, and she

released a small sigh and dropped her head against my shoulder.

"We ran into Esco earlier," I said, and when she didn't respond, I continued. "They're gathering people near the town hall to try and center the positive energies. The few people we found we guided there, and we were discussing going there ourselves. If we're going to do something, it makes sense to do it there."

Mother nodded slowly, and I lifted my gaze to find John watching her carefully.

"Where are the others?" John asked, his eyes firmly on Mother, even though she wasn't looking at him, and continued to stare at her hands. When she shook her head in response, John moved next to her, touched her chin, and forced her to look at him. His gentle touch was in contrast to the rough edge of his voice. "Where are Cael and Roger? Are they okay?"

"John, she'll tell us when she's ready. I'm sure everything is okay." But his glare cut right through me. There was no way to know everything was okay, but I couldn't believe Mother would be here if Dad were in danger. I reached out to take Mother's hand, but John snatched my wrist and gripped it before he flung my hand away.

When a flare of anger surged from me, John met it with one of his own, and for the first time, his Tenebrian essence crawled along my skin. "We don't have time for this, Samael. Ana won't break simply because I ask questions." My stomach flipped, but I said nothing, and when John looked back at Ana, she stared at him insolently. "Where are the others, Ana?"

Mother's tone was flat as she answered, "They're in Lucidis, training the half-breeds to control their powers."

"So, they succeeded in getting some of them together?"

"Yes."

"Why are you here and not helping them train?"

She stared at him, but something shifted in the air around her. "Because I'll do more damage than I help. I can feel my power clawing at me from the inside. It's unstable, and given my emotions at this point, *I'm* unstable too."

"You talk about your power as though it isn't part of you."

Mother scoffed. "It's difficult to accept it as part of me when it was so easily used against me and everyone else. I don't see the point in my being there."

John bristled. "You fucking *what?* You don't see the point?" His tone changed, and grew harsher with each passing moment until he forced the final word through gritted teeth like a parent scolding a child. Mother frowned at him, and my brows raised. This wasn't a side of John I'd seen before, and I shoved down the urge to shove him away from us. John's eyes flickered to mine briefly, as though he felt my intent. But when I didn't act, he returned his hard stare to Mother and waited for her to answer.

She slumped next to me, and a sick sense washed over me. It was as though all her energy had abruptly been drained.

Or hidden.

"What's to stop the Tenebrians from doing what they did to me to someone else? If we succeed in correcting the Shift, what's to stop another rebellion from rising and trying to tip the Balance again? The world will repair itself only to have all this death and destruction happen all over again. And even *if* they don't get this far again, the Tenebrians *will not stop*. They'll always be there, hurting and killing. There will always be Rogues, and they don't care. We're promising a life of ongoing pain for so many people. What kind of world is that to save?"

“There are plenty of things worth saving,” John growled out.

Mother’s eyes flickered to mine, but she said nothing.

“Like your family for a start.” John scowled when she didn’t answer.

“I’m not sure I can save anyone.” When she met my eyes, I wasn’t able to hide my disappointment at her words, and a sharp pain cut through me, a pain which echoed from her until I felt it as clearly as though it were my own. Mother looked back at John. “I’m sorry, I just can’t be a part of this. I’ll only make it worse.”

John looked as though she’d slapped him, and dropped his hand from her face. “If it all comes down to you, you’re saying you won’t help?”

The dark cloud around Mother strengthened, and John glanced up at the ceiling as he felt it too, assuming it had come from outside. But no, he followed the trail of negative energy, and it led back to Mother, and his brows furrowed farther.

“I don’t know if I can,” she whispered.

I watched my mother as she retreated into herself, and no longer fought the urge to hug her against me. With a gentle touch, I pushed at John’s shoulder, and while I felt the brunt of his rage for a moment as he glared at me, he moved away. Conflicting emotions and desires tore at my insides. I didn’t want to use Mother or her powers as the Tenebrians had, but what if she was our only hope? I knew John loved her, too. It seemed he was stronger than I was, and maybe he would push her to unleash if he was forced to.

But if she couldn’t shift the cloud of negative energy around her, I had my doubts she’d be able to help. John’s jaw was tense as he watched her, no doubt filtering through the same thoughts and conflicting feelings as I was. There was a greater good here, but it didn't make pushing someone you loved into the center of it any easier.

I stood. "I think we should go to the city center."

"What about Cael and Roger?" John asked.

"If they come here instead of honing in on our essences, we'll leave them a note."

"I should stay behind and wait for them."

I glanced at Mother, who was still staring at her hands, and then back at John. "I'd rather you come with us."

John nodded, stood, and held out his hand to Evelyn. She and David were sitting at the small dining table and had remained silent throughout the entire conversation. As she stood, John squeezed her hand, a comforting gesture that didn't go unnoticed. "You up for a bit of a walk?"

She glanced around uncertainly. "Can't we drive?"

"Sorry," I said, although I wasn't looking at her. David was staring into my eyes, and breaking away from his gaze was difficult. I wanted to read him so desperately because I wanted to know what he was thinking. But not only would it feel like an intrusion when I'd promised him time and space, but it was an unnecessary use of powers when I couldn't afford to waste them. "Driving would attract too much attention."

Evelyn nodded. "Alright. I'm sure I'll be fine."

John squeezed Evelyn's hand again. "Don't worry. I got 'ya, love."

A moment of amusement passed across Evelyn's face. David didn't see it because he was still watching me.

What are you thinking?

I held his gaze. "Are you ready?"

David's eyes expressed worlds of things for which there weren't words. "As ready as I'll ever be."

Silently, we gathered the remaining food and the most suitable clothing we could find. Evelyn found some sneakers in the box, which was usually reserved for providing clothing to Guardians, something more comfortable than her heels.

For extra measure, we took some moonstone blades with us.

There wasn't much to say as we walked through the streets, so we mostly walked silently. Although we were always on high alert, scanning every shadow and corner. What did you talk about at the end of the world? David kept glancing at me from where he walked a few paces ahead, and every time I would scream internally *Talk to me!* As though I could silently will him to do so. I wanted him to say something, *anything*, to break the silence that pounded against my eardrums. Even from the small periods I'd spent here, I missed the sounds of the city now. The people, the vehicles, and the music—it was all gone. Save for the occasional scream of tires or terror.

I needed David to make the first move to reestablish communication between us, because every time I had tried to break the silence following David's revelation about what I was, I'd been met with one-word answers. I understood, as much as I could, but not talking to him strained me.

And worse still, I could feel it strained against him, too. As though we were attached through some invisible thread, and every step we took without physical or emotional contact tugged against our chests. Even without trying, I could sense his feelings. Once we were out in the open, they'd hit me harder, and I wondered if the protection on the building had dulled them.

The more disturbing thought was how *strong* Mother's essence was. It swirled around her, and as easy as I imagined it would be to pick up on, somehow, I doubted many Tenebrians would approach. She felt dangerous, and I squeezed my eyes shut for a moment, thankful David wouldn't recognize the sense for what it was, even if he could pick up that something was wrong.

When I couldn't take the strain anymore, I lengthened my stride and came up next to David. David was more patient than I was, and not talking wouldn't solve anything. I could almost hear David's thoughts as they ricocheted around inside his head, and arguing with himself wouldn't help him deal with all this information. If anything, it would only compound it until he gave up trying to make sense of it and shut himself down.

"Are you angry?" I asked.

David shook his head. "Not angry. I'm confused."

"I'm sorry—"

David stopped walking and pivoted to face me. "You're not *human,* Samael," he hissed out, as though he were simultaneously trying to keep quiet while releasing all the pent-up emotion. "You do realize how weird that is, right?" The outburst came abruptly, a surge of emotion in the air without much forewarning. I pressed my lips together, glad I'd gotten him to talk and broken his flimsy control by asking a question. But how could I make it better?

Can I make it better at all?

David sighed and looked down the street, his expression blank as he took in the collapsed buildings and cracks that crept across the pavement and deep into the roads. "I felt a connection with you, and I really, really liked you, Samael," he said with another sigh. "This is hard."

My stomach dropped. "Liked, past tense?"

"Don't look at me like that." David rubbed his face. "*Like.* I *like* you. But..." His eyes swam with pain as he met my gaze. "I feel like I don't even know you."

"You do know me, I'm still the same me."

David eyed me momentarily, and when he started walking again, I moved to keep pace with him. "I'm trying, Samael, I am trying. I feel if I can get past *this*, then I'll start to feel better." With a hollow laugh, he gestured vaguely around the street. "But accepting who and *what* you are is only the beginning, isn't it? You've lived your entire life knowing about *Guardians,* hell, being one. And you knew about humans and different realms and this *Balance* and all this crazy shit." He dragged a hand down his face again and looked sideways at me. For a moment, something sparkled in his eyes, almost recognition, and I couldn't successfully squash down the hope that flared in my chest.

"I'm not trying to rush you," I said quickly. "I just need to know you're okay."

David held my gaze, and I tried to look past the dark hues of his irises, wanting to soothe the confusion and hurt behind his eyes, wanting him to look at me the way he did before any of this started.

When David reached down and took my hand, I sucked in a breath. He gripped my hand for a moment before he let go, and his arm fell to his side while my hand found my pocket, needing to do something to stop myself from retaking David's hand.

"I'll be okay," David said.

"I never meant to hurt you."

David almost smiled. "I know."

We walked together in silence, but my chest felt lighter.

I could handle the silence. Now we had made small steps toward repairing our connection.

Maybe there was still hope for us.

Chapter Nineteen

Esco

The child's voice drew my attention as she tugged on Lynn's hand. "Mommy?"

"Yes?"

Louise yanked again until Lynn stopped and bent down next to her. I, too, stopped a handful of paces back as Louise whispered in her ear. Lynn straightened and cleared her throat, drawing a questioning look from Penny.

"Louise needs to go to the bathroom. Can we stop for a minute?"

Drawing level with them, I assessed our surroundings. "Yes, but go behind those bins there."

Louise's face scrunched in distaste, and Lynn sighed before she patted her on the shoulder. "Sorry, sweetie, it's the best we can do," she said before she led her off to the side.

"I'm going to go see what street that is ahead, so I know how far away we are," Penny said.

I reached out to grab her arm, but stopped short of making contact. "Wait," I said, and my words were enough to draw her attention. As Penny turned, my eyes widened. Her gaze shimmered with tears, and her lips were pressed together in a fine line. I could almost see her reliving her interaction with the dying man as her gaze bore desperately into mine. She needed a moment of space, and although I understood, I hesitated before continuing, "Do not leave my sight."

Penny nodded curtly before she turned away. My fingers twitched with the urge to follow her, but Lynn and their child also needed protection. The child, more so than her parents. Watching Penny slowly saunter down the street felt like I was being forced to choose between two lives, and while there was no immediate danger I could recognize, it itched against me to run to her and drag her back.

But her emotional needs were strong at that moment, and my duty was to protect them.

Humans were so complicated.

When this was all over, I wondered if I'd be better at my duty given my understanding, or at least my awareness of these internal conflicts, or if I'd simply long for how I was before everything started.

A little ignorant, perhaps. Under-educated by Guardians who, it turns out, knew little more than I, but unaware of what it felt like to have emotions stab at my chest.

The best I could do was settle for staying near Lynn and Louise, and not allowing my gaze to wander from Penny as she made her way down the street, her steps measured and steady. I'm almost certain that Penny would usually have a more carefree and natural gait. It wasn't a stretch of my imagination to picture her walking down this street with Lynn, holding hands, or perhaps each holding a hand of Louise and swinging her between them. Maybe she'd have had a slight skip to her step.

A crack emanated from my jaw, and I released it, realizing I'd been clenching my teeth.

What had been wasn't relevant. All that mattered was now.

So why did my thoughts keep straying?

Both women were quite beautiful, both physically and within their emotional imprints. They were an interesting and conflicting match, but there was much love there, and I was glad Louise had parents like them. When another pang hit my chest, I raised a hand and placed it over my breast. I think I missed my parents, and it wasn't something I'd ever thought about before.

I didn't even know if they were safe.

"Are you almost done, sweetie?" Lynn asked as I watched Penny come to the corner and, with a heavy sigh, lean against a wall, reading the street sign.

"Yes," Louise squeaked.

"Lynn." She turned when I spoke her name. "I need to bring Penny back."

Panic immediately gripped Lynn, and her entire body tensed. "Where is she?"

"She went to look at the street name. I will get her. Stay here, and hide if needed."

She nodded, and I looked at her for a moment more before Louise retook her attention. Quickly, I moved to the end of the street, and Penny looked up as I approached.

"Only a few more blocks," she muttered, and stretched her arms over her head. With a soft groan, she rolled her head to the side to face me. "I shouldn't have rested like this, it's like..." She lifted a hand to wave it slightly. "The moment I stopped moving, all the fatigue caught up with me." She slumped against the wall.

My senses tingled, and my brows pulled together.

Someone was coming.

A human? It was difficult to tell, and I didn't like that I couldn't tell.

"I understand. We need to keep going."

"I know, I know." Penny glanced at me with a slight smile that appeared forced. "I'm a nurse. I'm used to pushing myself to keep going even when I think I have nothing left. I gotta tap into that part of me again." She pushed herself from the wall with her palms.

As Penny came upright, she collided with someone as they came around the corner. I hissed in reaction until I recognized her, and, caught off guard, Penny was knocked to the ground.

She kneeled beside Penny and started to help her up. "Oh shit I'm sorry, I..."

Penny's eyes grew wide, and the color drained from her face as she stared at the woman above her. My stomach dropped, and all at once, I understood the gravity of the situation. But what could I do? Penny had already seen her.

Ana raised her eyes to mine, and I shook my head slightly, wishing I could offer something helpful. But Penny's pain and confusion radiated off her, mingling with Ana's and growing like a black hole. Penny reached up slowly, as if seeing a mirage, and touched Ana's hair, which she'd dyed brown and cut short since Penny had last seen her. She stopped short of touching her hair, and instead, Penny's fingers drifted to her face and brushed gently over the fine lines around her eyes.

Penny's jaw trembled, and she barely got the word out as she sat up slowly. "A-Ana?" she whispered.

They stared at each other, Ana's arm still around Penny's back from helping her, and her fingers twitched with indecision as we all froze. When Penny let out a sob, the moment shattered. Ana looked at me as I opened my mouth to speak, and shook her head quickly.

I understood and shut my jaw. It would do no good for Penny to realize Ana knew me. The ache in my chest grew as I watched Ana lift her hand to touch Penny's face. She hesitated a hair's breadth from contact, then pressed her fingers to Penny's cheek, wet with tears and flushed with emotion.

"I'm sorry, Penny." Ana's voice hitched as she choked on the words, the confusion in Penny's eyes broke my heart, and I could almost feel Ana's shattering as the shards dove deep into me. "I'm so damn sorry. I never meant for any of this."

Penny was still shaking, and she touched Ana's hand on her face with trembling fingers.

Penny's voice caught in her throat as she repeated, "Ana?" before she fainted into her arms. Ana caught her as her weight hit her arm and lowered her to the ground. She looked up and met my eyes, and I gaped at her. The sound of pounding footsteps broke the moment, and Ana's eyes widened as she spotted Lynn running toward us. She stood, hastily glanced around in indecision again, and cast a regretful look at Penny before she turned to me.

"I'm sorry," she croaked out, and I lifted an arm to reach out to her before she spun on her heel and bolted back around the corner.

Lynn kneeled next to Penny and took her in her arms. "Penny? Penny?" She patted her cheek gently. "What happened? Is she okay?"

Louise came up next to me and gripped my hand, her small fingers curled around mine, and her eyes wide as she watched her mother. Penny's eyelids started to flutter, and her hand came up to touch Lynn's face.

"Ana?"

"Are you okay?" Lynn wrapped her fingers around Penny's hand. "What happened?"

Penny's brows pulled together slowly, and she closed her eyes again before opening them and staring at Lynn. "Ana. I saw Ana."

Lynn glanced around before she looked at me. I opened my mouth to respond, but unable to find the words, I stared. Her brows drew together, as if she could tell there was something I wasn't saying, before she turned her attention back to Penny. "That's impossible. Ana's dead."

"It was Ana. I swear it was." Penny managed to hold back one sob before another came, and the tears tumbled down her cheeks before Lynn pulled her against her chest and cradled her for a moment. "I know it was her," Penny repeated, over and over again, as Lynn shushed her gently and brushed her palm down the back of her head.

After a few moments, Lynn encouraged Penny to stand and looked at me. "What happened?"

My insides twisted. "We need to keep moving," I said, holding Louise's hand as I indicated to Lynn to start walking. Lynn threw a frustrated look at me, and when I offered nothing, she turned and walked with her arm tight around Penny's waist.

OUTLET

Chapter Twenty

Ana

Penny.

For the love of fuck, it had to be Penny.

When I thought the black hole inside me couldn't open any further, I broke all over again at Penny's voice. There was pain and confusion in her eyes, as though our hearts were shattered together at the same time. Penny was an innocent victim, and I was the cause of all the pain she was living through. Of course, I'd often thought about seeing her again, but as much as it carved into my soul, Cael was right, and it was too complicated. I'd have to explain to her the existence of the other realms, the Guardians, and my role in it all. The Elders barely accepted me as it was. I can't imagine how I'd even be allowed to stay in the community if I broke the most sacred of rules without what they considered a valid reason.

But when I imagined seeing Penny again, she would wander into my thoughts with her smirk as though she were about to rip on me for something. It was never like this.

I didn't imagine the look in her eyes when the very sight of me drew all her grief to the surface. I didn't imagine it would be at the end of the world itself, where each of us was fighting for our lives, while the Guardians fought to keep the fabric of Earth together.

None of it was her fault, and without even trying, I triggered the suffering of someone I loved all over again. Like a coward, I ran, because what else was I supposed to do? Stay and try to explain to her that while I had died on Earth, I lived in Lucidis?

The truth would hurt even more, and it was my burden to bear.

Samael whipped around as I ran past him and grabbed for my arm. I shook his hold free. "Please, I need a minute," I managed to say before I jogged down the road. I didn't go far, turned into the first corner I found, leaned against the wall, and took staggered, heavy breaths as tears streamed down my face.

My breath caught in my throat.

I wasn't alone.

"Hello Anahera." My tears stopped abruptly as Cascus stepped into the light. I glanced behind me, but the lane was empty. He smiled, and the effect was unsettling. "You're supposed to be dead."

I glared at him. "I guess the Tenebrians are cowards like you are."

His smile dropped, and without another word, he advanced. I shook my head as I backed up in equal measure, and the tears fell again. My heart had been ripped open, my soul destroyed, and I had no time for this asshole.

"Leave me alone," I said, and put my hands out as if I could create a shield between us. Cascus grinned as he mistook the tremble in my voice for fear, when it was instead grief coming to the surface.

Penny.

As the vision of her face swam in my mind, Cascus stumbled backward and almost lost his footing after the wave of energy that had pulsed from me.

Samael came around the corner and skidded to a stop when he saw Cascus. "You."

Cascus ran, and I lowered my hands and dropped my head. There was no point in chasing him. Samael pursued Cascus for a few paces before he stopped, and after watching him retreat, he sighed and turned back to me. I stared determinedly at the sky and tried to blink away the tears. The warmth of his hand when he reached out to touch my arm drew a shaky sigh from me, and I squeezed my eyes shut as the tears began anew.

Fuck that guy.

"What did he want?" Samael asked, his fingers squeezing my shoulder.

"I don't know. Probably to kill me," I said flatly.

"What?"

I shrugged. It didn't matter.

I didn't want to feel this. I didn't want to feel any of it.

No matter how hard I tried to shove everything down and mask myself as the Guardians did, it all kept bubbling to the surface. Each time, it snowballed and collected more and more until it became an avalanche of emotions.

Each time I shut it away, I was afraid the next time I'd lose control entirely, and I had no idea how to stabilize myself.

Cascus had been physically pushed away from me when there had been only a crack in the wall I'd built around myself. What would happen if it shattered? How many more people would be hurt or die?

"Mother, are you okay?"

"I'm sorry, Samael." I sniffed and turned my watery gaze to him. My son. God, he was so strong. Cael would say he got his strength from me, but I wasn't so sure. "I'm sorry for everything."

"We keep telling you it wasn't your fault."

Looking at the ground, I shook my head. "I turned the corner and just... there she fucking was." When Samael's eyebrow flickered upward, but he said nothing, I continued, "Penny. She was an old friend of mine, and she recognized me. She thought I was dea—" I stumbled over the word as the pain in Penny's eyes swam in the forefront of my vision. "The suffering she must have gone through when I died, and now she's suffering again."

"Oh, Mother..."

Stifling a sob, I raised the back of my hand to my lips. I moved my gaze to Samael, my eyes shining. It wasn't lost on me that the attempt on my life by Cascus had meant nothing to me. It was like he barely tried, and the moment I had shown the slightest bit of power, he'd backed off.

Coward.

"It's been hard since I came to Lucidis. Don't get me wrong..." I pleaded with my eyes for Samael to understand. "I love you and your father more than the world." I'm sure the desperation leaked through my voice, and when Samael squeezed my arm, my panic eased slightly. "But I've missed Earth, I've missed *Penny,* and I've missed knowing who I was." I sighed and rubbed my face. "Although it turns out I didn't know who I was at all."

"I understand." I met his eyes, and his gaze was steady. Of *course,* he understood. He knew what it felt like to not quite belong in either realm, but somewhere painfully in between. Samael reached out, and I clasped his hand in mine as he leaned against the wall beside me. We stood there for a few moments, sharing our essences through touch. I wonder what he felt, and if the whirlwind of horrors and guilt and uncertainty inside my mind and soul was tainting him. When I tried to pull my hand from his, his grip tightened slightly, and I met his gaze with wide eyes. He stared at me as his essence touched against the darkness inside me.

I was lost in a fog of my thoughts and dread, and I didn't know what it would take to bring me back.

I didn't know if I could ever come back.

Without me, none of this would have happened.

"Come on." Samael pulled on my hand lightly, and I straightened. "Let's keep moving."

Chapter Twenty-One

Esco

The church's spire was visible. We were so close.

Penny released an audible sigh of relief, and I twitched with the urge to use my calming influence on her. Her nerves were frayed, ripped edges that snagged on every sound and shadow as we walked.

With Ana no longer near, my senses became clearer after they'd become muddled when she approached. I frowned as guilt churned in me, not wanting to wish for Ana's absence, but I needed a clear mind to protect Penny and her family, and I knew Ana would want that.

Feeling things was so complicated.

My arm shot out and stopped Penny in her tracks, and she grunted as her shoulders hit my forearm.

"Wha—"

"*Shh.*" I cut her off, and battled between releasing my senses to confirm what I suspected I'd felt, and drawing them back in to hide my position. I chose to explore the area with my senses because if Tenebrians were near, they'd already be able to sense the humans, and cloaking my presence would not help.

Perhaps if they realized a Lucidian was close, they'd move past us without causing trouble.

A rush of air released as I snorted quietly. It was too much to hope.

Shoving Penny to the side next to Lynn, I ushered them a few feet away and threw my arms open. They watched me with wide eyes, unable to see anything yet.

But I knew someone was close.

The Tenebrians were aware of our actions and plans, and they'd most definitely be able to feel the mass of humans gathering in one spot. If they couldn't get to them there, they'd try to pick them off as they got close. With a groan, I released a rush of power and hoped it was enough for the Tenebrians to think twice before they approached.

These humans are under my protection.

There was silence, and Louise approached me and wrapped her hand around mine again. "Stay with your parents," I said.

Movement caught the corner of my eye, and I released Louise's hand and shoved her to the side.

The Tenebrians were cloaked with decades of experience over me, and they were on me before I'd realized how close the threat was. I grunted as one ran up behind me, grabbed me around the waist, swung me around, and then tossed me against a wall. Dust exploded as I hit the bricks, and I cried out as my arm fractured before I sank to my knees and gasped for breath to replace the air crushed from my lungs.

Dread washed over me. It started in my stomach and filled me as the shrill cry of Louise hit my eardrums. The two Tenebrians approached Louise, and she stood rooted to the spot, screaming.

"Esco!" Louise cried as Penny looped an arm around her and slung her behind herself and Lynn. While I'm sure the child recognized the similarities between these beings and me, she could tell they differed on another level, aside from the noticeable color differences.

They *felt* different.

They felt like terror and death, and their raised spikes, which quivered with anticipation of violence, only heightened this effect.

A high-pitched cry of anger sounded, and I shoved myself to my feet as I realized the sound came from me, fueled by a protective nature I didn't know ran so strongly through my blood. I charged toward the Tenebrians as Penny grabbed Lynn and shoved her toward Louise. Lynn swept Louise up in her arms, turned, and ran. I collided with the Tenebrians, my shoulders hitting them under their ribs. The impact pulled grunts from them and exploded pain in my arm as pressure was applied to the existing bone fracture. I ignored it the best I could, and gritted my teeth against the sharp pain as I fought to move the Tenebrians away from Penny and her family. In the brief moment I had to raise my gaze to check Penny, I noticed she hesitated, and was looking between me and Lynn.

"Run!" I yelled. The Tenebrians were on their feet and lunging at me before I had time to catch a breath, and when Penny continued to hesitate, I snarled and pushed influence into my voice, "*Run.*"

Penny's eyes widened before she pivoted and bolted, and Lynn paused long enough for Penny to clasp her outstretched hand. Together, they fled toward the town hall, and as I wrestled with the Tenebrians, I tried to ignore how my body grew weaker.

I hoped someone would help. Would they sense the disturbance, or was the Shift keeping things too muddled?

The Tenebrians continued toward Penny and Lynn, and each time, I pushed them back. But they advanced faster than I could stop them. My strength waned, and I was no match for both of them, and I gritted my teeth and refused to cry out as I was flipped and landed hard on my back. The sound of my pain stopped the humans, and when I opened my mouth to shout at them to continue running, one of the Tenebrians placed his foot on my chest. I sucked in a sharp breath as he applied his weight and snarled out a laugh. The ground rumbled beneath me, and as the Tenebrian swayed, I grabbed his ankle and took advantage of the moment to shove him from me. He didn't fall and regained himself quickly while I clutched a hand to my chest, certain my ribs too were fractured. There was a silent exchange between the two Guardians before he aimed a kick at my already injured arm, and this time, no amount of willpower could keep in the cry which burst forth from my lips.

The other moved away, and I rolled and lunged for his leg, but my fingers swiped uselessly against his scales as he strode toward the trembling humans. There was no air in my lungs to shout, and the Tenebrian above me grabbed the quills on my head and slammed me back into the pavement. A burst of lights exploded across my vision, and when he did it again, I tasted copper as I bit my tongue. After the third time, he lost interest in me, turned, and followed the other Guardian as Lynn cried out. The ground trembled again, and I rolled over, crying out at the sharp pain in my arm and chest, as my vision swam.

"No," I pushed the word out, as Lynn was struck on the

side of the head as the Tenebrian slapped her with the back of his hand. Louise's hand was still clutched in hers, and fell with Lynn as she collided into the side of a building, turning her body to protect her child from the impact and take the brunt of the force herself. Lynn sank to the ground, and Louise scrambled to her and grabbed her clothes and hair to rouse her. The two Tenebrians advanced on Lynn and Louise, and I caught Penny's eye as she turned to me. Desperation flared in her gaze, and I reached out and dragged myself forward an inch. Every movement was agony, and in the split second Penny met my gaze again, something inside me crumbled.

I can't help you.

The ground shook with another tremor as Penny bolted toward her family. She stumbled from the quake and fell to one knee before she made a hasty correction and continued running. Penny grabbed Louise's arm as she reached out, flung her to the side, and flinched at Louise's pained cry. But she was away from the Tenebrians enough for me to crawl to her. I attempted to stand, but collapsed onto all fours. Louise's small hand found my shoulder as I spat blood onto the ground. One of the Tenebrians glanced at me before they both laughed as Penny tucked Lynn behind her.

They were cornered against the wall.

"Do you feel it, Ristka?" one cooed, and I scrambled against the ground, hissing through my teeth as one of my claws snapped. The child grabbed at my face and arms as tears streamed down her face.

"I need to help them," I hissed through my teeth, but a wave of nausea kept me on my knees as I tried to stand. When I touched the back of my head, my fingers came away bloody, and

I hissed quietly.

Another tremor made the Tenebrians stumble, and Lynn covered her head with her arms as a few bricks from the building behind them came loose and landed around her feet.

Penny held her arms wide, holding herself between Lynn and the creatures. "Leave her alone," she screamed, and her voice broke as they laughed before she'd even finished her plea. Lynn scrambled to her feet and gripped Penny's shoulders as her back hit the wall. "Get to Louise," Penny cried out.

I needed to help.

My body won't cooperate.

Why aren't I healing faster?

There is no energy to draw on.

Louise's hand gripped my shoulder as I lurched forward again, and guilt and anger clawed at me from the inside. When one of the creatures snatched Penny's arm, she spun and struck it on the side of its head with her elbow. Its neck jerked to the side before it turned back to her with a foreboding sneer.

"Are you okay?" Louise whispered into my ear.

Though I wasn't, I nodded and shot my hand out to grab her wrist. Louise cried out in surprise but didn't struggle, and with a sigh, I drew on her energy, hating myself as I did it. It wasn't enough to heal fully, but it was a start. She was only a child, and I shouldn't be drawing her from energy at all. It wasn't happy energy. The poor child was terrified.

But it was the only way.

"*Run,*" Penny screamed as the other Tenebrian lunged for Lynn, and she grabbed its wrist and kicked at its shins.

"Penny—" Lynn was pushed off her feet as another tremble rocked the ground, and I stumbled, my stomach churned, and my vision swam as I desperately tried to blink away the spots and keep my sight clear. Penny and the Tenebrians stumbled together, but she didn't let go of them, nor they her. Lynn's eyes fell to me, where Louise quietly sobbed by my side. Lynn's entire body twitched in a physical manifestation of her hesitation.

"Go," Penny cried out again.

Lynn ran for their daughter, but the relief that swelled through me at Louise being with her mother was short-lived. The quake increased and rumbled out from underneath our feet in ripples. Lynn staggered and dived forward, knocking Louise out of harm's way as the building behind her came down and bricks hit her calves. I shielded my face as the dust stung my eyes from the collapse, and rolled over to shield Lynn with my body as she curled herself around Louise, wincing every time we were struck with falling debris.

The energy in the air shifted, and I sucked in a grateful breath.

There was silence.

Flexing my fingers, the pain in my arm had reduced, but the fracture hadn't healed yet. Lynn shifted next to me, and Louise whimpered as she was released from her mother's tight hold. I rolled onto my back, and pain radiated throughout my body, exploding in a sharp point when I rolled onto broken glass. When Louise's small hand came to my face and pried my eyelid open, I stared at her.

"Esco?" Her voice was small, and I nodded slightly.

Gritting my teeth and using my good arm, I pushed myself into a sitting position and raised my gaze to where Lynn stood behind Louise. She was facing the pile of rubble where the building had once stood, and her entire body almost vibrated with tension. The energy around us shifted again, and on instinct, I grabbed Louise and pulled her closer to me.

Lynn screamed, and I flinched.

The scream carried on as she stumbled forward and ran. Blood streamed down her legs from the bricks and debris, but she ignored it as the scream morphed into a wailing cry which grated against her throat and my ears.

The sound carried her pain with it, and I wished I could bat the energy away as it pounded into me and through my skin, magnified and stronger than anything I'd felt since arriving on Earth.

The pain was so vivid that it was almost as though Lynn wished for death.

For surely, death would be less painful than the way her heart shattered.

Pushing myself to my feet, my stomach dropped and chest constricted, and I stumbled forward a step as I clutched my chest.

Only a pile of rubble remained where Penny and the creatures had been. The impact had destroyed the road beneath it, and Lynn disturbed the settling dust as she clambered over the pile of rubble. She pulled at rocks and bricks until her fingers bled when she couldn't move them.

She shrieked, "*Penny!*"

"Mom?" Louise looked at the bricks and then at me. "Mom?"

"Stay here," I whispered, gently ushering the child behind me before forcing myself to walk. The pain was still there, but the physical pain was nothing—*nothing*—compared to the emotional pain radiating from Lynn. She threw her head back and screamed at the sky, a wordless sound. There were no words for the ache that flooded her body and built itself to something that could only be expressed through an animalistic cry. I flinched again as the essence pounded against me the closer I got, and the ache in my chest increased. How had I become so attached to these humans in such a short time? Was this what it was like to feel love, loss, and empathy firsthand?

It hurts. It hurts so much.

Lynn collapsed against the rocks, banged her hands on them, and buried her face in the rubble as though breathing in the resulting dust would bring her closer to the person underneath.

Lynn twisted around to face me as I neared. "Do something," she cried as her fingers flexed against the bricks and glass. "Do something. *Please.*"

Lowering myself to my knees next to the pile, I placed my hands against the dusty bricks. Sucking in a breath, I forced the pain of my body to subside enough to focus what little energy I had through the remnants of the building. My essence found its way through cracks where even the air barely managed to break through, coursing through the maze left by the destruction and seeking, searching, desperately hoping to find a life force. When I felt nothing, I held back an uncomfortable lump which formed in my throat—*was I crying?*—and searched for a heartbeat, an imprint, for *any* sign I could cling to in the hope life was still there.

I needed to find any hope I could give Lynn and Louise.

Dropping my hands heavily to my knees, Lynn looked desperately between me and the pile, slapping the rubble's side with her palm.

"Again!" she cried, and I raised my eyes to her.

We both knew they were no hope, but I tried anyway.

As I placed a palm on the fallen bricks, I glanced back at the child standing in the middle of the road, lost and defeated. Wide eyes I wished weren't filled with the comprehension of what had happened, and what she had lost.

"I can't find her," I said finally. I wanted to lie and tell Lynn it'd all be okay, just as I'd witnessed Penny do. I wanted to watch her eyes fill with hope, and know I had given her that hope. However, giving false hope would only result in a more crushing pain later.

I couldn't do it.

Lynn's eyes widened as her lip trembled. "Please." She started pulling at the pile again and dislodged a few bricks before she stopped as her shoulders shook. I suspected she didn't understand what powers I was utilizing, but she knew I was trying. Lynn begged, "Try again, *please.*"

Relinquishing, I released an uneasy breath before I closed my eyes and pressed my hands against the bricks again. Forcing myself into the moment, I let warmth tingle through my fingers, the lingering heat from the sun escaping into the air. I thought of Lucidis and wished I could tap into its power if only for a moment.

"Give me your hand." Lynn didn't question and held out her hand immediately. When I took it, I hissed sharply through my teeth as her pain radiated into me. "Think something happy," I said, and Lynn tilted her head at me as anger flashed through her eyes. I met her unwavering gaze. "I need positive energy to be stronger. Think of something good, and give me that energy." Lynn closed her eyes, and slowly, the energy coming from her shifted. I continued to watch her face, and her eyes closed as tears rolled over her cheeks.

I didn't need to ask who she was thinking of.

The energy was bittersweet, but it was enough, and with a small grunt, I forced it into the air between the rocks and bricks and toward the ground, leaving no space unexplored. I sighed. For a moment, I could almost forget about the Balance and remember what it was like to be home and do my duty.

My senses reached a space under the fallen wall, and even though I wanted to withdraw, I pushed forward and forced myself to continue until there was no doubt.

Because the only sense that came back to me was death.

My voice was quiet. "She's not there anymore."

"What do you mean? What do you *mean* she's not there?" Lynn shrieked as she tugged her hand from mine. "She was right there. She is *right there!*" Lynn pointed at where Penny had stood.

"I mean..." I pulled in a shuddering breath. I could feel everything Lynn was feeling, and my pain mingled within it, and it was tearing me apart. I resisted the urge to touch a hand to my chest, as if I would be able to feel a physical representation of the pain. "She's *not there.* She's gone." The effort of raising my gaze to Lynn's was a physical strain. A thin layer of tears was swimming at the bottom of her eyes, which spilled over and joined the paths the tears minutes before had left. "I'm sorry," I whispered, "She's de—"

"No," cried Lynn, and swiped a hand toward me. "Don't you *dare* say it." She started pulling at the rocks again and threw her weight behind them, but there wasn't a hint of movement of the larger pieces, and she collapsed to her knees. "No, *no, no, no.* Take me instead. *Take me instead.*"

The effort of standing was beyond the physical pain that had returned threefold once I lost Lynn's energy from my fingertips. I touched Lynn's shoulder, and my fingers twitched as I tried to force my mind to remember a more comforting gesture. My voice hitched as I said, "We need to go."

"I'm not leaving her." Lynn angrily shrugged off my touch and continued to pull uselessly at the debris.

When she didn't stop trying, I increased the pressure on her shoulder and physically pulled her to her feet. "Go to your daughter."

Lynn's expression shifted as she spun around and wiped away the tears on her face with the back of her hands. Her skin was streaked with dust and blood as she closed the gap between her and Louise, knelt, and pulled her against her in a crushing hug. Louise's cheeks were blotchy red as she cried silently. "Mommy?" she whispered, her eyes on Lynn, before her gaze traced to the destruction. "Mom?"

"I'm sorry, baby," Lynn said, a sob raking through her. "Mom's gone."

"Was it my fault?"

"No." Lynn pulled back, grabbed Louise's arms, and looked into her daughter's eyes. "No, and don't *ever* think that. The only ones at fault were the creatures who attacked us. It is *not* your fault..." She took a deep breath and pulled Louise against her again, "... and it's not my fault either."

She squeezed her eyes shut as if trying to convince herself.

"Mommy." Louise sobbed and grabbed at Lynn's top as Lynn cradled her small face against her shoulder, hushing gently.

My breathing was ragged, and I struggled to keep the emotions I was feeling at bay.

This was too much. Everything swirled inside me, as though all it took was *one* thing before decades of emotions unfelt came rampaging forward and forced themselves into my soul. I approached them, placed a trembling hand on Lynn's shoulder again, and squeezed. Lynn nodded, stood, and took Louise's hand as she wiped at her face with the other.

Lynn paused and looked me up and down. My body was covered in blood and dust, claw marks marked my arms, and a trail of dried blood ran from the wound on my head. "Are you okay?" she whispered.

No.

"I will heal."

Lynn's expression twisted. "I won't."

Lynn and I stared at each other for a moment, and as we started to walk, Lynn took my hand. The slight squeeze I gave her in return was enough for her to know I understood her pain.

Even if I couldn't do anything to take it away.

Chapter Twenty-Two

Ana

Walking with John and Evelyn, I dragged my feet as we remained paces behind Samael and David. We'd taken a slight detour to abate my fear of running into Penny again, although I knew that it was likely we were all heading toward the same place anyway. How could I explain to Penny that while I had died on Earth, through a twist of fate, I now lived on in another realm? Would she believe I hadn't faked it? Would all the current devastation and strange events help to convince her and make her understand? Or would they confuse her more?

All I wanted was not to hurt Penny anymore. I didn't want to hurt *anyone* anymore. Would it be more painful for Penny if I told her everything, or if I hid and said nothing?

There was no correct answer.

Her eyes had been glazed, perhaps she'd think I was a waking dream.

Or a nightmare.

In an attempt to shake the thoughts from my head, I watched Samael. He and David walked close together, shoulder to shoulder, with their arms touching. Occasionally, their hands would brush against each other, and Samael's fingers would flex as though with the effort of holding back the urge to take David's hand. Then David would glance at Samael as though he *wanted* him to. I pressed my lips together, holding back the desire to get involved. This was *beyond* a complicated situation, and they needed the space to sort it out for themselves. Focusing on the air around them, I felt the love that mingled with their beings and physical closeness. Real love, which made my chest ache as I absorbed it, and I mourned for the loss of their chance to have a normal relationship. Something normal outside the different realms, the Shift in the Balance, and all the chaos and violence. Simply two beings who shared a connection.

That was my fault, too.

Out of the corner of my eye, I saw Evelyn watching me, and I turned to look at her. Her entire world had been turned upside down. I wanted to offer words of comfort or an apology, but when I opened my mouth, no words came.

"It's real, isn't it?" she whispered.

"What is?"

She indicated David and Samael. "Their feelings for each other."

With a tilt of my head, I analyzed Evelyn's face. Her cheeks were a blotchy red from crying over her lost husband, but she only cried whenever she thought no one was paying attention, and pretended she was stronger than the need to release her grief. Now she watched David and Samael with a mixture of curiosity and sorrow, and I knew her mind strayed back to her conversation with David before he left their home.

"Yes, it's very real," I said. Evelyn stayed silent, so I continued, "Samael told me what happened between David, you, and your husband."

Evelyn sucked in a breath before she cleared her throat to hide the sob which rose in her chest and threatened to escape. "I never meant for... I didn't understand."

Linking my arm with Evelyn's, a gesture I'm sure younger Ana would've baulked at, but Penny would have approved of, I patted her hand. "Their love is as real as your love for your husband and son."

Evelyn nodded, and she squeezed my hand briefly before moving away to walk next to her son. David glanced at her as she came level with him, and opened her mouth to apologize, but David shushed her gently, put his arm around her shoulders, and pulled her against him.

John shuffled next to me. "Their love is something worth saving, don't you think?"

"I never said it wasn't."

"When the time comes, Ana, they might need you."

"I'm not strong enough to control it, John."

"You are stronger than you think."

"So everyone keeps telling me, but look at what I've done. I wasn't strong enough to stop this." I glanced at him briefly from the corner of my eye before I stared ahead as we approached the town hall's edge.

As we entered the courtyard, we were greeted by Lucidians, and I found myself searching for Penny's emotional imprint. Whether I was doing this to see her or avoid her, I wasn't sure yet. Maybe I was being selfish and needed to know she was near, even if I couldn't, or wouldn't, talk to her. My brows drew together when I couldn't find it, and I looked around quickly, my head moving back and forth until I located Lynn's bright red hair.

What do I do?

But as I stared at her back, as if sensing someone watching her, Lynn turned. When our eyes met, Lynn's jaw dropped, and her eyes filled with tears. She slapped a hand over her mouth to stifle the emotion that rose in her chest and filtered into the air around her.

Lynn and I were never that close, so I couldn't figure out why she would react to my presence with such a visceral emotion. No doubt it would be confusing to see me, but an emotional reunion is not what I expected.

Unless...

Panic bubbled in my chest, and I glanced around again, and my cropped hair fell in front of my face as I searched frantically for Penny, both visually and with my senses.

No, no, no, no, no.

My panic increased, and tears threatened to take hold and break me yet again when I found nothing.

"Not this." I didn't think my heart could take any more, and Samael looked down at me as a sob raked through me. "Anything but this."

"What's wrong?" he asked as my panic rose like a tidal wave, only to come crashing down into grief that settled over me like water on the sand.

"I can't find her." My emotions rose, starting in my stomach with an uncomfortable squirming as though I was going to be sick, and growing in my body. Uncomfortable sensations filtered throughout me until the ache in my chest was too much to bear. By the time Lynn approached me, my hand was clutched over my chest, and I was breathing rapidly. I shook my head and stepped back as if physical distance could keep the words I didn't want to hear away.

Lynn opened and closed her mouth a few times but said nothing.

I didn't want to know.

Please, God, no.

"Penny?" I whispered, my voice croaking out as it mingled with the black hole inside me. The only response I got from Lynn was a slow shake of the head, accompanied by tears that ran down her face to match mine. "No." I choked, doubled over, and clutched at my stomach.

As I collapsed to my knees, Lynn kneeled with me, placed her hands on my shoulders, and waited for me to look at her. When I finally did, no other words were spoken between us. They didn't need to be. Lynn and I bonded for the first time under the worst circumstances. I leaned forward and pulled Lynn against me, and as her arms came around me, both our emotions toppled over the edge, and we held each other until our sobbing subsided into silent mourning.

I squeezed Lynn against me. "I'm so sorry," I whispered repeatedly, desperate to atone for my sins. "I'm so so sorry."

Lynn leaned back, but as she opened her mouth to speak, a small child approached her. "Mommy?" she asked quietly. My eyes darted from Lynn to her daughter, and when Lynn looked back at me, her eyes filled with silent tears again.

I choked again and clenched my fists so tight my nails dug into my palms. With a tilt of my head, I indicated Samael. "My son." I barely managed to rasp the words out.

Lynn nodded and tried unsuccessfully to force a smile before turning to the little girl. "Sweetie, this is Ana, a friend of your

Mom's."

"Hello," the girl said quietly.

"Ana..." Lynn hesitated, and there was a look in her eyes I couldn't read. "... this is Ana-Louise."

The ground dropped out from underneath me, and my chest hollowed. I stared at Lynn, the realization hitting me as Lynn nodded slowly and shrugged slightly with one shoulder, making another unsuccessful attempt at a smile. "Penny wanted to name her after you."

"Lynn, I'm—" My voice shattered with my soul, and tears broke through again. There was nothing else I could say except "I'm sorry." But the words felt empty.

I couldn't make any of this better.

"It's not your fault." We stared at each other again. There was nothing left to say. Ana-Louise tugged on Lynn's shirt gently, and she rose to her feet. "I'll, um, see you soon," Lynn said as Ana-Louise gave me a sad smile and wave before they moved back into the crowd.

My jaw ached from clenching my teeth. My chest ached.

Everything ached.

"But it *is* my fault," I whispered.

Chapter Twenty-Three

Heather

"You... um, have a very menacing resting expression."

"What do you mean?" Ferox looked down at me, his lip lifted into that almost permanent scowl he wore, and I pursed my lips to suppress my laughter. It didn't work, and I watched with delight as his scowl morphed into a small smile. Ferox didn't always understand what I was laughing at—and honestly, it was mostly *him*. It was difficult not to, in his grumpy way, he was adorable, and the butterflies that fluttered in my chest when I looked at him had only increased since we'd made love.

But he smiled when I smiled, because like an absolute sweetheart, he liked it when I was happy, even if the joke was at his expense.

"Like that," I said with a giggle and pointed to his face. "Before you smiled, you looked like you wanted to rip someone's head off. Maybe humans will respond a bit better if you look a bit more... friendly?" I offered. Ferox's brows furrowed as he looked ahead. Before he returned his piercing gaze to me, I continued, "You've expressed your annoyance that humans don't trust you, despite all your work to protect them."

"And now I need to *look friendlier,* too?"

With a quiet laugh, I reached up and rubbed my thumb over the furrow between his brows. My smile widened as his face relaxed, and his shoulders slumped as his entire body seemed to follow suit at my touch.

"Yes!" I clapped my hands together. "Much better."

Immediately, the furrow returned to his brow, as though he was trying to figure out what he'd done differently. I tutted and brushed my fingers over his face again in the same manner, and when his face relaxed, realization dawned in his eyes. As my hand paused, so did his steps, and we stood there looking at each other. His hand came up to grasp my wrist, and after a beat of silence, he pressed his cheek into my palm.

"It's you."

"Yes." The word that left my lips was breathy. It *was* me. It was I who relaxed him.

Things were getting incredibly intimate between us, on a deeper level than physical, and I swallowed around the emotion that welled in my throat. Ferox wasn't human, and I had to keep reminding myself—not because it bothered me any longer, but because eventually he would have to go home, wherever that was, and I would have to let him go.

With a thin smile, I shook my head slightly. "How about you try smiling?"

Ferox bared his teeth, pulling back his top lip as he raised the corners of his mouth and dropped his chin. The effect was mildly terrifying, and I immediately felt guilty at the burst of laughter that escaped me. He dropped the expression, and his eyes searched my face.

"I'm sorry..." I stifled my laughter, "... that would look like you wanted to eat them."

"I could devour you again."

My smile dropped as quickly as his had, a flush rising on my cheeks. This time when he smiled, his eyes flashed with the depraved thoughts he was no doubt having, and I sucked in an unsteady breath. "That smile," I whispered as I clenched my thighs together. "I like that smile."

"I can only do it that way when looking at you."

My chest warmed. "So, look at me."

Ferox snarled as his arm came across my body, and he pushed me behind him. I squealed and gripped his arm as glass shattered across the sidewalk, and a Tenebrian fell backward onto the pavement in front of Ferox.

My fingers gripped his arm as we both stood in shock.

The Tenebrian had a stiletto heel buried in each eye, and blood leaked from his face as he lay, dead, at our feet.

"Holy shit," I whispered, and Ferox tensed in front of me.

One by one, four women emerged from the building, and I glanced up to see the neon sign announcing the name of the strip club. I barely registered the letters as my gaze returned to the women before me. Three wore everyday clothes, while one wore only a thong bikini and high heels. The glittery tassels of her outfits seemed obscene as we all stood, staring at each other in shock and silence.

"He's one of *them,*" one of the women shrieked, bent, and ripped one of the shoes from the Tenebrian's body, before she flailed it threateningly in front of Ferox. He growled, and I stepped out from behind him.

"*No.* He's with me."

The woman lowered the shoe, but her eyes narrowed as she

studied me. "Is he holding you hostage?"

Before she'd even finished her question, she'd raised the shoe again, and I glanced uneasily at the Tenebrian's body at our feet. The reds and oranges of his scales were beginning to fade, as each of the puncture wounds on his body continued to bleed.

The puncture to the eyes may have been the fatal blow, but there was *rage* in this kill.

I swallowed. "Did he hurt you?"

"He tried," the woman with the makeshift weapon held her chin high, and the girl behind her in the bikini sniffled. "We grabbed the thing closest to us that could be a weapon and used it."

"All of you?"

"Together."

My lip twitched as I held back a smile, which felt as though it would be inappropriate. The ill feeling I'd had in my stomach after I'd killed a Tenebrian rushed back, and whatever amusement I'd felt fizzled and died within me, and was replaced with horror at what these women, and countless other people, were having to do to survive. I licked my dry lips, and when my fingers curled around Ferox's, the girls followed the movement. "I was going to say we're here to help, but it looks like you may not need it." My lip twisted as I glanced at the dark building behind them. "Were you hiding?"

The woman finally lowered the shoe and used her other hand to run it through her long hair. "Yes. I'm Rose, by the way."

"Heather," I said, and I indicated Ferox with a nod. "Ferox."

Rose hummed as her gaze dropped to our intertwined hands before continuing, "The floor manager told us to hide, and he was going to get help, but he never came back. We were discussing if we should try to leave and find help ourselves when this fucker came through the door."

"We can't stay here now. Not with the window smashed like this," another of the girls said, and when I looked at her, she touched a hand to her chest. "Regina." Then she indicated the other women. "Alysia and Brandy."

"This asshole tried to attack Alysia, fucker's cock was hard, sick fuck." Rose spat onto the body, and Brandy's lip curled.

"So, what now?" Alysia wrapped her arms around herself, seemingly determined to forget what had happened, and what had almost happened, and move on.

"Humans are gathering in the city center. We will take you there."

There was silence after Ferox had spoken, and he glanced at me before he pulled his lips back into a smile. Unfortunately, it wasn't the nice smile I liked, but the terrifying one. The girls stepped back, and I pressed my lips together and prayed for the strength not to laugh.

"Come on, Brandy, put on some clothes, and we'll wait with Heather and uh... Ferox."

Brandy followed Regina back into the club, while Alysia and Rose stared at us.

"Do we need to bring anything?" Alysia asked.

"Weapons?" Rose said as she held up the heel with a manic grin.

"If it makes you more comfortable," I said tightly.

Regina and Brandy returned, after which followed a bout of awkward silence.

"You're alright?" Brandy asked, directing the question at me.

Ferox's forced smile dropped, but to Brandy's credit, she

didn't shrink under his gaze. I squeezed his hand as I waited for her to look at me again, before I answered. "I'm fine. Ferox has been protecting me."

My gaze was drawn to Regina, who was staring at Ferox with an unreadable expression. Ferox locked eyes with her, and something unspoken appeared to pass between them. His grip on my hand tightened and released briefly, and when I glanced up at him with a question in my eyes, he didn't look down at me, but continued to stare at Regina.

"What is it?" I whispered as impatience ate at me. I wanted to know what he knew.

Was she dangerous somehow?

It took him a moment to pull his gaze from Regina, and when he finally met my eyes, his expression was cloaked with confusion. "Let us go," he said to the group without turning away from me, pointing in our intended direction. Under the pretense of brushing dust off my clothes, he kneeled before me and kept his lips close to my ear. "She is a half-breed," he whispered.

My back stiffened. "You mean?"

He nodded curtly once before standing, and we stepped behind the group of women. I didn't understand the significance of Regina being half-Guardian, but from Ferox's demeanor alone, it was important, or at least, rare.

I wondered if Regina knew.

We'd only been walking a short while before Ferox stopped, and again placed his arm in front of me. "Stop," I called out to the girls in a stage whisper, and was thankful they turned and stopped immediately without further question. Following Ferox's gaze, I noticed movement as it flitted down an alleyway, and my body tensed.

"What is it?"

"Tenebrian."

When I followed his line of sight, I couldn't see anything anymore, but he continued to stare down the alley as he drew himself to his full height and placed his body in front of mine.

"What do we do?" I whispered.

"Stay behind me."

The girls came and stood near us, but didn't gather as close to Ferox as I was, and Rose held up the bloody stiletto. After a beat, the Tenebrian strolled out from between the buildings. While like all other Guardians he was naked with his cock swinging proudly, I imagined if he had been wearing pants he would've had his hands in his pockets and casually sauntered in front of us. His eyes never left my face, and a chill ran down my spine. Ferox edged closer to me as an involuntary whimper left my lips, and Rose glanced at me with her lips pressed into a fine line.

I'd encountered Tenebrians before, and while none of the interactions had been pleasant, something about *this one* curdled the acid in my stomach.

He leaned forward, splayed his arms out wide, hissed, and then laughed as two of the girls screamed and shuffled closer together. His gaze traveled back to me, and a wide, unsettling smile spread across his lips, almost cracking his face and diamond-like skin as he laughed.

Recognition tapped at the back of my skull, but I didn't understand.

Who is he?

"We meet again, my little whore," he said, delighted, and his darkened eyes flickered to Ferox as he snorted in rage. "Oooh...

and you have yourself a protector."

My brow furrowed even as my stomach lurched violently, and I swayed slightly as fear crawled across my skin.

"Don't you remember me?" he said, and tilted his head dramatically. "Oh, that hurts. Maybe I didn't fuck you hard enough." He took a few steps toward us, and I backed away equally fast, my hands clutching Ferox and taking him with me. I didn't want this Tenebrian any closer. My skin already crawled with his proximity, and I felt that if he came too close, I'd vomit. Ferox continued to snarl until his low growl was constantly in the background. His arm muscles under my fingers twitched as though he wanted to attack, but I found myself unable to release him.

"Joel," the Tenebrian said with delight, and slapped himself on the chest. "Well, you knew me as Joel, but it's Culo." He laughed again, and with another intentional step closer, his expression darkened. "Don't you remember what it felt like to be under me while I fucked you, and you begged me to slow down. You really wanted to tell me to stop, I could feel the regret and pain seeping from your skin." I choked on my fear as it rose with the bile in my throat at the memory of him on me, *in me*, and of how he lulled me into a false sense of security and then used it to his advantage. Ferox's chest rose and fell rapidly as my fear increased, and reality seeped back into my mind when I remembered he could feel what I felt. With uncertainty, I gazed up at him, expecting disgust in his eyes, but all his hatred was directed at Joel... Culo.

He doesn't blame me.

Ferox took a step forward. "Leave before I am forced to kill you." Though the twitching of his fingers told me Ferox wanted to kill Culo immediately.

"You would like it to be that easy, wouldn't you, coward?" Culo spat at him.

Ferox was on him with a speed that took my breath away, and with one hand on his throat, Ferox pounded the back of Culo's head against the pavement with every strike of his fist into his face. My hands flew up to cover my mouth, and when I went to take a step forward, Regina came up next to me and gripped my arm. I knew Culo didn't deserve to live, I knew what he'd done, and I could only imagine all he may have done to other people. But the display of violence from Ferox still took me by surprise—the rapid movement of his hands and the sheer strength he displayed. Blood spurted from Culo's nose as well as the back of his head, and his eyes rolled.

Rose looked between me and the fight. "Did he hurt you?" she asked with disgust dripping from her voice.

My voice shook. "The orange one, yes." I gasped and reached forward through the empty air as Culo landed a punch to Ferox's jaw and managed to launch Ferox off of him.

"Oh, that repulsive freak." With a scream, Rose was on him and stabbed at Culo with the heel, her weapon of choice. After a brief moment of hesitation, the other girls followed suit and banded together, and each began striking Culo with all the force they could muster. The stilettos were sharp, and I'd never considered stabbing someone with a shoe before, but how it punctured his skin had my stomach lurching again. Culo screamed in rage as a heavy bottle was broken across his face, and he covered his head with his arms when a shard of glass embedded in his cheek.

Ferox stood and roared in rage. He gripped the back of Rose's top but released her when she turned and swiped at him. Culo tore himself away from the group, cast a dirty look at me before he turned to run, and stumbled with a heavy limp. Ferox roared again and tried to get past the girls. I could tell he was holding his strength back, and while he could shove them all to the side with a simple sweep of his arm, he didn't, and when Culo managed to find an awkward, lopsided gait and disappeared around a corner, Ferox snarled at Rose. The girls breathed heavily and backed against each other again as Ferox advanced on them.

"Why did you put yourself in danger? Foolish *humans,"* he spat the last word out, and I flinched.

"We were protecting her from that creep," Rose said.

"*I* was protecting her."

"You don't need to get all possessive. We were only trying to help."

Ferox halted himself from responding when I placed my hand on his arm. He rounded on me, and all the rage in his eyes melted away and was replaced by something much more disturbing.

Fear.

He placed a hand on top of mine, looped his other arm around my waist, and pulled me close. When my hand landed on his chest, it was sticky with the Tenebrian's blood, and I closed my eyes against the onslaught of emotion. This was too much all at once—the polar opposites between the love and care and the utter violence he was capable of.

The violence that the other women were also capable of.

And me too.

This Shift Ferox spoke off—I could have sworn I felt it in the air now, as though the atmosphere itself buzzed with change, and every deep-seated emotion that lingered inside people was being drawn to the surface.

"Let's keep moving," he snapped at the girls, and slowly they trickled away. Ferox didn't move and stared down at me. "I scared you."

When I shook my head, he remained tense under my hands. "No. I was scared of you being hurt."

"You are lying."

I met his eyes, and my vision blurred with tears. "There was so much blood."

"He hurt you."

"I know. I know you did it to protect me, I'm not mad, I promise, I'm just... scared." I ran my palm down his cheek, and winced when it left a bloody streak. "Sometimes I feel so strong, but when he hurt you..."

"He could not hurt me."

I huffed out a laugh through my nose and smiled at him. When my smile dropped and my lips pursed, he tilted his head. "Stop trying to read my feelings."

"I do not have to try. They come to me anyway."

"What am I feeling now?"

Ferox opened his mouth to respond, but no words emerged. I knew why without having to ask. With a slight nod, I placed my palm on his chest and waited for him to bend so I could gently kiss his lips.

"I feel it," he whispered against my lips.

"Me too."

Slowly, he turned to follow the girls and held out his hand until I took it, and we fell into step together. There were no words, because words weren't enough.

I love you too.

Chapter Twenty-Four

Cael

Focusing our energies on the dying realm around us became increasingly difficult. As Gateways continued to open and remain open, the lines between Earth and Lucidis grew increasingly blurred. The same thing would be happening to Tenebris. Eventually, only one realm would survive after the devastation—a combination of all three, and suitable for no beings to inhabit comfortably. Roger's knuckles whitened where he held my hand and squeezed, and a sharp pain interrupted my focus as we stood as one with Sasha and the half-breeds. We stood in a circle, as we'd been doing for hours, and each time I could feel the energies of the group sharpening and forging together. The sliver of hope that lived in my chest strengthened.

Keeping my eyes closed, I tapped into the essence of the half-breeds, and tried to guide them to where they needed to be. "Focus on something positive in your life, a memory if you need to, but try to capture the feeling. Feel it in your gut, in your core, and let it radiate out from you. Picture the positive energy as ink flowing through your bloodstream and let it take you over, then force it outward."

My eyes shot open as Roger nudged me with his elbow. When my gaze found his, he tilted his chin toward Emma and Floyd. I had to squeeze his hand to keep the tremble from mine under control, as Emma's and Floyd's skin took on a bluish glow which radiated outward from them and began to surround the group.

I continued hastily, "Now, focus on each other. Bring your emotions into line together. Feel where your hands meet, and your essences join, and make it the only thing you can feel."

Each time we tried, we got closer, and while I could see the fatigue beginning to creep in to the half-breeds, they hadn't given up. Each attempt required rest we didn't have time for, so I walked a delicate line between allowing them time to recharge and teaching them as much as I could in such a short amount of time. These were things Guardians grew up learning. There were no secrets, and they knew their powers and purpose from the moment they were able to understand. These beings had been thrown into it and forced to undergo the same training in a fraction of the time.

We didn't need them to be perfect. They only needed to be able to align with each other.

But each time I forced them to move forward when they sought rest, I was met with resistance and a hint of resentment.

When the dome of positive energy increased around us and fluttered Sasha's hair, the air of Lucidis in the immediate area returned to its usual warm light under the invisible dome. My eyes widened. I had dared to hope it would work, and now the evidence was in front of me, displayed and pushing aside the doubt that lingered.

We might have a chance.

The half-breeds still had their eyes closed, but when Emma felt the rush through her as her energy connected with Floyd's, she opened her eyes and gasped as she saw the blue glow to her skin. Her reaction drew Floyd's attention, and when he opened his eyes, the link broke, and the change in energy was like a heavy blanket thrown over us, casting us back into the murky shadows where the light had once been.

Emma pulled her hand from Floyd's and turned it in front of her face, again in her natural tone. "I'm sorry," she said, her voice shaking. "I wasn't expecting..."

"That was closer than before. We're getting better."

Roger pressed his lips together. "I'm not sure how much more time we have to practice. If we leave it too late—"

"I know," I held up my hand, before I rubbed my brow. "I know. But we have to keep trying."

"Is Ana coming back?" Grace asked.

My hesitation drew a suspicious glare from her. "No, I don't think so. We'll meet her on Earth."

"Why did she go? She didn't seem convinced this would work."

"It's not that, she's been through a lot." When Grace continued to look unconvinced, I approached her. "The doubt and fear inside you could potentially be our undoing." I allowed my gaze to drift between the others. "You have to be completely in this, or not at all. Cast aside any doubt and focus on being one with each other."

Grace's smile didn't extend to her eyes. "This is all sounding a bit like some cheap meditation class."

"However it may sound, this is our only hope for survival, and you need to understand the importance of that." I'm sure my expression was as grim as my tone. "This is life and death. Are you in?"

"I'm in, but—"

"Let's try again."

Grace held up her hand. "Don't get me wrong, Cael, it's not that the existence of other realms and beings doesn't *wow* me. But are you seriously trying to tell me positive thoughts will save the day?"

Impatience crawled inside me, and I stamped it down, reminding myself that humans were not born into the knowledge of the Balance and its powers. I had somewhat expected this sort of resistance earlier, but it had been bubbling beneath the surface, and every time I pushed the group, their uncertainty grew, even as their success did. Grace spoke all their questions, and the others watched the exchange between us, eagerly awaiting the answers to the questions they were too afraid to ask.

"Yes and no. Listen..." I rubbed my head again, and Grace's expression softened slightly. "I am sorry we don't have the time for me to give you the explanation you deserve. I know Roger has explained to you the purpose of the Guardians, and how all the positive and negative energies driven by humans' emotions affect the Balance." Grace nodded slowly, but said nothing. She wanted more clarity. "This is about more than that. It's about every action having a reaction. It's about light and dark. You've seen this *every day* without even knowing it. We're simply trying to push things back in the right direction."

"Has it been done before?"

Once again, my hesitation was the answer. "No."

"So, we're supposed to, what? *Happy* our way to a better

future?" She turned, her arms extended, trying to muster agreement and backup from the others. "What's going to happen, really? We've gone this long as a species without knowing about the Balance, so why is there now a great rush for us to protect it? Why can't you do it without us?"

My hands shook, and anger grew within me. I wanted to remain calm and gently explain to Grace all the things she needed to know, the way I had with Ana all those years ago.

Ana.

The feel of her memory hit me like a blow to the stomach. I had been trying so hard to concentrate on what needed to be done, and I brushed off any mention of her as though it didn't bring her to the forefront of my mind. But the vivid memory that exploded in my mind now was too much—the way she'd collapsed to the floor after returning from Tenebris, and the panic at what she'd seen and experienced. How she had looked at me with wide eyes like a child seeking comfort, and I wished I could lie to her and make all the hurt and confusion go away.

Ana brought me to my knees every time.

This was about more than doing what was right by our duty. This was about saving lives.

Saving *her.*

Saving *us.*

Grace leaned back as I took another step forward and entered her space. The way her pupils danced across my face told me she'd felt the shift in my demeanor, and when I reached for her, she took a half step away from me.

"Give me your hands."

Grace complied, but slowly, each move speaking her hesitation when her mouth was dry as she licked her lips. She didn't break our eye contact, and tensed as though she were waiting for any sign to indicate I was going to hurt her.

Snatching her hands together, I focused on the sensation of the fleeting realm of Lucidis—my home, and the place where Ana and I had raised our son. The realm that brought Ana back to me when I had almost lost her. I allowed the grief, which never quite left, to open up inside me—how I'd felt as though my chest was going to crack open from the pain as I held the weight of Ana's lifeless body in my arms.

Grace's hands twitched in mine, and I increased my grip.

If she wanted to know what life would be like without Balance and why it was so important, she was about to find out.

All the things I had pushed aside so I could not only do my duty but also live and love Ana and Samael, without the fear that I would lose them creeping into my mind every moment, I let them go now. Focusing on all these things, I relived the pain etched across Ana's face when she was in Tenebris and the Balance began its Shift. That moment of absolute realization when she knew what was happening and that I wasn't there to save her.

I channeled all the negative energy into a fine point, and with absolute precision that only years of experience and power could offer, I drove it into Grace's being.

She cried out and recoiled, her entire body jolted as though she'd fallen from a cliff and had landed on a rocky outcrop, and her neck snapped backward as she gasped. But I held her hands and tugged her toward me as she tried to pull away. Her eyes widened as mine glazed over white, and when her hands grew warm and felt as though they might burst into flames, she kicked out at me, and finally, I let her go.

Grace stumbled away and almost tripped before Arin caught her. She clutched at her chest and allowed Arin to support her as her legs grew weak. Tears sparkled in her eyes, and her cheeks were flushed. Her entire body probably felt as though she had been crying for days—those heavy, racking sobs which took the energy out of your muscles and tore at your abdomen, and left you feeling empty except for the sense of complete and utter hopelessness.

My hands flexed by my sides as I watched her recover. I was aware that everyone in the group was looking at me, but they needed to understand the importance of what we were doing and the potential power that lived inside them. Sasha stared at me, and in my peripheral vision, the look of distaste on her features was clear.

I didn't look at her even as she spoke, "Was that necessary, Cael?"

"I've never seen anything like that..." Roger's eyes were wide.

My voice shook as I stared at Grace. She was on her feet and held my eye contact even as her lip trembled. "Imagine that feeling..." My chest heaved as I forced myself to calm, and locked away the feelings again. "But in everyone, everywhere. Hopelessness, nothingness. No love, no happiness, just absolute emptiness inside." Grace swiped angrily at a stray tear from her cheek as I continued. "This is why the positive energies are so important. They are the *only weapon* we have against the Shift. The *only thing*. So, despite how silly you think it sounds, how horribly unlikely and hopeless, you must put *all* that aside and focus, because we have no choice but to try."

Everyone's eyes continued to follow my movements as I indicated for Grace to resume her place in the circle. She did, and patted Arin's arm as she returned to her place on shaking legs. Floyd leaned over to ask if she was okay, and she brushed him off impatiently. Grace sniffled and held my intense eye contact for a moment before looking away. She was frightened of me now, which wasn't ideal, but while the others hadn't experienced what she had firsthand, they'd have felt the ripples from the negative energy. Hopefully, it was enough for them to realize the importance of what they were doing, if they hadn't already, and the magnitude of the consequences if we failed.

Emma cleared her throat, barely holding back from crying herself, and sniffed. "So, Ana is going to help us, right? You said she was more powerful than us."

I turned my back as I took my place to reform the circle. "Ana will meet us on Earth and help us then."

I'm certain only Roger saw the doubt on my face.

My eyes snapped open as I experienced a surge in energy from the group around me.

We had been in complete synchronicity for a moment, and there was a shift.

It was very minor, but it had been a shift significant enough to touch the Balance itself. The slight tilt was so small I doubt even another Guardian would have noticed had they not been looking for it. But it was *there.*

Hope.

But shortly after, something else stirred in the air around us, and the hope flickered, but didn't die.

"We need to go back to Earth," I said.

Sasha nodded. "You felt it too?"

There had been a stirring from Earth, so close it was almost as if I could've reached through the thinning veil which separates our realms and touch it. Whatever it was, it was near John's, where we had departed Earth.

A battle was looming.

The energies of large numbers of Tenebrians and Lucidians close to each other, and the excited ripples through the air of impending violence.

"Are we ready, though?" Emma asked.

"As ready as we can be." We shifted our positions so that Roger and Sasha were on either side of the chain, and we held hands again, with me in the center. I turned my head to face Sasha. "Focus in on Ana and Samael. They'll be together." I squared my shoulders as the Gateway opened in front of me. "Let's go."

Chapter Twenty-Five

Ana

It had been a good plan at some point.

For the short term at least.

Maybe.

As the crowd in the town hall square grew, they began to run out of space. People made themselves as comfortable as possible, but we didn't have the food or resources to keep everyone here for an extended period. The plan had been to centralize their energies, but everyone was frightened and without direction. With nothing to hope for and many unsure where their loved ones were, the atmosphere around the area was bleak, and it seemed to be working against the Balance in a way that was counterproductive to our needs.

Additionally, Tenebrians were gathering outside the town hall's walls. Monia gathered a group of Lucidians, and I sat next to Samael, listening in. "I think we need to be ready to fight," she said in hushed tones, as though every Guardian here wasn't already aware of the impending threat. No new people had arrived in over an hour, no doubt unwilling to come too close given the number of Tenebrians running around.

"You believe the Tenebrians will attack?"

"I know they will attack, and we must be ready." She looked up as Samael stood. "This is war."

"But war will negatively affect the Balance," Samael muttered, and when he glanced at me, I pressed my lips together in a thin line and looked at my feet. Perhaps I should have stayed with Cael and the half-breeds, but I was convinced that my presence would be a hinderance more than a help.

I'm not sure I was any more help here either.

"I know, but we have no choice. The Tenebrians are actively trying to force the Balance beyond the point of no return. While the Shift has already begun, they seek to expedite the process. An act of terror within these walls will be devastating, and not only for the Balance. I fear that we have made it easier for them by gathering the humans here."

"We need more Guardians."

"Yes," Monia agreed with a sharp nod. "Those still out gathering survivors, as they return here, instruct them to stay." Before the group separated, she added, "Be aware, not all Lucidians are friends, and not all Tenebrians are foes. Make physical contact if you can and try to find out who is who before anyone passes these walls."

Samael crouched in front of me. "I'm going to find Esco and tell her the plan. Wait here." I nodded without looking up.

Time passed slowly, and as Lucidians gathered, they came with reports of Tenebrians circling the town hall area and attacking humans as they tried to make their way to safety. Something in the air continued to change, and while I knew I could feel the Shift, I squeezed my eyes closed and wondered if I could convince myself it was something else. But everyone could feel it, including the humans, even if they didn't understand it. The area was filled with the constant sounds of sobbing and screaming, over a background of whimpers and fearful chatter of those missing family members.

Some who came through reported that a handful of Lucidians stopped outside the town hall and instead opted to join the Tenebrians. I toyed with the fabric of my top and wondered how long so many of them had felt like this. Was it a feeling that had built inside them? A resentment of the system and how things *had always been,* which slowly simmered until it boiled over? Or did some of them understand that there was no coming back from this, and they may as well join, instead of fight.

The feeling of impending conflict was strong in the atmosphere, and it strung tense lines between the Guardians within these walls. I glanced up at the large stone blocks that surrounded the town square gardens and wondered how the sky could remain so blue when the world below it crumbled.

Would it still be blue after the Shift?

The hair on the back of my neck prickled when a Tenebrian entered, and several Lucidians dropped into a defensive stance.

"Wait." Monia held her hand out as she strode confidently between them and the Tenebrian. "This is Vena, he is on our side." While the Lucidians relaxed their stances, suspicion was still clear in their eyes. I watched Vena as he had a hurried conversation with Monia, and when the others continued to stare at him, he huffed out an angry sigh.

"Get it over with," he muttered, and held his hands out.

Three Lucidians reached out at once and touched his outstretched arms, and Vena allowed them to read him while he gritted his teeth against what I'm sure was the feeling of a hundred tiny needles going into his skin where they touched him.

Opposites, and yet, the lines between Lucidians and Tenebrians were blurring as much as the lines between the realms themselves.

If we made it out of this, would everything return to how it was?

I didn't see how it could.

Vena sat next to me, and I glanced at him out of the corner of my eye while letting my hair fall in front of my face to cover my curiosity. His skin appeared to be almost crawling with the way the sunlight played across the deep reds of his scales. He was on edge.

"Are you ready?" he asked me, staring straight ahead.

"For what?"

"To reverse this. You are the key." When I hesitated, the moment filled with conflicting thoughts and emotions that I could no longer put into words, a flare of anger pulsed from Vena. His voice grated as though he were no longer speaking to an equal, but someone who needed to be schooled. "Everyone can see it but you. Why are you being difficult?"

"I'm not being difficult, I'm just struggling with this... with *all* of this."

"*Everyone* is struggling, but we need to make things right. You had the power within you to begin the Shift, do you not believe you have the power to end it?"

"I don't feel I can control whatever power I have effectively enough."

"You are so blinded by your self-pity that you cannot even see what is right in front of you..." He turned to stare at me and waited until I returned his gaze. "... and what is inside you."

"I—"

"No, enough of your excuses. If I were raised in Tenebris to believe that humans are nothing but tools to be used and discarded, but even I can see the value in saving humanity, why can't you?"

"He's right, you know."

I looked up as John sat on my other side. Their combined presence made me feel cornered, and the Tenebrian in John was clearer now that he was close to his kind. Briefly, I wondered if Vena recognized him for what he was, then just as quickly, I discarded the thought. It hardly mattered. The lines between good and evil were so blurred now that it was nearly impossible to tell which side anyone was on. They acted as though I were intentionally being difficult, as though I could easily flick a switch and save the world as quickly as I had set it on the path to its doom. But inside me was turmoil. I knew there were things worth saving—love, family, and life's joys. Not to mention my son and the life he had yet to live, or the time I still had left with Cael.

I knew all these things, I wasn't blind to them.

But when I reached inside myself to find the power, it was locked away. I had closed it off intentionally, not because I didn't want to save the world, but because I no longer wished to harm it.

If I joined hands with the half-breeds and Cael, and we tried to restore the Balance, what if there was something within me that only pushed it farther with explosive force? Then the world would end before I could even turn to Cael and Samael and tell them I loved them one last time.

"I do not need to be lectured by Tenebrians on the value of humanity," I said through gritted teeth. John winced at my words, and then guilt was added to the swirling of emotions inside me. There were so many different things, it was a vortex instead of a black hole now, one pain and fear unable to be separated from the next.

Vena looked at John, and a flicker of recognition passed across his face as they stared at each other. "What did you see on Earth that made you stay?" Vena asked him. John didn't answer straight away, and Vena tilted his head. "A human?"

John's jaw was tense, and my chest stung when I realized he had a story before I had ever existed. Something he had been through, which led him to be in Dad's path. A story I didn't know, and may never know. "Initially, I wasn't even sure what it was," John said, not breaking Vena's eye contact. "Something in the way humans loved with reckless abandon, the way they opened themselves up again and again after being hurt, the way they reached out to help strangers." His gaze slid to mine. "And unconditional love, in every sense of the word, where nothing someone said or did could stop you from loving them as much as you did the moment you first saw them."

I squeezed my eyes shut.

There were too many feelings, and I didn't need my love for John, as well as the reminder of love lost, abandonment, and what could have been, to be added to what was already a confusing mess. A mess I would have to sort out if I had a chance of helping Cael save the world and being the key everyone seemed to think I was.

Where do I even begin to sort this out?

When I opened my mouth to respond, I stopped when a familiar emotional imprint entered the area. Looking up, I watched as Ferox entered with a group of women. All but one of the women left his side the moment they were within the bounds of safety. But one stayed near him and stood so close they were touching. As she curled her hand around his, Ferox looked down at her with affection—a look he quickly replaced with stern indifference as he faced back toward the crowd.

When he saw me watching him, we held eye contact for a moment, allowing our experiences from the past hours and days to wash over each other, mutually understanding that everything had changed.

Ferox, of all Guardians. I would never have guessed.

Everyone seemed to be finding themselves through this tragedy, and all I was doing was losing myself further in it.

As the walls of the realms came down, so did the walls the Guardians had put up within themselves to block out the part of them which was open to emotions. My lip twitched in the semblance of a smirk, and I wanted to declare *I was right,* gleefully in front of them all. I *knew* they all had the capacity within them to *feel.* The merging of the realms and the upset of the Balance had blunted their ability to keep themselves indifferent. Ferox was not the only Guardian I had seen today with an apparent connection to a human, but he was the one that had surprised me the most.

All this love and realization in the air, and yet I still struggled to see past the obliteration of the two worlds I had called home, and one I had called hell.

Even if Vena was right and I was the only one blocking myself from my recovery, how do you even reason with yourself when the only voice inside your mind is your own?

Turning, I watched as Samael stood close to David. Every movement he made was born from hesitation, but he still couldn't help but touch David, and brushed his fingers on David's forearm before he held his hand. I tried to draw something positive from them to clear the fog within me, but they were surrounded in their own cloud of confusion.

"I must fight," Samael told him.

"I want you to stay here with me." Through all of this, David had struggled with his internal battle, one I'm sure almost all the humans here felt too, but with the added complication of loving a Guardian. He was trying to figure out where he fit into a world he no longer understood.

But when it came down to this—face to face with Samael as the sounds around them drowned into nothing—his eyes were on only Samael, and he squeezed his hand back.

He didn't want to lose him.

"I can't stay. I'm sorry. I need to do my part."

The pain radiated across the short space between them and me, and my chest constricted. Even love couldn't save them from being hurt because, in the end, there were always tough decisions to be made. I touched my chest and remembered the feel of the arrow as it pierced my skin, and the look on Cael's face as his finger compressed the trigger.

I had done that to him. I caused him all that pain. I was the reason Samael felt out of place in his own home.

Cascus had been right—without my human influence, it would have been different for Samael.

The Balance would have remained safe if it weren't for me.

They kept telling me I was the one who could fix this.

But how?

Chapter Twenty-Six

Vikt

They knew, of course, they knew.

The commotion within the town hall area had intensified. It was not an audible stirring, though the cries and wails of the pathetic, confused humans never ceased, but a change in the air once the Lucidians began to rally themselves for a fight as much as we were.

The Shift was happening, and they needed to accept that.

If it meant fighting so they would give up their pathetic attempts to rectify things, then so be it.

We were looking forward to it. The negative energy from a physical battle would only help our cause and harm theirs. They could *feel* us gathering, and they were preparing themselves for the inevitable.

The new world created after the Shift would be uncomfortable for everyone, and then all beings would experience the discomfort we had lived in for generations.

Holding up my hand, I halted the procession of Tenebrians behind me as I stopped mid-step and narrowed my eyes. Straightening, I opened my senses to the air around me. They couldn't have rallied so many in such a short time, but the Lucidian imprint was stronger.

Was *she* here?

Spinning on the spot, I swiftly lifted my hand to strike as a Lucidian approached from my left. When I brought my arm down, I was met with the strength of his resistance as the scales of my forearm slapped uselessly against the inside of his palm.

"Do not be stupid," he hissed out.

"Right, it's you." I sneered at Cascus as he shoved my arm away. "I thought you were waiting for Cael and Samael. Or did you run away from them, too?" I was no longer bound to him. His role in our plan was done, and although I wasn't stupid enough to challenge his power, he seemed to believe that he still had some authority over me, over *us*. We would have eventually achieved the Shift, though his information was valuable when it came to the placement of attacks and Ana's usefulness, he was nothing to me anymore.

These Tenebrians weren't his army. They were mine.

"I waited, they didn't emerge." He lifted a shoulder, and my brows furrowed at the gesture. It was as though he were trying too hard to appear casual, but the tenseness of his jaw and the way his quills raised told me a different story.

"You know what I think happened?" I asked.

"I do not care what you think."

"I think Cael returned, and you are still scared of him. You ran before, and you ran again."

Cascus's eyes flickered to the crowd of Guardians behind me, and I smirked. I was pushing him harder than I would dare if we were alone, but I wasn't alone, and none of these Guardians were on his side.

"I decided to enjoy myself as you no doubt have been. But the energies here shifted, and they will try to stop us."

It was my turn to shrug, though I achieved the gesture with more nonchalance and attitude than he had. "We are aware of their intent. They can try, but they won't succeed."

"They mean to undo the Shift in the same way we created it." His eyes narrowed. "Why did you not kill Ana when you had the chance after the Shift began?"

I snarled at him. "I wasn't there. Why didn't *you* kill her and that lover boy of hers?" I didn't care to tell him the involved Tenebrians had left Ana alone and lost interest in her the moment the Shift began. They had been distracted by the tantalizing consequence-free pleasures Earth held once all accountability was void.

"Because she lives, she might be able to undo all of this."

I spat at his feet. "You're a coward. You have only acted behind the scenes, pulling strings rather than taking action yourself. *You* didn't kill her, nor did you kill Cael or their offspring. We did everything, while you stood behind your protective bubble in Lucidis and watched."

Cascus's eyes narrowed as the Guardians behind me jeered. He stepped forward and entered my space, but I didn't back down. "Kill her before she dooms us all." He glanced at the town hall walls, the pulses of conflicting energy between us and them were almost visible in the air as they pressed against each other. "If this does not succeed, we will not be allowed to live. There is no going back."

"They have no chance. The Balance is too far gone."

He said nothing but huffed out an impatient breath, and I narrowed my eyes at him. He had been drip-feeding us information all along, and I was tired of it.

"Kill Ana—"

"You have no power here anymore. We will not do your dirty work, nor will we protect you from your kind. If you want her dead, you kill her." With a snarl, I grabbed his shoulders and ignored how my fingers burned from the contact between our species and the power which pulsed beneath his skin. "*You do it,*" I snarled out between gritted teeth.

His eyes darted between mine and the group behind me, and while I could feel his rage, he said nothing. With a lurch, he pulled himself from my grip and disappeared into the crowd.

As he stalked away, another Lucidian approached. I didn't recognize them, and while she didn't look poised to fight, the quills on my back rose in defense.

"Relax..." The Lucidian chuckled. "I'm on your side."

I looked her up and down, her ice blue scales splattered with blood.

"Are you injured?" I asked without concern. If she was hurt and therefore too weak to fight, she was useless to us.

The Lucidian grinned and held up her hands. Her teeth were stained with blood, and her claws were caked in torn flesh. "It's not my blood."

Chapter Twenty-Seven

Cael

We were met with screaming as we passed through the Gateway and into the space within the courtyard walls. Humans scattered from the area as we stepped out, and several watched with confusion as Roger landed calmly next to Emma and Grace. I had no idea what each of the humans had seen when the Gateway opened—had the rules changed with the Shift, and they had seen it in its proper form and knew it was a Gateway to another world? Had they expected Tenebrians to step out?

Looking up, Monia ran toward us, followed by two other Lucidians from our community, ready to face whatever threat had drawn a response from the humans.

Sasha stepped gracefully forward, and Arin and Floyd fell into place behind her. Monia rushed to me, stopped a foot from me, and paused with uncertainty crossing her features. Her expression twisted, and I tried to offer her a smile, unable to muster the expression before she pulled me into a tight hug. My arms remained motionless for a beat before I raised them and held her. I couldn't remember a time when she had hugged me.

I pulled away. "Have they started fighting?"

"Not yet, but I fear it will begin soon."

"Do we have enough to fight?"

"I do not know."

Sasha and Roger worked to close the Gateway behind us, and when they were done, John approached and took Roger's hand in a handshake that sounded with a loud clap. Turning, I found Samael and Ana waiting for me, and closed the gap between us before I pulled them both into my arms. Ana ducked her head against me, and Samael patted me on the back. There was a confusing rush of emotions from both of them, and I squeezed my eyes shut, wishing I could make it all better for them.

I can.

Leaning back, I looked them up and down, and Samael offered a small smile. "We're okay, Dad."

I studied Ana's face and wasn't sure she *was* okay. She had been crying, and whatever had happened since we'd separated had only deepened the black hole within her that I'd hoped she'd be able to pull herself free from. The wall she had built around herself was cracking, but behind it wasn't the strength I knew she was capable of. Instead, a mixture of all emotions from pain and grief to love and hope swirled within her, cancelling each other out and crushing her spirit. I feared that even if we made it out of this, I would no longer be able to find the real Ana beyond everything she had endured.

I could touch and hold her, but she wasn't the Ana I knew.

"Samael, you need to come with us," I said.

"Dad, I need to go fight."

"No, you have the human part within you that makes you stronger, and we need that."

Roger approached. "Regina, the other half-breed is here. I can feel her."

"Go get her," I said, and Roger nodded, then disappeared into the crowd.

"We need a place away from here."

"There's an empty hall around the back of the square," John offered.

Emma, Grace, Floyd, and Arin stood listening to the conversation with nervous energy running through their bodies. This entire situation must still feel unreal, and I imagined that if they stopped to think about it too long, how the world's fate weighed on their shoulders, they might collapse under the pressure. Grace kept glancing at Ana, and I wanted them to trust her. But how could I build that trust out of nothing when, to them, it appeared that Ana had abandoned them in their time of need?

"I feel nothing from her," Grace muttered to Emma.

"What do you mean?"

"These readings we're meant to be able to get from others. If I try it on Ana, I get nothing."

Emma's brow furrowed, but she said nothing further, and my stomach dropped. But there wasn't time for this doubt. We needed to act.

Ana watched Grace watch her, and I'm sure she could feel the younger woman trying to probe her essence. No doubt Ana was reading her in return, and maybe if she found something good inside of her, Ana would have something else to hold on to.

Or at least, a small bit of clarity.

Roger came back through the crowd with a young woman following him, her eyes wide as she held on to the back of his shirt so as not to get separated as they wound their way between the cluster of people.

Roger made the introductions hastily. "This is Regina."

She gave a small, awkward wave. "Hi."

My skin prickled. She had the essence of death around her and was splattered with blood. When Regina noticed me scrutinizing her, she glanced at her clothes before sliding her hands into her pockets. Slowly, she returned my gaze and cocked an eyebrow at me, her lips pressed together. Without breaking eye contact with me, she whispered out of the corner of her mouth to Roger, "Is he reading me?"

"Yes."

"You feel like death," I said, wishing I had chosen different words immediately.

Regina looked at her feet. "We were attacked, and we... had to kill it."

Her tone did not reflect pride or pleasure in the act, and for that, I was grateful. I nodded and muttered, "I'm sorry. Are you okay?"

"I didn't get hurt."

"That's not what I asked."

She looked up at me and was about to answer when Sasha spoke, "We need to get away from this crowd," Sasha said, pressing her palm to her temple. "They won't be able to focus their energies here. I barely can."

I followed her gaze toward the group of half-breeds, and when Arin met my gaze his expression was pained. "I never liked crowds, but here with you all..." He winced. "It's like I can feel every emotion from all these people, and I can't separate them from my own."

The others nodded, and while the spark of hope in me flared at their ability to have opened their powers up enough to read the area, Sasha was right.

"First, I think we need to shift the energies within this area," John said.

Before I could object, John shouted to draw the attention of the people closest to us, before he pressed his fingers to the corners of his lips and produced a sharp whistle. Slowly, the dull murmur of thousands of voices silenced, starting nearest to John and spreading across the area like a shadow being chased by lights. When the blanket of anticipation reached the corners of the square, all eyes looked in his direction, waiting for answers they had been denied since this all began.

John stood on a retaining wall for one of the small garden beds in the courtyard, and held his hand to shade his eyes as he looked out at all the faces gazing up at him. Amongst them, and surrounding the area, were Guardians. Mostly Lucidians, with the occasional Tenebrian dotted throughout. Those were the Tenebrians who understood the importance of the Balance and knew that even though they might lead an uncomfortable existence at times, there were things of greater importance than their pleasures, and a world without the Balance would be far worse than a balanced world.

John cleared his throat, and the sound carried across the area, echoing off the tall walls surrounding them. "A battle is going to begin soon, and it's going to get worse before it gets better." His words were met with silence, though the air shifted uncomfortably. "You will hear, feel, and maybe see things that will frighten you."

John glanced down at Ana before looking at the crowd

again—all those faces stared up at him, seeking reassurance that everything would be okay. I could feel the desperation that ate him from the inside, and how badly he wanted to give them the security they sought, but lies would help no one. For now, all he could offer them was a sense they weren't alone, and knowledge that perhaps they could help somehow. "But we need something from you. I know you don't understand what's happening, but I need you all to work together. What we need right now is positive energy." He paused, and I expected scoffs, murmurs of disagreement, or a series of questions, but everyone continued to stare up at him. They had all seen and experienced things they didn't understand and, at this point, were willing to accept anything without argument if it could help. "We need you all to look inside yourselves and find that piece of you that still has hope, find that memory, or think of that person who makes your life worth living." He looked back at Ana. "That makes life worth saving."

Ana's chest heaved as she held back her emotions.

"I know some of you have suffered great loss, and I'm truly sorry. But think of those you have lost, think of the love they had for you and the love you have for them, and feel it grow within yourselves. Hold hands with those next to you, find togetherness, find peace, and let it flow through us all. Humanity is worth saving, and if you believe you are worth saving, you need to help us."

There was a pregnant pause, and John waited, nodding slightly at those near him when he sensed the uncertainty coming from them. The Guardians around the perimeter channeled their energies. They began to fill the area with a positive influence, enough to rid the humans of their uncertainty and allow them to start the work they needed to do.

Ana turned slowly as she felt it, and her eyes met mine as the air vibrated and shimmered around us. People took the hands of those next to them, found those who were there alone, and welcomed them into their families. I saw Lynn, her eyes shining with tears as she clung to her daughter, and together they felt their love for Penny, which was now stronger, as they had to keep it inside them like a treasure. Samael and David looked at each other across the grass, and David squeezed his mother's hand while she closed her eyes, no doubt thinking of her husband.

And there was Ana.

I watched her take it all in, and I saw how her shoulders relaxed and her eyes widened as she observed the scene around her. When our eyes met, everything I felt for her flooded my being. Every moment we had shared, all the heartache and the pain. But stronger than all those feelings was the memory of us dancing together in the bar all those decades ago. In my mind, the image melted into how we would dance under the stars in Lucidis. I wondered if these memories were entirely from me, or if Ana was the driving force behind them. Through our eye contact, was she directing this movie, which played out in my mind? I could hear the music, a soundtrack to our falling in love and our lives together. While far from easy, I wouldn't trade it for anything, and all I wanted was for Ana to look inside herself, beyond the black hole of pain, and realize her strength was always in our love and the love of our son.

Her eyes fluttered shut, and I knew she'd found it.

When she opened her eyes, she looked at Roger, and he held her eye contact. All the love he couldn't express with words, and all the apologies and regrets he's had since, flooded past the blue of his irises and filled the air between them. My chest swelled as I struggled to contain all the emotion, as it mingled with everything around us. We were completely open to the senses and essences of those around us and allowed ourselves to become filled with them. I tapped into Ana's imprint and marveled as she allowed the energies to permeate the darkness that had opened up within her, letting it bring her back to herself, and us. Tears streamed down her cheeks as her eyes snapped open, and she snatched my hand and gripped it.

"He was right. I was too blind to see it before," she whispered, and my vision blurred. Ana placed my hand on her stomach. "What is in front of me, and in me, and is worth saving."

She was pregnant.

It had seemed so long ago, when we were together in Lucidis as one, and I had lost control. I was so filled with fear at the concept of losing Ana that I hadn't maintained the discipline of my body and controlled my instinctual mating urges.

Within her was another child—a sibling for our perfect Samael.

We held eye contact.

It was working.

The energy within the area was shifting.

I watched the expressions of the half-breeds, and my body relaxed at the look of pure joy and contentment which settled on their faces. They felt it—the true experience of being a Guardian—but on top of that, they were also human and felt those emotions themselves. They were lost in it.

John closed his eyes, opened his arms, and encouraged everyone to keep going. "Yes," he said, and his voice broke as though he too was holding back tears. "You're doing it."

The feeling was shattered by a cry, sharp and serrated with rage, and as though glass had been broken, the shards of the elation crashed around us. John had the wind knocked from his lungs and rolled as he was tackled from the retaining wall by a Lucidian whose internal power outweighed his physical presence.

"You will *not* succeed," Cascus snarled as he pushed himself to his feet and stood over John. A dome of power surrounded him and pressed us back as we advanced to protect John. "You are all weak." Cascus pointed to the humans with a sweep of his arm as they backed away from the power they didn't understand. "You will *all* perish. You have brought this on yourselves. Humans do nothing but fight and mourn, and all we do is clean up your messes. No more."

He looked at John in disgust as he scrambled to his feet, his fists clenched and a glint of rage in his eyes. John's eyes clouded over black for a moment as his Tenebrian pushed to the surface. "And you..." Cascus bared his teeth, "... will die before her."

Roger and Ana cried, "*No,*" as they moved forward.

The dome of power surrounding him shattered.

Cascus drew a moonstone blade and sliced it through the air toward John's stomach before he snarled as he was yanked backward by his quills, and with a scream of rage, Monia's hands were around his neck. Her claws dug into the sides of his throat as she strangled him with both hands pressed against his windpipe. Even as the cartilage crunched under her strength, his eyes narrowed at her, and only a hint of fear showed through as her unbridled rage kept him from escaping her clutches.

"You are weak..." The words from his throat were stunted

and awkward. “Cordus was, too.” His lip lifted into almost a smile, and he pushed out, “I am glad I killed him.” With a shriek, Monia bore down on him, the sound of the taut muscles in his throat crushed under her hands and echoed in my ears before she snapped his neck, and he slumped beneath her.

Chapter Twenty-Eight

Ana

The snap of Cascus's neck broke my shock, and I whirled around.

No.

His hands clutched his stomach where the blade had sliced him, clean and deep. The blood that soaked his shirt spread across the fabric in a grotesque artwork, and it steadily flowed across his flesh. Slowly, he lifted his hands in front of his face and examined them as the deep red liquid dripped from his fingers before he collapsed to his knees.

John's eyes met mine as I choked on my words.

John knelt behind Roger, blood on his arms as he cupped his hands over the wound in Roger's stomach, attempting to stop him from bleeding out when it was already too late.

No!

"Dad!" I cried, covered the short distance toward him, and landed hard on my knees by his side. Placing my hands on his shoulders, I moved to hug him against me, and at his pained groan, I dropped my hands to cover John's before moving them back to Roger's shoulders again.

Desperate and rapid movements of someone cornered with nowhere left to turn.

Pressure on the wound. Pressure on the wound.

But his body was slippery with his blood, and when he coughed, a stream shot out and hit my arm.

"No, no, *no,*" I cried out, and pressed my hands to the wound to try to stem the flow of blood, which continued to ooze between my fingers. He winced under my touch. "Somebody help!" I cried out in a broken voice, then whispered, "Help…."

Roger grabbed my fingers, both our hands slick with his blood. "Ana." He coughed, blood spraying on his chest.

"No." My voice was nothing more than a desperate wail. I didn't think I had any tears left after Penny, but all my sorrow flowed through me now, and shunted away any positive energy which had filled me after John's speech. The light left my being and was shoved to the side to make way for the darkness to open up within my soul and consume me once more. "You can't leave me, Dad, I only just got you back. We didn't have enough time."

"Bloody hell, Roger…" John whispered as his friend's weight fell back against him, "… what the hell did you jump in front of me for, mate?"

Roger laughed, a single wet *hah that* resulted in another cough of blood. "You're welcome."

"Dad, please, *please* don't leave me again. I'm sorry I didn't forgive you. I'll do better, I promise. We'll work it all out. Please, I need you."

"Everyone needs *you*." He smiled and touched his fingers to my face, and I closed my eyes at the sensation as streaks of blood were left on my cheek. "I'm so happy… I got to be with you again." He gasped with the effort of talking.

"Dad, I love you."

"I never stopped loving you."

As his hand dropped from my face, I lifted it from his lap and shook his arm. "Dad?" I shook his hand with increasing desperation when he didn't answer. "Dad!" My hands found his shoulders, and I shook him like a child trying to wake a sleeping parent. My grief morphed into rage, as though it were a personal insult he wasn't answering.

"Ana," John's voice was gravelly. "Ana, he's gone."

"Don't you say that!" I glanced back at the group of half-breeds who stood behind me. "Can't somebody do something? Somebody must be able to do something!"

Cael approached and kneeled behind me, and all at once, the weight of Dad's arm was too much to bear. Twisting on the spot, I collapsed against Cael and curled his shirt between my bloody hands. Cael nodded at John, and I turned after I felt the motion of his chin against my head. As John went to lift Roger's body, I spun around and grabbed my father's limp arm. "Where are you taking him?"

"Somewhere more private," John said, his voice broke before it dropped to a whisper, "Ana, *please.*"

I didn't only lose my Dad, *again,* but John lost his friend. The history between them had cemented their relationship into something special, and I sobbed as I dropped my hand and allowed John to take my father's body away. This wasn't fair, none of this was fair. All these people here had lost someone, their homes, or at the very least their sense of stability in a world already scary enough. The black hole inside me was back, bigger than before, and with its appearance it sucked away the oxygen from whatever small flame of hope I'd held.

An explosion rocked the foundations of the buildings surrounding the courtyard. Samael looked sharply at Cael. "That wasn't a Gateway."

"No." Cael threw a glance at Monia. "They're attacking."

As Monia moved away, Cael and Samael gathered the half-breeds and ushered them toward the far end of the courtyard. Until Cael's arms came under mine and I was pulled to my feet, I didn't move. John came around my other side and curled his arm around my waist. Between them, I was guided through the crowd as people looked at us desperately, seeking answers we had neither the time nor information to provide.

John rubbed his hand down his face and paused, pulling Cael and me to a stop with him. Halfway through dragging his hand down his face, he pulled his fingers away and stared at the blood stains on his skin. He dropped his head, shoulders shaking, before he looked at the crowd again.

"Everything I said before..." he called as his voice cracked, "... still stands. Now more important than ever." He paused, glancing pointedly behind him. "The man who saved my life was my best friend, the one who taught me to see the good in people. Think positive, spread the word."

I glanced up at him, certain the doubt I felt shadowed my eyes, and even though he didn't look directly at me, his arm tightened around me.

"Come on," Cael urged.

John nodded to the people closest to us. "Try to ignore all the sounds from outside these walls and focus as you did before, on yourselves, your family, and any love you can find within you."

Lurched forward by another explosion, the three of us followed after Samael, Sasha, and the half-breeds.

Chapter Twenty-Nine

Vikt

They had to be credited for trying even when the situation was hopeless.

Outside the high walls of the town center, the positive shift had been visceral.

I smirked.

The shift they'd managed had been as obvious as its abrupt end.

A group of Tenebrians cheered as a nearby car exploded, the fuel igniting quickly.

I couldn't help but laugh. We were gathered, Tenebrians and a small handful of Lucidians alike, ready to fight until the Shift had completed. There wasn't much time left, hours, perhaps minutes. The world around us was blurred as the Gateways, which never closed, expanded, and both Tenebris and Lucidis were visible through them. The buildings were already unstable with the quakes increasing in duration and regularity, and it wouldn't take much to fight our way through to the group of hopeful humans relying on the Guardians inside to protect them.

We would slaughter them all, and their combined fear would be enough to give that final push.

There was no going back.

The rush of pure excitement that pounded in my chest skipped a beat as I felt our enemies gathering. The stamping of feet increased as the Lucidians came to meet me and the army I had assembled. Vena stood at the front of the Guardians, still intent on defending humanity, and shook his head at me with slight movements as though he were a disappointed father. I rolled my eyes, and with my army behind me, we slowly approached each other until Vena and I were toe to toe.

"I take no pleasure in killing my kind, but I will not hesitate to do what is right."

"Our pleasure in what we do makes us strong," I responded.

Vena's eyes flickered to the gathering over my shoulder. "Yes, but most of your army is indifferent to the cause, fighting for only selfish reasons. That makes you weak."

"We have Elders on our side."

"Cascus is dead."

His words absorbed into my skin, and I feigned disinterest. While I was done dealing with the coward, his power would have been helpful during this battle. "He was only one."

Vena smiled. "His power was useful to you. Now, it is just you and me."

She smiled back. "And my army."

"And our armies."

There was a pause, a moment thick with anticipation, and I wondered if similar battles were occurring across the country and the globe. Everywhere, all at once, Guardians would be aware the end was near, were they too trying to rally the humans to be *happy* as though it would be enough to undo the Shift? Or had they given up and accepted their fate and left the weakness of humanity to defend itself in the new world?

I let out a war cry which echoed across the street, and with a smirk, I opened the metaphorical gates of Hell as the legion of Tenebrians moved forward.

The two sides met in an explosion of violence.

Guardians didn't spend their time training from a young age to fight physically. It was a skill we did not believe we needed. We could rely on our influence and superior strength against humans, and if it came to it, against other Guardians, we relied on wit and a battle of powers.

But at that moment, I channeled into the part of me which was still animal, still *beast,* and I fought with instinct. My eyes widened briefly as a deep blue Lucidian with shocking white streaks picked up a Tenebrian and broke its spine over his leg without hesitation.

We were all fighting instinctively and using brute force, and it was a messy and unpredictable affair.

Vena had stealth and years of experience on his side. While he buckled as a blade swiped across his calf, he was fast enough to snatch the blade and lunge it into the eye socket of the Tenebrian that had attacked him. Kicking out, I shattered the kneecap of a passing Lucidian and relished in the sharp cry of pain as they collapsed.

The city continued to change as the walls of the realms came down as we fought, and those who ventured too close to the Gateways, which shimmered from the ground into the skyline, were taken by them. Whether they were transported to whatever remained of the realms, another part of the world, or destroyed by the compressed power of the Gateway, I couldn't know.

But they didn't come back once they disappeared.

Two Gateways expanded, their boundaries moved closer together, and a burst of energy gave me only seconds' warning to leap out of the way as a Gateway to Tenebris collided and crossed over one to Lucidis. A crack opened in the street and weaved its way jaggedly across the block, swallowing those who were not fast enough to move out of the way, and screamed on their way down into the abyss.

Chapter Thirty

Ana

With stumbling steps, I followed Cael to where the others had gathered. Skidding to a stop, I took in the large stained-glass windows—the scenes portrayed in the intricate images cast colored light across the group as we stood near the pews.

"A church?" I glanced at the cross, which towered over us and almost touched the top of the peaked ceiling.

"It's an empty space, don't overthink it," John said.

Cael almost looked as though he was trying to suppress a smile, and when he met my eyes, I lifted my lip slightly in an attempt to return it.

Yes, I had been thinking about movies, because that's how my mind worked.

No, I didn't think it meant I was fine and back to myself enough to have a clear enough head to do this.

Sasha ushered the group into a circle. "Did you all feel that shift out there when John talked to everyone about positive? That's what we're aiming for here, but on a bigger scale."

"But there's only five of us," Regina said.

"Cael, Ana, and I will be helping guide your powers, and

we will focus the energies you channel. The people out there are doing their part, and you can draw on that, but try not to overreach. If your senses reach beyond these walls..."

"What?"

Sasha paused, and I squeezed my eyes shut. The cloud of pain from the war outside was hovering around this building, and I tried to block it out.

"Just focus on each other," Sasha said.

They held hands, and as Cael and Sasha worked on clearing the air around them of negativity, the half-breeds closed their eyes as they focused on their internal energies. They undoubtedly thought of their families, the feel of their hugs, and the smell of home-cooked meals. Of helping strangers and cuddling pets, of watching someone they loved opening a gift, anything that would bring that spark of warmth inside them.

I searched inside me too, but when I closed my eyes, all I saw was Dad's body.

Or the fear in Penny's eyes.

When I opened my eyes, Cael was watching the half breeds, and nodded to himself as he noted the slight shift in the air. It was a slow build, and they needed more, but it was something nonetheless.

How could it be enough?

With Sasha and Samael on one side of the semi-circle, Cael clasped hands with Regina and held his hand out to me. I took it and gasped at the flow of positive energy through me. Pressure built behind my eyes, and I desperately wanted to cry, but I shuddered in a breath and held it back.

We are going to save everyone.

We are.

We can.

Another gasp sucked past my lips as doubt slammed down on my energies. Cael gripped my hand, and I opened my eyes to look at him.

"Help us, Ana," he pleaded.

"I'm trying," I whispered.

I tried.

I imagined the energy as a glowing orb that hovered in the air between us. It represented the spot within the universe where the Balance rested—that one spot where everything sat in perfect, or not so perfect, equilibrium.

"More," Cael whispered.

"It burns," Emma whispered, and I focused on the buildup of warmth between my palm and Cael's, the feel of energy transference we were used to. I wondered how uncomfortable it felt to them.

There was a give and take, a push and pull of energies between us as we simultaneously tried to recharge and release. I reached out and tried to cling to whatever essence of Lucidis I could feel through the air, but the realm barely existed anymore, and I grasped at the fabric of the air itself as it melded with Earth. I found a thread, drew from it, and turned myself into a battery, allowing the others to draw from me. I sensed Sasha doing the same, and I watched as she struggled to keep her back straight when her body tried desperately to pull her into a slump and protect itself from the abuse.

Each of their individual energies had its distinct pattern, and through the connection, I could sense where each one began and ended, as well as where they blended. I would have cried from the beauty of it if I weren't trying so hard to keep my fear at bay.

What if I ruined it and caused more damage?

As the thought crossed my mind, Cael squeezed my hand again.

Try. You have to try. For Cael. For Samael. For your family. For love.

Grace faltered, and Regina squeezed her hand when she felt the drop in energy. “Don’t give up on me now. I need your help,” she muttered, and Grace pulled herself through, the exertion draining her as much as her energy recharged us. The two women had been drawn to each other, something in their past they had not discovered linking them together.

I raised my gaze to John as he watched us work, knowing it wasn’t enough. We could feel the energies building, and blue and white vapor drifted around us, making our skin glow and pulling us together into one force. I knew John desperately wanted to help, but despite his feelings toward humanity and how far he had come, his Tenebrian heritage would be a hindrance.

We tried.

I tried.

But still, it wasn’t enough.

Something was holding them back.

Me.

Every time I linked the energy together and tried to force it into a fine point, my senses would falter, and internally, I tripped over the grief that rested inside me. There was no way around it, and pushing *through* it only resulted in everything positive being eaten up by the black hole that resided in me. Again and again, it tripped me up, and Cael’s grip on my hand grew painful as he tried to balance my powers with his.

To avoid the black hole, I started holding back. The demanding grip of grief, which crushed my heart, couldn't be penetrated, and so I blocked it off, and with it, most of my lingering power.

I jumped at John's voice next to my ear, having not even heard him approach. "You know all I want to do is protect you, right?"

I nodded and bit my lip hard enough that I thought I would draw blood as I tried to hold back the tears.

"But you have to let yourself break, Ana."

"Last time I did that, I ruined everything."

There was no fighting the tears now, and I could almost feel John's arm twitching as he resisted the urge to place a comforting hand on my arm. His touch could interrupt the cycle we had formed, and by the time we built these energies again, it may be too late.

Maybe it already was.

"If I break, it'll all be let out."

"So let it out, it's your power."

"I can't." My voice trembled and broke, and I squeezed my eyes shut. I didn't need to see Cael's or Samael's face as they realized we wouldn't make it, and it would be my fault.

Again.

"They need your power, Ana. You don't have to hold up the positive energy yourself. Just add your power."

"I don't understand."

"You never had to deal with everything alone." When I didn't reply, he moved closer. "Ana," John whispered against my ear. "You need to find that place in yourself, find that love, and let it go. They will stabilize it, I promise."

"I'm trying," I whispered back, my voice barely a breath against the air.

"Feel Cael next to you, feel Samael across the room. They are your family."

Tears streamed down my face. "And you?"

"I'm your family too."

"I'm afraid." My voice shook with the effort of holding myself together. My power was pushing against the inside of me, swelling with grief, gratitude, love, and injustice. Everything was a harsh mess of emotion, topped with the expectation bestowed upon me when I felt I had nothing left to give. "I'm so frightened I'm going to make things worse, like... like last time."

"It's not like last time. We're here now, and we are all here for you. We're together. Release your power, I promise they will direct it where it needs to be. You're not alone."

"Uncle John..." My voice was that of a frightened child, clinging to someone and wishing to be told it will all be okay.

I swear I could feel his heart as it broke with his voice. "Just a little more angel."

Cael started humming, and my chest constricted.

I remembered.

Of course, I'd never forgotten, and although I'd relived it less than an hour before, now I could see the shadows of our forms dancing in front of me. Cael's and my memories were so real, they resembled the Reflections of Lucidis and Tenebris. The Reflections' gaze was glued on each other, and I glanced around the circle. Everyone else's eyes were closed except mine and John's. I watched as our Reflections danced to the song Cael hummed, and my mouth opened in a silent laugh as I watched myself collide awkwardly against his chest. We barely knew each other then, but somehow, we knew all we needed to know.

As we swayed, my Reflection rested her head against Cael's chest, feeling his heartbeat, and without realizing what it was at the time, feeling the essence of him.

After that moment, we were already intertwined and destined to spend the rest of our lives together.

The image in my mind merged with what I saw unfolding before me, and as they swayed together, explosions of light echoed the stars in Lucidis.

Then we were lying in the grass with Samael, imagining shapes in the galaxies beyond.

Then Samael was a teenager, still making me laugh even as he struggled to find his place in the world.

These memories, always these same memories that held the potential to bring me back.

But still, the black hole resided within me.

John sucked in a breath as the blue glow strengthened around the circle, and everyone gripped the hands of those beside them harder. They struggled to maintain connection as the power I'd released surged through them all, amplifying what they already had, while at the same time threatening to tear them apart or bring us all crashing down together.

"That's it," John whispered. "That's the part of you that you need to channel into. It never went away... it was always there, no matter how dark you felt."

It was almost enough, and I sobbed.

"I'm so afraid..."

"Save your family, Ana," John said, and Cael's hand gripped mine. "The way your father saved us all."

The grief came back.

And I broke apart.

Crying out, I gripped onto Cael's hand so hard I felt his bones crack under my grip, and he roared as the pulse from my energy traveled through the group. A shock of electricity seized my muscles, and I couldn't have broken the connection if I'd tried. The energy spread through them all in one rapid movement, causing each to jerk as it hit them in turn —a surge and a shock passed down the line. Sasha gasped, and her hand gripped in mid-air, where she clung onto the feeling of Lucidis with her being, desperate not to let it go and disappear forever.

A wave of blue vapor grew from me and surrounded the group. Their skins amplified the bluish glow, and their Guardian halves came to the surface and dominated. As it moved, the energy vapor drew all their inner power and strength, projecting it toward the circle's center, toward the Balance's focus.

I screamed as the humanity within us merged with the Guardian, as we became one.

With a final blast of energy and an inhuman cry pulled from my lungs, a blinding white light expanded outward faster than sound and threw us all off our feet.

Chapter Thirty-One

Ferox

The ground tremored, a surge so deep it felt like it ran through the tectonic plates themselves. Fighting stopped as Guardians held still to steady themselves against the onslaught of movement, but there was no standing under such power. I fell to my knees and spread my fingers against the warm asphalt, turning my head to glare at a Tenebrian as he attempted to lift his fist to hit me, only to be thrown onto his face under the tremble of the Earth.

Was this it? Was this the final Shift?

Where there had been open Gateways, explosions followed. They sucked the air in from around them in a vacuum that had me groaning as the air rushed past my ears, before they expelled an outward blast powerful enough to slide parked cars away from them.

The Gateways vanished, and the air on Earth changed.

Thicker, more difficult to breathe, but almost sustaining. Glimmers of hope from the humans inside the town center pushed at my senses, and I opened them up to let the energy in.

Fuck. I hissed a breath through my teeth at how good it felt.

I found Heather's essence amongst them, and almost wept.

I sucked in a deep breath, and almost became light-headed at the sensation.

Somehow, Cael and Ana had done it.

The Balance was back.

Elation filled me, and I bellowed out a laugh as the sound around me died down. But my smile dropped as I stared at my hands, covered in a mixture of blood from the Tenebrians who had tried to destroy us. My first thought was of Heather. I wanted to go to her, to make sure she was okay, but also to lift her into my arms and bring her lips to mine.

But with the return of the Balance came a rush of reality.

Heather couldn't come with me to Lucidis, and I couldn't stay here.

I'd have to let her go.

Chapter Thirty-Two

Cael

Arin groaned as he pushed himself up on his elbows, and the sound drew my attention as I rubbed my lower back where I'd collided with one of the wooden pews. My hand throbbed, my fingers broken. Arin stared at his hands, and I let my gaze trail across the group of half-breeds. Their skin was returning to their usual tones, the blue fading, but it was a slow transition. Their bodies clung to the remaining glow surrounding them before their Guardian halves eventually submitted to the dominant human form.

Raising my hand to my chest, a ball of energy burned behind my heart.

We did it.

Floyd sat up with a groan. "Did we do it?" He turned to me as my gaze fell to Ana.

"*Ana.*" Her name was a strangled cry as I stumbled in my rush to stand and forced myself toward her. She lay in a heap on the floor, her arm twisted awkwardly behind her back, and blood dripped from her nose.

She was still, too still, a motionless body vacated by the being inside.

I dragged her onto my lap and bundled her into my arms. "Ana, *breathe.* Talk to me, my love. Blink, move, *anything*... just *wake up!"* I shook her shoulders, raising my voice with each plea as though she wasn't responding because she couldn't hear me.

John fell to his knees beside me as Samael clawed his way across the floor to be next to us. His leg appeared broken, though he ignored it as his wide eyes fell on his mother.

"No, no, no, *no!* Not again, *please*, not *again."* An inhuman cry clawed up my throat as I shouted, and the sound morphed into a moan. "Ana, I can't lose you again. Not again. *Please."*

Samael stared at me, and as the cavern opened up in his chest, I felt it too as his grief met mine through the air.

"Dad—" he croaked.

"No." I rounded on him. "No. This is *not* over!"

Lifting Ana under her shoulders, I released a low moan as her head lolled against her chest when I stood. Cradling her limp body against me, I buckled under the weight of the pain that threatened to break me apart. There was no time to recharge, and I stumbled as I focused, shook my head, and squeezed my eyes shut to clear the tears before they could escape.

I drew on the energy from the room.

Realizing what I was doing, Sasha held out her hands and directed energy toward me. Her power faltered as her body rebelled against the overuse, barely having anything left to give, but she forced it toward me anyway. Balancing Ana on my arm, I drew out a Gateway, and released a shaky sob when the Gateway formed, easier now that the Balance had been restored.

I went to pass through it, but I didn't go all the way to Lucidis.

I stayed within the Gateway.

"Come on, come on," I muttered.

Holding the Gateway open was draining whatever remaining power I had, and as I lifted my head, I saw through the blurred swirling light as Sasha sank to one knee with the effort of keeping the Gateway charged. She struggled, but didn't break, and I drew from her will and energy. My guilt at weakening Sasha was secondary to my desperation to help Ana.

To bring her back.

To heal her.

I could only pray the Gateways' healing powers had returned with the Balance.

As the light of the Gateway stole my energy, I fell to my knees. Sasha buckled as gravity became too much, and she too came to her knees, one palm hitting the ground, and her outstretched arm shook with effort as she continued to transfer her energy. Samael's hand landed on Sasha's arm, and there was an additional pulse.

I cradled Ana next to me in the swirling light and screamed as the Gateway whirled around me, enveloping me in its cold embrace as it tried to force me either forward to Lucidis or back toward Earth. The Gateway shifted and rebelled against being held open.

But we fought harder.

My scream echoed, and the sound faded in and out before it grew to encompass us both, moving around with the Gateway. There was nothing but the light of the Gateway and the sound of my grief, and even as my energy drained to almost nothing, I stubbornly stayed.

My body was about to give out on me, I could feel it, but my soul would not.

Take me. Take me and save her.

Take all my energy if you have to, give it to her.

I would give anything and everything, fight until my dying breath if I had to, if there was even a chance...

The first breath she took was the sweetest sound I'd ever heard.

Collapsing forward onto my hands and knees, Ana tumbled to the floor in the church as the Gateway slammed shut, and she rolled onto her side and gasped for air as she shuddered intermittently. Crawling toward her, my arms and legs shook as I whispered, "Ana..."

"'Mmm... okay," she mumbled, curled over, and coughed. "I'm okay."

Relief flooded me, and my chest was so tight I thought my heart might give out. Crying out, a sound with no words yet all meaning, I was almost pushed off balance as Samael swept me and Ana into an overwhelming hug, pulling us together and sharing his remaining energy.

John went to Sasha's side and called the others over to help bring back her energy. She kneeled with her head bowed, swaying slightly, all the color drained from her face.

Samael held Ana and me closer, drawing on the home realm that we could feel was repairing before the veil between the realms thickened, and used it to recharge his family.

I knew what he felt in me, though.

"Dad..." he whispered.

I patted his arm gently. "I know. It's okay."

"But... your powers."

"It's okay."

I had nothing left.

Nothing.

I didn't know if my power would ever come back, even when we went home, but with Ana in my arms, her brow furrowed even as she pressed her face against my chest and inhaled my scent, I didn't care.

"Did you hum that song to save the world?" Ana mumbled.

"For you," I said as I squeezed her against me. "It was always for you."

Chapter Thirty-Three

Esco

The quakes had stopped, and the Gateways were gone, but the devastation remained.

Standing, I took in the destruction around me. I was not proud of the fighting which had taken place, nor proud that our species, who so often claimed to be better than humans, had resorted to a bloodied battle.

However, what had been done was done, and all we could do now was find a way to move forward.

I turned, still in a daze, when Monia shouted across the crowd as the remaining alive stirred. "The Balance is restored. Those who resist returning to their home realms will be killed."

Her words cut through me, and the promised further violence cleared some of the haziness in my mind. The constant shifting of energies we could and couldn't draw from, the push and pull of the world and air around us during the Shift had left me feeling foggy, even though things were restored.

My gaze shifted to the Tenebrian next to Monia, Vena, and his eyebrows raised at the brashness of the statement. He knew as well as I that she was right to say it, but clearly hadn't expected her to.

Vena addressed the Guardians, "Tenebrians, you have much to learn. Tenebris was such a horrid place to live because of the negative energies you built there yourselves. If you let the Reflections be, the realm will still be Tenebris, but it will not be as unpleasant for us. You would not long for better and will be able to go about your duties." He looked at Monia again. "Those who refuse to comply *will* be killed. No chances will be taken again."

Vikt brushed herself off and drew herself to her full height across from me. "Won't killing us go against the Balance?" She said it as though she were proving a point, and my brows pulled together. She was behaving like a child. After all the damage she had done, all the countless lives which were lost because of her, and *this* was her reaction?

My lip twisted. *Pathetic.*

These beings have no right to look down upon humans.

Vena stared hard at her. "No, because there will be no grief for your loss."

Vikt screamed in rage and glanced around her. "Come on. We can *fight* them." But there was no response. The few who had been her followers turned away from her, unwilling to sacrifice their lives for a cause they had barely believed in. They relished in a future without consequence, but when they realized they had lost, they simply gave up. Vikt's gaze searched the area, and she moaned when her eyes fell upon a fallen Tenebrian. "Culo," she whispered, and stared into his eyes, open wide and unseeing, with his neck twisted at an unnatural angle.

I glanced up to find Ferox following her gaze, and his lips curved into a smirk. I suspected that kill was his.

Vikt looked hopelessly around at the Tenebrians who surrounded her, pleading for help without words. But Tenebrians weren't known for their loyalty.

"What is it to be, Vikt?"

As she turned back to Vena, her gaze jumped between him and Monia, and her eyes clouded black.

"You're a fucking traitor," she snarled at Vena, and though she twitched as if she were going to make a move to attack him, instead she chose Monia as the weaker victim, and ran toward her. Vena ducked and met her run head-on, his shoulder crushed her solar plexus, and he stood as she bent over the impact. Flipping her over his shoulder, He tossed her carelessly into the large crack behind him. Her scream was of rage and not fear, and ended abruptly as she collided with the jagged edges of the rocks on her way down into the abyss.

A sharp snarl and the breaking of bone broke the silence following Vikt's death, and Ferox dropped the lifeless body of a Tenebrian who had attempted to attack, and slowly his gaze travelled through the crowd. "Anyone else still want to pursue this ridiculous plot?"

Silence followed again, and I took the time to examine each of the Guardians in the crowd. The few Lucidians who had turned sides had disappeared, and I assumed they'd found their human forms and intended to live on Earth, knowing they'd never be welcome in Lucidis, and Tenebris was a painful existence for them.

I found Monia's gaze. "What now?"

"We rebuild."

As many Guardians created large Gateways, they didn't bother to find a discreet place. The humans had already seen so much, and perhaps it would do them good to see the creatures they didn't understand leaving their world. As long as they never saw them return, they need not know how close our realms are and how close they came to utter destruction.

Short of running, I rushed through the crowd into the town center building as the people started to move out, blinking and looking around as though they'd been hidden in the dark.

Metaphorically, they had.

Lynn's bright red hair caught my eye, and I moved toward her, slowing my steps as I came closer. Unsure what to say, the moment of deciding how to greet her was taken from me when Louise rushed toward me and wrapped her arms around my legs. I stared at her dark hair momentarily before touching her head as she pressed her face against my legs.

"I'm glad you're safe," she muttered.

Her face turned up toward me, her wide eyes found mine, and any words I had thought of saying were pushed from my mind as my chest cavity filled with emotion instead.

It was too much, all of it was too much.

Raising my eyes, I found Lynn. There was no accusation in her gaze, and as I could read clearly again, I couldn't sense any hatred or fear.

Only grief.

With my palm pressed gently against Louise's hair, I

whispered to Lynn, "I'm sorry I could not save her."

Lynn shook her head, and her hair cascaded in front of her face. She let it, I supposed she used it to cover the tears which flowed freely.

"I don't cry," she said as she swiped at her cheek.

"It is okay to cry."

She huffed out a humorless chuckle. "Penny cried all the time. Even the slightest sad scene in a movie, or a sad song, and she'd cry. I think it was her way of purging the difficult things she dealt with during her job." Lynn sniffled as if to shake the thought from her mind. "It's not your fault."

"I am still sorry. Penny was special."

"Yes. She was."

Kneeling in front of Louise, I had intended to apologize to her as well when the child threw herself forward and wrapped her arms around my neck. I froze before I very slowly wrapped my arms around the girl. "I will miss you, child."

"Will you come and visit?"

"Maybe."

As I stood, I made eye contact with Lynn as Louise reluctantly unwrapped her arms from around me before she moved to cling to Lynn's hand. I smiled sadly, and with a curt nod, I disappeared through the crowd, heading toward a Gateway.

I'm certain Lynn knew as well as I did that *maybe* meant *no,* and while I couldn't bring myself to outright lie to the child, I couldn't tell her the truth either.

Chapter Thirty-Four

Cael

"Come." I turned as Monia brushed her hand over my shoulder and looked back at Ana, who leaned against John's shoulder. She was either asleep or passed out, I wasn't sure, but her breathing was steady. Yet part of me still feared that if I took my eyes from her for a moment, she would disappear.

"Go, Dad," Samael said. "We'll wait here."

After Monia and I passed through the Gateway into Lucidis, my chest heaved as I tried to hold back tears. The air was revitalizing and fresh again, and the setting sun's warmth was on my face. My shoulders trembled.

"Are you okay?" Monia asked.

I released a heavy breath. "I'm just wondering if I'll ever forget how it felt to almost lose home."

Monia nodded. "I understand. But right now we have something to do."

With Cordus gone, and the revelation of Cascus' betrayal and ultimate death, the Elders of our community were in disarray. Scae was the remaining survivor of the Elders, and she stood proud next to Monia as together they opened Portholes, one after the other, creating a patchwork in front of us, ready to communicate with Elders from communities across the country.

Tenebrians had killed the rest of our Elders in targeted attacks to remove the biggest threats to their cause, and although Scae wouldn't tell us one way or the other, I suspected Cascus had a hand in more than one of the Elders' deaths.

However, it seemed more his style to have others do his dirty work for him.

Scae's voice was quiet, and I wondered how much responsibility she felt she shouldered. Guardians had been trapped in our *old ways* for so long that we were entirely unprepared for the eventuality of a rebellion. "Cordus had been considering you for the role of Elder," she said, turning to Monia.

"Who else will fill the roles?"

Scae lifted a shoulder, then stared at her arm as though the gesture had surprised her. Her lip lifted into a small smile, and I wondered what she'd experienced while on Earth. Perhaps she, too, had bonded with humans. "Whoever else will be voted in later. But much passed-down knowledge has been lost with the deaths."

It was my turn to shrug. "Maybe a fresh start isn't such a bad idea."

Scae observed me, but said nothing.

We all turned as Monia finished creating the Portholes, and there was a moment of heavy silence between the Lucidian Elders. Our community and country had been at the center of the Shift, and we had been privy to information that other areas were not. To most of the Elders, the Shift had come out of nowhere. One day soon, we would tell them the whole story of what had happened and how we stopped it, as well as the communication needed with the Tenebrians to prevent it from happening again.

But, a little bit at a time.

"The Reflections have not reappeared," one started.

"They might come back, and they might not," Monia said as she looked between the Elders. "We do not know what long-term effects the Shift will have on the Balance. We will have to be open to adapting." She looked around. "But I have some suggestions."

"Who are you?"

I arched a brow at the aggressive tone, but Monia seemed unfazed, though I felt a brush of irritation from her through the air.

"She is to be our new Elder," Scae said.

The other nodded. "Proceed."

"I have been in discussion with a Tenebrian Elder, and it is our opinion that the upset started because of the state of Tenebris. He will meet with the Tenebrians and explain to them the link between their behavior and the environment of their realm."

"They should have known," I muttered, and Monia looked at me. "The unrest was building for generations, we simply didn't care to see it."

"All it takes is a seed," Scae noted.

"They will still have their duties," an Elder said, and although he was across the country, he was crystal clear through the Porthole.

Monia smiled. "I do not think we have to worry about them

becoming a positive force. They still seek enjoyment from their duties, and hopefully, they will be more cautious. Secondly..." she continued, pausing to wait for an interruption which didn't come. My eyebrows raised. It was amazing how facing the near end of the world made everyone more open to change. "Humans are no longer to be viewed as only tools to correct the Balance. This was the other part of our problem."

"This is how—"

"If he says *this is how it's always been,* I'm leaping through this Porthole," I muttered.

Monia coughed quietly, and my eyebrows shot up.

Was that a *laugh?*

I ducked my head as I smiled.

Scae added, "An Elder of our own hated humans so much he chose to try to wipe them all out, and assisted the Tenebrians." She ignored the looks of shock that the other Elders failed to hide.

"I hope by now you have all realized how strong humans are and how powerful they can be. Maybe we can resolve to learn more about them, and perhaps even integrate some of those learnings into ourselves."

There was a general murmuring in response, neither affirmative nor negative.

I guessed it was the best we could hope for at this stage, and I withheld from commenting—one small step at a time was better than nothing, but I hoped Monia would become pushier if needed. Too slow to move and change, we risked the same happening all over again.

"One more thing." Monia paused again, and when there was no interruption, I felt a ripple of surprise from her. I struggled to maintain a neutral expression and demeanor around the Elders. Still, I was shocked that Monia could take command of this discussion without much resistance from the other communities' Elders. "It has been brought to our attention that for some generations now, Guardians have been cross-breeding with humans."

The silence that followed hummed with energy, and I almost laughed when guilt was also included amongst the shocked responses. *Of course,* they knew, and I scoffed quietly. I'd met half-breeds from around the world, and unless all of them were the result of Guardians falling for humans then leaving, there *had* to be Elders who knew and likely directed the acts.

Scae cleared her throat. "If monitored correctly and done so as not to upset or hurt humanity... this may be a good way to keep our numbers up to keep pace with the growing human population."

I clenched my fists, and Scae shuffled a step to the side.

"Do you have something to add, young one?" an Elder challenged me.

"No."

There was another beat of silence before Monia continued, "We have learned the power of humans and Guardians combined, but we have much to learn about this and the potential for maintaining the Balance, but also instability if not monitored." Monia risked the smallest glance in my direction before looking across the Portholes. "I ask that you each contact other communities, and that way, we will reach everyone across the globe. The message for now is simple—we need to work together and build communication between communities and realms. We will meet again soon."

The portholes closed one by one. They were not ones for goodbyes, and they terminated the conversation without saying anything further.

Monia indicated for me to follow as we stepped back through to Earth. "You could help you know," she said.

"I am not old enough to be an Elder."

She watched me out of the corner of her eye. "Perhaps age will not matter so much as we adapt."

I lifted a shoulder. "Maybe."

"I want you to continue with training the young Guardians."

"I had no intention of stopping."

"And train the other trainers," she added.

Vena had been waiting, and before I could answer, he stepped forward. "How did it go?" he asked.

"It was a small step, but it was in the right direction, and at least it opened the doors of communication."

"Why was inter-community communication not stronger before?" I asked. Questioning Elders didn't seem like much of a crime anymore, considering.

"It never needed to be."

I huffed. "We were so caught in our ways, and there was so much we could've changed or done differently. There was zero planning, because they never considered that some Guardians disagreed."

"We know this," Monia said with an edge of impatience.

"I'm not blaming you, I'm simply pointing out we're *not* better than the humans, as many thought."

I couldn't read the look in Vena's dark eyes, though it almost appeared to be amusement.

"How can we stop this from happening again?" I asked.

"Maybe we cannot," Vena said as he glanced around the emptying streets before meeting my look as my eyebrows furrowed. "Not entirely, there will always be rebellion, and Rogues. But if Tenebrians stop fighting against their homeland, their quality of life will improve, and we can conduct our duty without being tortured ourselves."

"I'm sorry it was like that for you," Monia offered. Vena shrugged her words off as she watched him. "Perhaps you and I should stay in touch also."

The corner of his mouth twitched as he replied, "Perhaps we should."

Chapter Thirty-Five

Ferox

As the humans vacated the town center, Heather and I sat off to the side of the crowd as they shuffled back out into the streets. They would return to their homes—if they still had one to return to—and hopefully find their friends and families alive. Without their communication devices working, I doubted the humans were aware of the potential global damage and death rate. This would not be something they recovered from easily, and I could already feel the prickle of the shifting energies against my skin. Lucidians would have our work cut out for us as we kept things balanced while they rebuilt. Everyone was hurting.

Guardians were also moving out of the courtyard square, and while some shook hands with or hugged humans as they left, others walked away without a backward glance.

Some of them hesitated considerably.

It would be interesting once we got back home.

Heather turned back to me after watching an emotional exchange between a male Lucidian and some children. Most of the emotion was on the children's side, though while the

Lucidian's face remained impassive, the pain he experienced at leaving cut into his heart. Heather dabbed at my wounds with a scrap of fabric ripped from her sleeve, soaked in bottled water.

My eyes fell to her as she cared for me. Heather didn't need to tend to my wounds, and I think she knew this as much as I did. With the Balance back and the energies restored, I could draw on them to heal. But I let her, and she cleaned them, as though there weren't a thousand things we weren't saying lingering in the air.

She hadn't spoken since I'd returned from battle, but she had thrown herself into my arms and I'd lifted her off the ground as her relief had flooded between us.

"You need not tend to my wounds. The Gateway will finish healing me," I said finally when she continued to dab at a cut she had already cleaned twice, and she paused, but didn't look up. "I can stay." I blurted the words out, and Heather stilled.

Her hand remained hovering over my arm as her eyes slowly lifted to mine. "Can you?"

She knew the truth before I had spoken, and a weight dropped in my chest. Lucidis needed me, the humans needed me. They would face months, years, perhaps decades of rebuilding the damage and loss, and I needed to do my duty from home, not on Earth.

Heather smiled, though it didn't extend to her eyes. Instead, it died on her lips as she shook her head. "I know. You have to go home where you belong. You have your duty."

I frowned, and a sensation swirled around in my gut.

I told myself it was anger, as though I could deny it was grief.

"You do not want me here." It wasn't a question, but when I'd spoken, Heather stopped dabbing and grasped my hand in hers, and absentmindedly flattened out the scales on the back of my wrist.

"That's not true!" Her voice was desperate, and my jaw clenched. "You know I want you." Tears leaked from her eyes, and I lifted my hand to brush them away. She tilted her head into my palm. "But we're different species from different worlds. We know nothing about each other."

"I know that I liked how you beat up those Tenebrians with your bag."

Heather laughed a quiet giggle that filled my senses with her essence, and I greedily I sucked it in. She looked at our hands intertwined together and sighed. "I don't understand how it can work. Your duty..."

"Does not seem so important anymore."

It wasn't a lie, and the way she gazed at me with hope and pain swirling in her irises in equal measure, I wished I could explain.

Cael got to have his human, why couldn't I do the same?

Heather was not a half-breed.

I didn't care.

"I wish things were different," she whispered.

"I do not."

She looked up at me with a frown.

"If things were different, I may not have learned so much. If things were different, I would not have known what love felt like."

She took my face in her hands and pressed her lips to mine, lingering long enough so I could feel the hesitation, sorrow, and regret as it seeped from her skin into me. As she went to pull away, I covered her hands with mine, pulled her toward me, and kissed her with all the passion I didn't know I had. Her cheeks were wet with tears, but she met my kiss with equal passion.

I love you. I love you.

"I want to ask you to stay," she said as she rested her forehead against mine. "I want to, but I can't take you away from your duty, can I?"

"Say what you want to say."

Heather stood, so her face was level with mine as I sat. She clasped my cheeks in her hands, and we shared intimate and intense eye contact. Could she read me, too? It seemed she might be able to, with how her pupils darted between my eyes. She was everything. How could I care for one being so much above all others? All the sex I'd had before I met her now seemed pointless, and she was the only one I wanted to touch forevermore.

Inwardly, I winced as I remembered my interaction with Ana in the early days.

I would apologize to her.

"I love you, Ferox," Heather whispered, and her bottom lip trembled as she kissed me.

The brush of her lips leaving mine was agony, and I wrapped my hands around her wrists as she cupped my face. "I will come back for you. I promise. I will not leave you waiting forever. We will figure out how to be together."

"Ferox—"

"No." I silenced her with another kiss. "The alternative is too painful, and I have decided I do not want to live it."

Heather released a watery chuckle. "Just now you've decided?"

"Yes." When I stood, she looked small as she smiled up at me. "Will you wait for me?"

"Yes," she breathed the answer out. She didn't ask how long she would have to wait or how I would find her because she knew I would not lie to her. Not ever.

The distance would be painful as long as I had to live it, but I would return to Heather. Breathing a heavy sigh, I had acute awareness that every interaction I had going forward would be a direct comparison to my connection with her. Every day of Lucidis would be less sweet because she wasn't near me. Squaring my shoulders, I turned to leave.

"Ferox," she called.

As I turned, she ran and leapt at me, and I caught her in my arms and met her kiss. She parted her lips, and I explored her tongue against mine, and groaned at the sensation. Heather was still crying, but while sadness swirled around us both, it was filled with hope and love. As she broke the kiss, she pressed her forehead to mine again, and I decided I liked it when she did that. My fingers flexed on her ass and I breathed in her essence.

"I love you," she whispered.

"I love you, too."

She released a watery chuckle as I lowered her to the ground, and I threw her a longing glance before I stepped through the Gateway. Heather offered a weak smile, and I waited until she couldn't see me before I gave in to the tightening of my chest. As the first tears fell down my cheeks, cutting a path between my scales, I swiped a finger through them and stared at the reflection of the warm Lucidian sun off the salty liquid.

As I arrived in Lucidis and the Guardians spilled out around me, I stopped and stared at the ground, a deep frown etched between my brows as I tried to rein in my emotions. When I looked up, Esco stood before me, and a small smile played on her lips. It wasn't a smile of happiness or amusement, but one of understanding.

"It was so much harder than I thought it would be to say goodbye," she said.

I grunted in response and stared back at the ground as though my feet were the most captivating thing I could find.

Esco cleared her throat. "I've seen some humans within this realm. They must have gotten trapped. Would you like to help me find them and send them home?"

She still had that slight smile on her face when I looked back at her, and her eyes glittered with the remnants of the tears she, too, was denying herself. We hadn't spoken much before the Shift, but whatever she had experienced on Earth was perhaps a mirror of the connection I had formed.

Maybe I would ask her about it.

One day.

Esco partially turned. "Are you coming?"

My face relaxed as I thought of Heather, and realized I needed only think of her until I could see her again, and with my own small smile, I followed Esco.

Chapter Thirty-Six

Samael

David's hand clasped mine as we stood facing each other. The movement of humans and Guardians around us had slowed after the first mass exodus, yet we didn't move. Everyone moved as though they were afraid of the silence, and were waiting for the next quake or explosion, which didn't come.

Which *wouldn't* come.

I didn't want to move.

"Samael—"

"I'll come to see you as often as I can, and we'll figure something out."

"I—"

"I should be able to live on Earth for a few weeks before I need to go home."

"I can't do this," David said.

My chest felt as though it had caved in. "What?"

"I..." David looked down and to the side before slowly bringing his eyes to mine. "I don't know if I can do this."

"What do you mean?"

"This is a lot. You living in a small country town is one thing, but another *realm*?" He shook his head. "You can't even be here for too long without risking your life."

"Not my life, just my powers."

David huffed and smiled, but there was no warmth in the smile. "You say *just* your powers like it's nothing. But how can I ask you to risk that for me? I don't see how this can work."

"But... we can try, right?" When David didn't answer, the hole opened inside me and pushed us apart in a way physical distance alone could not. "I know you love me," I whispered.

"Samael..."

"Say it, because we both already know it's true. I love you."

David's eyes blurred with unshed tears. "You know I love you, too."

"We can leave, and it'll be just the two of us."

"I can't ask you to do that."

"You're not asking," I snapped out.

"Could you leave your family like that?" David asked.

I clenched my teeth as my heart cracked, and squeezed David's hands as I turned to watch Mother and Dad. When I thought she had died... something inside me had broken, and the reckless part of me, which had been so intent on dropping everything, including my home, to come to Earth, had shifted. I loved David and knew we could make something work, but I couldn't leave home forever.

When my shoulders slumped, and I looked back into David's eyes, he pressed his lips together as he nodded tightly. Slowly, he withdrew his hands from mine, lingering when only our fingertips were touching as though he didn't want to break the contact either. David was doing what he thought was right, and while logical thoughts reminded me he'd been through a lot, I knew we could be together if he would *listen.*

When his hands dropped from mine, the loss of physical contact snapped a string in my heart and unleashed the full force of heartache—a pain I hadn't felt before, and wished I never did in the first place. The deep longing I had felt when I'd first seen David magnified with the sensation of him letting go of my hands, as the space where David had been in my soul was left empty.

"I'm sorry," he whispered.

"*I'm* sorry." My voice cracked. "But it hurts."

"It hurts me too."

Then don't do this. Come back to me.

All the words died in my throat because they were useless.

David needed to figure things out again. His entire world had shifted and would never return to its previous state. He had seen, and lost, too much.

I had to let him go, even if it destroyed me.

David reached toward my face, and when I tilted my cheek into the touch, it didn't quite come, and he brushed his fingers through my hair and tucked it behind my ear.

Turning my head away from David, I swallowed heavily. "Keep in touch with John. He will keep you safe. You can trust him."

David looked at John. "I know we can trust him, but I thought all this was over. What is he keeping me safe from?"

I stared at him until he returned my eye contact. "I need to know you're safe, if it's all I can have." My chest rose and fell rapidly as the tears fell, and I didn't care enough to stop them. David's eyes shone as I asked in a small voice, "How long does it take to get over heartache?"

A world of emotions swam across David's face. "It depends on the person, I guess."

"So..." I looked into the eyes of the man I had fallen in love with. "Forever then."

Chapter Thirty-Seven

Ana

Adjusting my position, I pressed my back against the wall where we sat, John on one side and Cael on the other, like guards protecting me from myself. Or perhaps they were afraid they would lose me again if they let me out of their sight.

I tried to think of what I'd seen when I'd died, but I couldn't remember anything.

I wanted to think Mom was there, though, reunited with Dad.

The sense of mourning shifted and flowed through the air, for the loss of family, friends, and homes, and the goodbyes. It mingled with the flickers of hope for the future from the Guardians, and dread for what the humans would find when they left this safe space.

Unease crept into my body, and my hand twitched against Cael's.

He turned his head to face me. "It's okay, it won't tip again that easily."

"This will be all across the world, though... this confusion and pain."

"So..." He stood and held out his hand. "I guess we have work to do."

John had arranged with some Lucidians to return the half-breeds to their homes. The safest way was the way they had come—through Lucidis—and given they'd been pivotal in bringing the world back from the brink of destruction, it didn't seem fair to abandon them in a foreign country with no way of returning home.

He stood as they approached, and Emma took John's hand in hers. "Bye, John," she said, placing her other hand on their clasped ones.

"What's the matter?" he asked as she hesitated.

I almost smiled at the expression that passed across his face. *What's the matter* seemed such an odd question given everything that had happened, and I could tell he thought it too, the moment the words had fallen from his lips. *Many* things were the matter, and some things would never be the same again.

"What if it happens again, and you need us?"

John patted her hand. "Let's just hope that doesn't happen. But if it does, we'll know where to find you." As she turned to leave, John didn't let go of her hand, and she turned back. "Just remember there is power in your actions, so do your best."

She nodded as Floyd shook John's hand before he hugged Emma to his side and guided her toward the Gateway. They left with Arin and Grace, all of them weighed down by the knowledge of the existence of the other realms and what it meant for every action they took and every word they said—for the rest of their lives and beyond.

John turned back to face me and Cael, and we stared at each

other for a moment. "Ana—"

"John, I'm okay."

"I know, I was going to tell you *I* was okay."

I chuckled, but it only lasted a moment. The weight of everything wasn't far from my shoulders, and while it lifted long enough for me to feel joy and hope sometimes, it hovered above me, waiting to come crashing down at any moment. I hoped the dark cloud would feel less imposing with time, and I could move on with the rest of the world.

"*Are* you okay?" I asked.

We stared at each other for a beat longer. "I think so."

I offered him a small smile, and before I could do it myself, John crossed the distance between us and pulled me into a hug. His arms encompassed my body, and his beard scratched at my cheek, but I buried my face into it and gripped him tightly. "I'm so sorry," I whispered.

He shook his head and squeezed me tighter. No matter how often they told me I didn't need to apologize, I felt I couldn't apologize enough.

"Don't be a stranger," he muttered.

"We won't." When John pulled away, he cleared his throat and sniffed before he looked at what remained of the crowd.

"What will you do?" I asked.

"Me? What I've always done." John smiled. "Hold the fort."

As I squeezed Cael's hand and stood before the swirling Gateway, I turned to him. "Do we tell humanity what happened and what caused all this?"

"We can't. Awareness of the Balance will make controlling it impossible."

"But all the people, so many died... so much pain... they won't understand."

He squeezed my hand in return. "It's a terrible loss, an incredibly high price to pay, but I've witnessed humans building love from grief before, and they can do it again."

"Yes, they can." I touched my abdomen and searched using my senses until I felt the pulse of our daughter.

Cael placed his hand on mine to feel the flicker of life beneath our fingers.

Another being, another child to bring into the world and raise as our own. Another miracle, a cross between Guardian and human, to be the best of both worlds, and teach us something new every day. I looked into Cael's eyes as we stood like that. He and Samael were everything, absolutely everything to me. Guilt swirled within me that I'd allowed myself to get lost, when all I needed to find the light again was standing right next to me the entire time. Cael and Samael never gave up on me, even when I had let them all down.

According to Cael, I never let them down. I was the only one who blamed me, but I felt as though somebody had to take this on their shoulders, and I would do it because I believed it was mine to bear.

Cael was everything I wasn't, and I was everything he said he needed.

"You're magic, Ana," he whispered as I got lost in the blue of his eyes. "Those lips that smiled at me at the bar and caught my attention. Those brows that furrow slightly when you're thinking, as though it's an effort every time to think straight." He chuckled as I swatted his arm. "Nothing short of absolute magic."

"How do you feel?" I asked.

He smiled because, of course, he knew what I was asking. "Whether I get my powers back or not doesn't matter. I can spend the rest of my life with or without them as long as it's with you."

"As long as we're together. You, me, Samael, and our daughter."

"Hope," Cael added.

I swallowed against the emotion in my throat. "Yes, Hope."

Epilogue

David

Four years later...

Earth was still recovering from the devastation that had rocked it and changed humanity's view on life itself. The creatures who had come to Earth, fought, and then disappeared had not been seen since, and there were thousands of theories as to where they came from and why they were here. Despite the shared experience globally, many theories were dismissed as conspiracies—an alternative universe, an alien species, or genetic engineering gone wrong. The most common themes seemed to be those of angels and demons, and of a Rapture that didn't come to fruition.

Of course, only a select few would ever know. But that would never stop the plethora of discussions and speculations, I'm sure, that would continue throughout history. Would the majority of humanity ever know what happened? And how could they stop it from happening again? Those who knew the truth and spoke up were dismissed as simply touting yet another theory. Every story intertwined and melded until there was a jumble of information, and no one knew the fact from the fiction.

Those who had been close to the creatures when rescued were met with a barrage of questions, but they didn't know much more about the true nature of the situation either. There hadn't exactly been time to talk history with these hardly forthcoming beings.

Sitting at my desk in my study, I marked the final bill as paid and turned it face down on top of the pile of paperwork. The light from outside was almost faded, and the branches from a tree I meant to prune but never seemed to get around to, scratched against the window.

I lived alone by choice and was single by choice.

While I had dated a handful of men over the years, I found that the connection I had formed with Samael had set the bar too high for anyone else to meet. What we had shared had been beyond spoken, and no matter how hard I tried, I had yet to find that with someone else.

Perhaps I never would, maybe it was Samael or no one.

I'd tried to ask myself how it had been possible to fall so deeply in love with someone so quickly, and to hold that torch for years afterward, but I had no answers. I loved Samael still, and that's all there was to it.

Early on in the rebuilding effort worldwide, I threw myself into my career and worked hard to open a bakery, employing four staff members.

It was an accomplishment I was proud of, as was my mother, and it kept me busy and happy.

Mostly.

While I had never denied Samael and I had formed a connection beyond friendship or a one-night stand, or that I loved him with a part of my heart that had felt newly discovered, the entire situation was too strange to get my head around at the time. Samael hadn't been in contact since, although I was certain I could feel his presence occasionally while out shopping or at the bar. But when I would turn around, he wouldn't be there.

Maybe it was wishful thinking.

Keeping myself busy had only proven so helpful, and I'd had a lot of time to think about things.

I tried not to curse myself too much for taking so long to get to a point where I was ready to see him again.

Checking the time, I smiled and pushed myself away from my desk, but didn't stand.

The best way to find Samael would be to talk to John.

Thankfully, I wouldn't need to look far, and my smile stretched a little wider, as I was meeting my mother and John for dinner in an hour. I was almost certain something was going on between them, but Mom was private and probably mad at herself for even considering being with someone else after Dad had died.

Making a mental note to reassure her that it *was* okay and she deserved to be happy, I stared out the window as I again got lost in a train of thought.

I *should* be getting ready to go out, but instead, I sat at my desk, with my pen hanging loosely from my grip as I continued to daydream. There were many times like this when I found myself thinking of Samael and unable to shake him from my mind.

It was stronger now, though, because the resolution had been firmly implanted in my mind. I was going to talk to John tonight and ask him to contact Samael for me.

My eyes narrowed because the new thought that occurred to me was foolish.

Maybe Samael *had* been watching me sometimes, but from his realm.

Maybe, if I thought about him hard enough, if I brought up the feelings that still stirred within me and let them come to the surface, maybe Samael would find me.

"I do love you, Samael," I whispered into the air. "I have missed you. I think I'm ready now."

I remembered the touch of his hands, skin, and lips. I remembered how he would get that half-smile when he had misunderstood something seemingly simple, and the child-like fascination in his face when he tried new foods. I remembered how he would look at me as though I were the only person in the room or the entire world that mattered.

He could see the sadness in my eyes past my smile, and he genuinely wanted to help.

The way he fell for me, before I even knew him.

Closing my eyes, I let the memories consume me.

If I thought about him hard enough, if I sent him a sign, maybe Samael would return to me.

Turning in my chair as the doorbell rang, my jaw dropped. "No way."

I felt it before I'd even moved. The shift in the air and a breeze brushed past my cheek, though the windows were closed. It washed over me, a wave of emotion that told me I wasn't the only one who had been waiting. The love I held in my chest came back magnified and encompassed me. The room was filled, and it spread into my soul.

"Are you going to open the door or what?" he called, and I choked back a sob.

Smiling, I stood as I whispered, "Samael."

ACKNOWLEDGMENTS

THIS WAS PROBABLY THE most difficult acknowledgement section to write, because what is there left to say that I haven't already said? So, I'll keep this short.

I say I'll keep it short, but anyone who knows me knows I never stop talking, so we'll see what happens.

I'm passionate about my work, I enjoy writing and bringing my characters to life, and even when it's hard, I never thought of giving up. Taking a break, sure, because sometimes if you don't take a breather and push through, you won't be happy with the quality of writing anyway. But even during those times when I'd stare at a blank document and wait for the words to come, I knew I'd return to writing. There was no doubt. It's too big a part of me.

As I write this, I'm just a few days past a large weekend-long event. Several people who had previously bought a book from me returned to purchase the next one, or in some cases, the rest of the series. There aren't enough words to express how amazing this feels. The conversations I have with my readers are wonderful, and it's somewhat surreal that my stories have impacted people in such a way that they're bouncing on their heels in excitement for the latest release.

Me? *My* books? Little ol' me?

So this acknowledgments section is dedicated entirely to my readers.

I want you to know that each and every one of you makes this an absolute joy. I *love* writing, but that feeling when others love my work? Beyond amazing.

I also want you to know I have more ideas than I can keep up with, so I can't imagine a time when there won't be a steady stream of paranormal and sci-fi romances for you. It's such a broad term, and I can't wait to explore every corner of it.

To my readers, near and far, whether online or in person, I want to express my gratitude.

Thank you, and love to all Xx

Connect with Me Online

ANGELS AND FIRE BOOKS

Find our exciting stories at:

www.angelsandfirebooks.com.au

READER GROUP

https://www.facebook.com/groups/588038442170571

NEWSLETTER

https://www.subscribepage.com/angelsandfirebooks

GOODREADS
https://www.goodreads.com/author/show/21761217.Stefanie_Dawn

AMAZON
https://www.amazon.com/author/stefaniedawn

BOOKBUB
https://www.bookbub.com/authors/stefanie-dawn

WEBSITE
https://www.angelsandfirebooks.com.au/

FACEBOOK
https://www.facebook.com/stefaniedawnwriter

INSTAGRAM
https://www.instagram.com/stefaniedawnauthor

About the Author

Stefanie Dawn writes steamy paranormal and sci-fi romances, as well as dark and urban fantasy. She strives to give her readers stories they can escape into as they become absorbed in the worlds created, and fall in love with the characters.

Stefanie adores creating romances that will keep you hooked, with HEAs and paranormal fantasy, elements of instant attraction, and of course lots of steam!

When she isn't writing, Stefanie might be painting, reading, or watching movies. She loves the process of producing films as another form of storytelling. There's also a good chance she'll be baking some delicious treats—pretending she won't later regret consuming them—or simply enjoying a cocktail with friends.

Stefanie Dawn lives in South Australia with her ever-supportive partner and a lovable gang of rescue cats.

You can stay up to date with Stefanie and her books at www.angelsandfirebooks.com.au

www.ingramcontent.com/pod-product-compliance
Lightning Source LLC
Chambersburg PA
CBHW020328030826
48979CB00021B/474

* 9 7 8 1 7 6 3 8 7 0 5 3 6 *